LORD MONTJOY'S COUNTRY KISS

"Samantha," Kevin growled and started toward her. "You are going to pay for this!"

Still nearly prostrate with glee, Sam took several steps backwards.

"I'm going to spank you like a child!"

Seeing that he appeared very serious and quite capable of carrying out his attack, Sam pivoted, hitched up her skirts, and took to her heels.

In time with the strains of laughter, Sam ran around the side of the castle, hoping to be able to dodge Kevin in the formal plantings, until she could reach the service door. She had almost gained the rose garden when an unforseen event occurred. A rabbit, hiding in the thick box hedge, was startled and hopped across Sam's path. It seemed like she fell for minutes before she actually struck the ground. She bounded onto her knees, but Kevin, too close and speedy to stop, tripped on her leg and plummeted onto her.

"Ow!" Sam yelped as she sprawled out for the second time. She tried to wriggle away, only to find herself flat on her back and staring into his face, which was only inches away. "You lummox!"

He looked back at her with a startled expression of surprise, then slowly grinned. "You are captured, Samantha."

"Let me up!" she wailed, flailing her arms.

He neatly caught her wrists. "I don't think I shall do that. Not yet, at least. Tell me, have you ever been kissed?"

"That is a very personal question, Kevin, one that I shall not answer!"

"Hm, maybe I can learn the truth in a different way." Leisurely, he lowered his lips to hers . . .

Books by Cathleen Clare

An Elusive Groom

Lord Scandal's Lady

A Priceless Acquisition

Lord Montjoy's Country Inn

Published by Zebra Books

Lord Montjoy's Country Inn

Cathleen Clare

Zebra Books
Kensington Publishing Corp.
http://www.zebrabooks.com

ZEBRA BOOKS are published by

Kensington Publishing Corp.
850 Third Avenue
New York, NY 10022

Zebra and the Z logo Reg. U.S. Pat. & TM Off.

First Printing: May, 1998
10 9 8 7 6 5 4 3 2 1

Printed in the United States of America

For Sharon Stevens,
With Many Thanks

One

Blinded by tears, Winifred Stiles let the single sheet of stationery slip from her lap and float down to the flagstone terrace, as she groped in her sewing bag for the handkerchief she knew she had placed within. The letter was all too sad. Who could believe that a small scrap of paper could impart such awful news? Just a few short days ago, she'd received word from her niece that the poor child's husband had died. Now she learned that the dear girl herself was gone, taken in a frightful cholera epidemic that had ravaged the American frontier. Winifred thought that her bosom would surely burst from the congestive pain of despair. Finally grasping the lacy bit of cloth, she dabbed ineffectively at her eyes.

Yes, it was all so very sad. Sweet, pretty, little Elizabeth had been her favorite of all her brother's girls. It was nothing short of devastating to know that there would never be the slightest chance that the vivacious young lady, with her snappy green eyes and bouncy brown hair, would return to her homeland. Winifred cursed the day that Elizabeth had left England's shores, but her niece would entertain no other thought than that of wedding the dashing American frontiersman, Nathanial Edwards. Elizabeth may have been charming and lovable, but she had possessed a mind of her own. If she determined to do something, then do it she did.

Winifred's shoulders shook, and her tears flowed more freely as she stared unseeingly at the rather overgrown flower garden of Montjoy Castle. The crocuses and snowdrops, the harbingers of spring, had always lifted her spirits and lightened her step, but this time their merry blooms failed to cheer her. Elizabeth was dead, passed away some time ago, according to the date on the unhappy missive. Nothing would ever be the same.

"Aunt?" Her nephew from a different branch of her family tree had silently come to the terrace. Laying a comforting hand on her shoulder, he knelt beside her. "Is there bad news from America?"

"The worst." She could not seem to staunch the flowing tears. Her whimsical handkerchief, good only as a delicate accessory, was sodden. Now her nose began to run as freely and profusely as her tears. She gave a mighty sniff.

"My darling Elizabeth is gone, Kevin," she managed. "I shall nevermore, in this lifetime, see her again."

"I am so very sorry." He produced a large, sensible handkerchief and pressed it into her hand, gently patting her back.

She wiped her eyes and noisily blew her nose. This time, she gained a measure of control. Blinking rapidly, she cleared her throat.

"Shall I send for The Connection?" he asked, using the term he'd coined for his elderly female relatives.

"No, I want to gather my wits before telling the other girls." She snuffled and blew again. "I wouldn't wish you to have a trio of watering pots on your hands, my dear boy. While they were not relatives of Elizabeth, we three seem to embrace each other's emotions."

"I've perceived that." He smiled sympathetically and picked up the fallen letter, placing it on her lap. "Would a glass of your medicine aid your recovery? I'll gladly fetch it for you."

"Why yes, child, I believe it would." She patted his cheek. "What would I do without you?"

He rose and impulsively kissed her forehead. "I am only happy to do whatever I can to ease your pain, Aunt Winifred."

"You are such a darling."

She watched the tall, straight young man walk briskly to the castle door. Known to the world as the Earl of Montjoy, and to her as her adorable Kevin, he was a fine, upright gentleman, who deserved far better than the cards circumstance had dealt him. His father had run through the family fortune, leaving his only son a poverty-stricken inheritance, and a name and position to uphold. The estate, consisting of a stalwart, picturesque castle of great antiquity and multiple acres of swampy lowland, offered little promise of financial improvement. The earl and The Connection existed on revenue from their meager investments. The only hope for a more prosperous future lay in Kevin's wedding a richly dowered lady.

Winifred sighed and shook her head. Why had life inflicted her loved ones such terrible blows? It just wasn't fair.

Kevin returned, striding proudly through the garden like the nobleman he was. He carried two glasses, one with brandy for himself, and the other containing her medicine, a healthy sample of Scotch whisky. He smiled kindly as he placed it in her hands.

"It won't cure the pain of loss, Aunt Winifred. Only time will do that. But it should soothe the rawness of the affliction."

"You are such a thoughtful boy, Kevin." She took a drink, closing her eyes as the strong, smoky liquor burned a path to her stomach. Almost immediately, she began to feel better, a haze of euphoria creeping through her veins to her head. She picked up the note from her lap and gave it to her nephew.

"Please, Kevin, read the rest of this missive to me. The medicine is making my vision somewhat blurry."

"Certainly, Aunt." He sat in the chair beside hers and perused the short document. "The letter is from your Elizabeth's daughter."

"Yes. The child has fine penmanship for her age, doesn't she?"

"How old is she?" he queried.

"I do not remember exactly. I would have to read past accounts. But she can be no more than a slip of a girl."

"Then she expresses herself quite well," he mused, "for an American."

"Such national snobbishness, Kevin!" she chided. "I cannot believe that all America is untutored. Besides, Elizabeth would have taught her. No matter how wild and savage that American frontier, my niece would have seen to her daughter's education."

Visions of deep, dark forests, rampaging rivers, and frightening red Indians raced through Winifred's mind. Elizabeth's little girl would be alone in that awful environment. What would become of her?

Kevin suddenly gaped openmouthed at the letter. "The child is coming to you."

"What?" Winifred cried. "Little Samantha is coming to England?"

"Apparently so." He looked up from the page, meeting her startled gaze. "On her deathbed, her mother begged her to seek your protection. It was her final wish."

Winifred began to tremble. "Oh, my. Ah, mercy me!"

"Now, Aunt," he soothed. "America is practically a world away. Making the journey would pose quite a challenge to one so young. Your Samantha might travel here sometime, but I doubt that she could manage it in the near future."

"Perhaps one of us could go to her." She eyed him hopefully, but saw a quick frown dart across his handsome features before he was able to compose himself. Her spirits plummeted. The cost of such a trip would be prohibitive, even if Kevin and all three members of The Connection made great sacrifices.

"No." She shook her head. "Such a venture is totally unrealistic. I am certain that there are those in America who are eminently suitable to care for the child. Elizabeth would have seen to that. What else does she say?"

Her nephew turned back to his scrutiny. Again, the letter seemed to bring him to a state of shock. "Lord God!"

"What is it?" Winifred shrilled. "What is happening?"

"The child is sailing—" he gulped. "She could be in Portsmouth even now, as we speak!"

She nervously kneaded the handkerchief. "What shall we do?

The child might be alone in this foreign land. Oh, my dear little Samantha!"

"Indeed." He grimly gazed at her.

Winifred read his thoughts. "My darling Kevin, she will not substantially add to our strained budget. She is just a little girl. She will not eat much."

"Aunt Winifred!" he exclaimed. "I would never begrudge her a bite of food! After all, you are contributing to our ante."

"Not as much as the others."

"That doesn't matter."

"I know." Tears returned to her eyes as she reached out to squeeze his hand. "But I also know how you worry."

He grinned lopsidedly. "Never fear, aunt. I shall soon wed a wealthy lady and save us from our sinking ship."

She did not laugh. It wasn't a matter for jesting. Winifred and her husband had shared an ideal marriage, which was ended all too soon by his death. She wanted her nephew to also experience such marital bliss.

"In fact," he went on, "I suppose that I've found her, but that is beside the point now. We must think of your little niece. I shall travel at once to Portsmouth to fetch her home. Do you wish to accompany me?"

She reached for the letter and rapidly scanned its contents. "She mentions traveling with some sort of cat. *Bob Cat*. That must be its name. No matter! Little Samantha mentions no other traveling companion, but I imagine she has one. No child could travel without a maid. So since she will have a chaperon, I shall remain at home. You will reach Portsmouth much more speedily without me as an added encumbrance. You will also save on the expense of the trip."

He nodded. "I am more interested in the speed. I wouldn't pinch pennies for such a matter of importance, so feel free to come if you wish."

"No, it's best that I stay behind to prepare for her. Poor child! I can just visualize her, pitiful and homesick, and hugging her kitty for comfort. As a species, cats are so notoriously aloof and independent. This Bob is probably representative of his breed and offers the girl scant consolation."

"She'll have a maid, remember?" he reminded.

"Servants are sometimes of small use in such situations," she adjudicated. "Often the mistress must bolster them!"

"Well, I shall rush to the rescue in no-time flat," he promised, "and I'll soon bring her home to you. You can coddle and care for her as much as you wish."

"Having the child here will ease the loss of Elizabeth." She smiled poignantly. "Lord Stiles and I longed for children, but we were not so blessed. This will be like rearing a daughter of my own."

"The rest of The Connection should enjoy her, too," he suggested.

"Yes. We'll pool our pin money and make her a new wardrobe." She frowned in consternation. "If, of course, that is all right with you, Kevin."

"Certainly, if it will bring you pleasure. We are not so stricken with poverty that we can't gown a mere wisp of a girl." His dark-lashed blue eyes sparkled charmingly. "I'm glad that my ladies will be entertained."

"Her dresses shouldn't require much yardage." She stared into space for a long moment, then giggled girlishly. "I'm so excited, my darling. I can scarcely wait!"

"Then I'd best hasten my travel arrangements." He rose. "I'll find Grandmother and Aunt Daphne and send them out to you. You can tell them what has occurred, and you can begin your plotting."

"Oh, Kevin, you are so good to me!"

"How could I be otherwise? You are so very lovely." He bent and gallantly kissed her hand. "That is why I'm finding it difficult to select a wife. She must measure up to the beauty and charm of The Connection. I'm beginning to think it's impossible."

"Fustian! Such words!" She laughed, then grew serious. "You must take your time. A marriage is forever."

"How well I know that!" He bowed and departed, crossing the terrace with his casually prideful stride.

Winifred gazed after him. Her dear Kevin was a heartbreaker. If he'd had a modicum of money, he could have had his choice among all the young ladies on the Marriage Mart. But alas, it was not to be. He must wed for profit.

She picked up Samantha's letter from her lap and reread it, deciding from the structure and content that someone older had helped her write it. Perhaps Elizabeth had dictated portions from her deathbed. Again, Winifred's tears began to stream, catching in her facial furrows like flood-swollen rivers. She would care for her dear niece's little girl, using every shilling of her tiny, self-imposed allowance.

"Elizabeth," she whispered, "I will cherish your Samantha as if she were my own. I haven't much money, but she will never want for love."

With a weak smile, Winifred straightened her shoulders and turned to meet her fellow Connection members as they rushed through the door.

England. The lump of sorrow in the pit of Samantha's stomach was joined by a host of butterflies, milling about and beating their wings in a mad, nerve-wracking frenzy. Taking deep breath after deep breath in a futile attempt to still her anxiety, she clutched the ship's railing and stared through a veil of tears at the busy port city. *England.* The island would become her home, until she could satisfy herself that she'd carried out her mother's last request. Then she would return to America.

There was a low, rumbling growl at her side. At that threatening sound of warning, Samantha quickly shifted her gaze from the shore to the deck. She smiled at the approaching ship's master.

He halted a safe distance away. "A good day to you, miss, and my best to the beast. I'll be missing you, young lady, but not him."

Laughing lightly, she bent to pat her big cat. Bob's defensive snarl turned into a rough purr, but he kept a wary eye on the intruder of his space. The captain would not emerge unscathed if he came any closer.

"Bob will be glad to set foot on dry land," Sam observed. "I don't think he's much of a sailor."

The man grinned kindly and shook his head. "I hope you won't find it a mistake that you brought him."

"I couldn't have left him behind." She scratched the base of an alert, tufted ear. "He's all I have left of my American family."

He nodded. "That may be, but most folks aren't interested in housing wild animals."

"Bob isn't wild," she protested. "I discovered him orphaned in the woods. He grew up in the midst of people."

"Child, child," the captain gently chided. "The cat is ferocious. If I came a step closer, you'd have a hard time keeping him from leaping for my throat. Bobcats just don't make trustworthy pets."

Samantha knew it was true, but she couldn't bear to admit it. Everyone in the little settlement on the Ohio River had advised her to return the lynx to the forest. They were probably right, too. Yet, whenever she looked at Bob, she remembered how his presence had comforted her during the sickness and death of her parents. She recalled how he'd lain close beside her, offering warmth when she'd shook with the chills of the cholera. Bob was loyal to her, and she was steadfast to him. He was unaccustomed to life in the wilds. If she'd sent him away, he might have died of starvation.

"Captain," she murmured, "I just had to bring him along. He needs me, and I need him. Besides, he will guard my aunt and me and keep us safe."

"He may keep you so secure that you won't be able to find a husband."

Sam gasped with horror. "I won't be looking for a husband here! I certainly wouldn't wed a weak-kneed, sisterly Englishman!"

His eyes twinkled. "You may find your preconceived notion of the British male is wrong. They were a force to be reckoned with during our recent troubles."

"They merely were lucky," she insisted. "No redcoat for me! I would choose an American gentleman any day."

"Well then, being an American man, I'm flattered." He bowed deeply, hurriedly straightening when Bob made a grumble of protest and showed his teeth. "If I were twenty years younger, I'd definitely come a-courting, even if your sweet kitty cat didn't appreciate my suit."

"There you have it!" Sam gaily retorted. "My bobcat will separate the cream from the whey. A gentleman who takes on his challenge is a worthwhile individual."

"Or an idiotic one," the captain said dryly. "But that is neither here nor there. What I really came to learn is your itinerary. Will someone be meeting you on the docks?"

"I don't know." She frowned lightly. "I wrote my aunt of my plans, but, of course, I could not be specific about my time of arrival. I truly am unsure of what to do. I . . . I'm rather lost, I fear. England suddenly seems like a very huge country."

"May I make a suggestion?" he offered.

"Please do."

"I have a friend, a widow woman, who owns an inn in Portsmouth." He flushed and eyed her sheepishly. "She'd take good care of you. You could send your aunt a note, telling her of your arrival, and stay at Polly's until she arranges your transport."

"That might be best," Sam agreed. "I probably shouldn't set out by myself to find her."

"No, especially not with that cat. I doubt they'd allow you to ride on a public coach."

She winced unhappily. "I hadn't thought of that."

"You probably would have to secure Bob in a strong crate," he told her.

"I've had to do that before, and he hates it." She smoothed

the lynx's silky fur. "I hardly know what to do. Will Miss Polly allow me to keep him in my room?"

He chuckled. "I believe I can cajole her into doing so."

Sam brightened. "Perhaps I can trick people into thinking that Bob is just an overgrown house cat. No one would expect me to have a wildcat on a leash."

"I hate to disappoint you, child, but no one would ever mistake that beast for anything but what he is. One can easily discern his evil intent."

She bristled inwardly. She wished that people could see Bob through her eyes. He wasn't wicked. He was just protective. He behaved in a manner that was natural for him.

She did not contradict the ship's master, however. He'd already formed his opinion of Bob. It would do no good to quarrel with him, especially since she needed his help. In a strange land, she would benefit more from Captain Greene's protection than from Bob's.

"I would like to stay at your friend's inn," she said. "It sounds as if I will be safe and well cared for there."

"It is a tavern," he stated, "but Polly won't put up with much rowdiness. As long as you avoid the taproom, you'll be just fine. Now, if you'll wait until I see to the ship's unloading, I'll take you there."

"Thank you."

When he strode away, she turned back to the railing and watched the busy activity on the dock. There was only a smattering of personal baggage aboard. The main cargo was tobacco. Bale after bale of the leafy, aromatic American export was taken ashore. The English must be quite fond of their smoking. The rest of the freight consisted of furs. They were mostly beaver pelts, which were used in the manufacture of gentlemen's elegant top hats.

Sam studied the scene with interest. It was amazing how much one could learn about a nation by noting its consumer goods. The overwhelming majority of the *Mary Frances*'s lad-ing were products for men. Were women ignored in British society? Or perhaps America boasted no products for them.

She watched her trunk being carried ashore and her speculations ceased. Her life was contained in that box. Probably, one could find out a great deal about her from the things she had kept, after selling the rest. There were her mother's treasured brass candlesticks, silver spoons, and mantel clock. From her father was a sleek Pennsylvania rifle, disassembled because of its length. There were assorted other mementos, nothing of very high value, and her small wardrobe, the only interesting piece of it being a pair of Indian moccasins.

When all was dispersed, Captain Greene came for her. "I would offer my arm, but I have to admit I'm afraid of that cat," he apologized.

"I shall keep my distance," she promised.

They debarked down the long gangplank. The crowd parted for them, giving them a very wide berth and staring watchfully. Sam realized that many of the timid onlookers did not even know what kind of beast Bob was, but instinctively stayed clear of him. Bob rewarded them with low growls and suggestive lip twitching.

The big cat was not the only one of the trio the company ogled. Samantha gained no small measure of the masculine attention. With her thick, glossy brown hair and wide green eyes, she was a fine-looking young lady, even in her plain blue dress and cloak, which never could have been considered fashionable. But she ignored the speculative stares. The gapes had been much the same in America. Not realizing that she alone could garner their regard, she blamed their inquisitiveness on the bobcat.

Captain Greene led the way through the rough cobblestone streets to a sprawling, stuccoed and half-timbered building which bore the sign of The Mermaid.

"You'd best wait out here," he advised, "until I can secure you a room and explain Bob to Polly."

"All right." She sat down on a bench by the door and gazed at her surroundings. The Mermaid was a clean and attractive inn. Its pale walls were freshly painted and boasted window boxes filled with bright flowers, for a pleasing contrast. The courtyard was neat and immaculate, the stable employees hastening to fork up the inevitable piles of horse manure. Miss Polly, the captain's friend, must be assiduous in keeping her establishment welcoming.

A large public coach swept through the gates, the horses immediately locking their legs in a jarring halt and nearly ejecting the driver and outside passengers from their perches. Recovering himself, the coachman snapped his whip, but the team only plunged, shied, and rolled their eyes. The man's whip-cracking was quickly punctuated by loud, colorful epithets.

"Get the 'ell out of here!" he swore at the top of his lungs.

Sam stiffened, seeing his attention fixed on her.

"Get that damned beast out of here!" he shouted. "He's scaring my horses!"

She leapt to her feet.

"I don't care if you are a woman!" he ranted. "If you cause me to wreck, I'll personally break your jaw!"

"You could have asked politely!" Sam fired back. "You go to hell, yourself!"

The coachman gaped at such unladylike rhetoric, then glared severely.

There was a brick walkway which passed through an arbor and gate at the side of the inn. Sam tried to whisk Bob in that direction, but he preferred to remain and take up the coachman on his challenge to fight. With a horrid amount of snarling and showing of teeth on the part of the lynx, and cursing and whip-lashing by the driver, she managed to haul Bob around the corner and out of sight.

"What am I going to do with you?" she moaned.

Bob sat on his haunches, smiling pleasantly.

"You scared those horses on purpose, didn't you? Maybe I should have left you in Ohio," she vowed, but she squatted down, hugging him. "You're all I have, though."

He soothingly licked her cheek.

"I hope we can go to Aunt Winifred's soon," she said. "You're not very good out in public, Bob."

He gave forth a deep, throaty purr, which many people would think was a growl.

Equilibrium restored, Sam stood. The small pleasure garden that she and Bob had entered was the perfect place to afford them much needed privacy. It was a pretty plot, enlivened with a large variety of late spring bulbs. A multitude of roses were coming back to life after the winter and would make a marvelous show as the season progressed. Charming stone benches were strategically placed for the viewing of the floral display. Obviously, the widow was interested in her outdoor space and was very talented in its design.

"Miss Edwards? Oh, there you are!" The captain strode through the garden gate. "Excellent! This is exactly what Polly suggested . . . that you take the cat to the garden and enter through the side door."

"Bob was scaring the horses," Sam admitted. "I do believe he enjoys such things."

"Enjoyment?" Captain Greene lifted an eyebrow. "More like he's wanting to dine on them, but his ambitions are neither here nor there. There were complaints against him, even before you became a registered guest. People are afraid of him, and he creates chaos wherever he goes. You should have left him behind."

Though she needed his help, Sam was growing a bit weary of hearing of his hindsight. He hadn't made such comments when she had booked passage, paying for Bob as well as herself. "What is past is past," she said, a trifle snippishly. "It serves no good purpose to speculate on what might have been."

The captain was not to be put off. "Did you stop to consider how you'll travel to your aunt's home if that beast scares the horses that haul him?"

"Bob rode in coaches in America," she stated. "Let us get to the point. Will your friend house us?"

"She will, but she wants you to keep that cat out of sight."

"I surely will do so," she said with relief.

He nodded approval. "Let us go inside."

Keeping the lynx on a shortened leash, Samantha followed him into the inn and down a long narrow passage to the back stairs, where a cheerful, buxom woman awaited them. Obviously taken with the landlady, the captain smilingly made the introductions. Bob merely gazed curiously at Polly Stone, but he lifted his lips to the captain.

"I believe he likes me, but certainly not you!" the widow chuckled.

Captain Greene grunted. "Don't press your luck, Polly."

"He does seem to prefer females," Samantha acknowledged. "My father was the only man he tolerated."

"Women must not be as threatening to him," Polly presumed, "but come now. I'll show you your quarters."

While Captain Greene went on his way, the innkeeper conducted Samantha to her own private salon/dining room where she would join her for meals, then she took her upstairs to a large, attractive chamber, with a little balcony that overlooked the garden.

"I want you to confine that animal to this room and the garden only," she told Samantha. "I can't have him frightening guests and ruining my business."

Sam nodded solemnly. "I will take great care to avoid others, Mrs. Stone. I do so much appreciate your taking us in."

"I am glad to be of service." She smiled and, skirting Bob by a wide margin, left the room. "Dinner at six!" she called over her shoulder and disappeared.

Sam closed the door and bolted it, then removed Bob's leash. The cat stretched luxuriously and began a sniffing exploration of the premises. Sam made sure that the door to the balcony was securely latched. If she went out there, she would have to put Bob on his leash. It wouldn't do to have him spring down upon the shoulders of unwary inn patrons. Satisfied that Bob could not escape, she lay down on the bed and napped, happy to be on dry land again, even if it was England and not America.

Two

Samantha's stay at The Mermaid passed in a quiet routine. On the morning following her arrival, she posted a letter to her Aunt Winifred, informing the lady of her coming. After that, she could only wait, but the days were not dull. In the morning, afternoon, and evening, she exercised Bob in the garden. In between times, she read or explored Portsmouth. Peering in the windows of the port city's shops was rather dissatisfying, however, when one had no money to spend. Not knowing when her aunt would come for her, she hoarded her coins to pay Mrs. Stone when the day came for her to leave. She also spent time caring for her room, since the maids were afraid of Bob. She took all her meals with the landlady and greatly enjoyed her company, especially in the evening when Mrs. Stone was able to linger over her tea.

"I wish I could help you," Sam told her one night when The Mermaid had been particularly busy, and the innkeeper looked fatigued.

"Thank you, child, but I doubt that your aunt, Mrs. Stiles, would approve of your doing menial work." She smiled wearily and sipped her tea. "As you know, we aren't often this lively. There's a cockfight nearby, which is drawing a great many young, high-spirited men. Our regular clientele is composed of the mature middle class, who do not expect frills and luxuries, only clean chambers and good, plentiful food and drink. These young bucks are requesting a bit more service, but if I catered to the aristocracy, I would have to hire many more employees."

"Why?" Sam asked.

"For the most part, our English nobility require coddling." She rolled her eyes. "I am glad that they do not come here, although our ordinary business would improve if a lord or two stayed here, now and then."

"Why?" Sam asked again.

Mrs. Stone laughed. "Many of our merchant class citizens, or their wives in particular, would come in droves if they thought they had the chance of rubbing shoulders with a peer."

"Really? I can't understand why." Sam wrinkled her nose. "Your nobility seems to me to be a useless, parasitic bunch."

"Spoken like a true, democratic American!" the landlady cried. "You sound like my good friend, Captain Greene! But mark my words, whenever Americans visit this country, they wish to lay eyes on a true nobleman. Your countrymen might have rebelled against our system, but they miss the glamor of our peerage."

"I do not," Sam protested. "I admire people who are shrewd in business. Like you, Mrs. Stone. Your ability to run this inn smoothly is far more impressive than an idle peer who gains adulation only through the accident of birth."

Still chuckling, Mrs. Stone refilled their cups. "You are a very attractive, unmarried young lady," she said. "While I appreciate your views of those who work for their bread, and especially for your nice compliment to me, I cannot believe that you would turn down a handsome young lord's offer of marriage in favor of that of a businessman."

"Well I would," she insisted. "I could not cherish a do-nothing, and I cannot imagine myself wedding a man I could not honor."

Mrs. Stone's eyes twinkled merrily. "Some of our young lords are heartbreakingly handsome. I know this from standing outside a London church, watching the comings and goings of an aristocratic wedding."

Sam firmly shook her head. "Looks are only skin deep. I would not succumb to a handsome man, and not to any Englishman. I would never insult your nationality, ma'am, but I plan to satisfy my mother's wishes and then to return home to America. That is where I belong."

"You don't hurt my feelings," the innkeeper assured her. "I know what it is like to long for home. In London, I worked in a shop that sold bed linens. That is where I met my dear Mr. Stone. He had just bought this inn and was seeking supplies. It was love at first sight, I suppose. So I came to Portsmouth, but I felt for a very long time that London was really my home. Uprooting can be an adventure though, if one is young!"

Sam smiled. "So you were dislocated by love?"

"Indeed I was, and I am tempted to do that, again. Over and over, Captain Greene asks for my hand, but I am an old dog now, and I don't know if I really want to learn new tricks. I like my life as it is. I'm not sure I want to move to America, and that's what he wants."

"But you would love it!" Sam enthused.

"No," she denied. "I have the rest of my life plotted out. In a few years, I will sell The Mermaid and buy myself a cottage by the sea. There, I will spend the rest of my days."

"Do you have any children?" Sam inquired.

"We were not so blessed," she wistfully replied.

"But won't you be lonely when you cease innkeeping?"

Mrs. Stone sighed. "Here at The Mermaid, I have had enough company to last a lifetime. I've even made some friendships that will remain. Yes, I even correspond with some former guests! I hope you will number among them. I'll be interested in learning what you do with your life."

"I'd like to know about what happens to you, too," Sam told her. "When I return to America, I'll come early to Portsmouth, so I can spend several days at The Mermaid and visit with you."

"I am flattered." Mrs. Stone reached out to squeeze her hand. "And of course, there will be no charge."

Sam lifted a hand in protest. "I will pay for my room and board. Business is business, and friends are friends. I refuse to take advantage."

"You are so kind," she said, "but if I am living in my home by the sea, you will stay with me at no cost whatsoever."

"I will share in the food expense."

"No . . . no!" She smiled secretively. "The Mermaid has already made me a well-to-do woman. I could sell it right now and live comfortably for the rest of my life, but I like my work. I like being in the midst of people."

"I do, too," Sam admitted. "My father owned a little outpost, a general merchandise store, in the Ohio country. There were very few people in the area, so we were terribly excited when new families came. Everyone had a story to tell!"

"That is what makes a business like this very interesting," she acknowledged. "Perhaps you would like to own an inn someday."

"It sounds interesting." Sam knitted her brow in consideration. "I sold Father's store to fetch the money for my trip, but I kept much of the land. As the country is settled, there will be more and more travelers. Constructing an inn could be a wise investment."

Mrs. Stone thoughtfully cocked her head. "England is already populated. Buying an existing inn here might be even wiser."

She dimpled. "Are you trying to sell me The Mermaid?"

"You could do worse." The landlady winked in confession. "But I am not yet ready to sell it. Allow me a year or two!"

"You will never wish to sell it," Sam scoffed. "You would miss people all too much."

"If I sold it to a friend, I could come and work, free gratis, whenever I wanted the bustle."

She shook her head. "I just cannot visualize your being anywhere but right here."

"Humph! We'll see about that!" Mrs. Stone rose. "I have tarried too long for such a busy evening. I must check on Old Gus and his serving girls in the taproom, and I believe you have a cat to walk."

"Yes, I do." Samantha finished her tepid tea and stood. "Have you time to join me for a glass of sherry at bedtime? I find that the wine makes me go to sleep easier."

"You're having trouble sleeping?" Mrs. Stone probed. "Is there too much noise from below?"

"Not at all." She flushed. "I must admit that I'm rather nervous about meeting my aunt and taking up residence in this country. I don't know what is expected of me."

The landlady surprised her with a big hug. "You are a charming, pretty, unspoiled young lady. You will be fine!"

"I . . . I just don't know. My mother was a sweet, gentle lady. She dearly loved her Aunt Winifred, so I should not be worried. But I am."

"Now, never you mind!" Mrs. Stone patted her back. "I am sure that your aunt is a fine woman. But on the outside chance that you are unhappy with her, just you come to me! You can be my assistant."

"Thank you, Mrs. Stone. You are too good to me."

"Not at all. I am selfish and enjoy having you with me. Even in this short time, you seem like the daughter I never had."

"I am happy to fill the role." Sam beamed. "And I wish you would call me Samantha, or better still, Sam. A friend and a daughter substitute should be known by her first name."

"I'll do that if you'll call me Polly," she responded.

"Thank you, Polly. I shall, indeed."

"Thank you Sam." She extended her hand and shook Samantha's in man-fashion. "I'll be glad to join you in a glass of sherry before bedtime. Meet me at ten o'clock."

"I'll be here."

The two ladies exited the room. Mrs. Stone turned toward the noisy taproom. Sam climbed the narrow servants' stairs to her chamber. Bob was anxiously waiting. While she fastened the leash to his collar, he rubbed his face on her leg and purred in his deep, rugged voice.

"There you are," Sam told him. "Now we're ready."

They softly padded down the stairs and out into the garden. Sam made certain that the gate to the courtyard was bolted securely, then unhooked the bobcat to allow him to roam at will, as was her custom during the past quiet evenings. Seating herself on a stone bench, she watched Bob meander gracefully round the flower beds in the dim light.

It was a lovely evening, balmy and calm, but there was a hint of rain in the air. Sam inhaled deeply. England was pleasant at this time of year, but even late spring weather was notoriously unpredictable. It would soon rain and most likely become damp and chilly for a short while. Then her sojourns with Bob would be swift and unpleasant, and she would enjoy a bright fire on the hearth. When would she hear from her aunt? She looked up at the dark, swirling clouds and the misty moon in the sky. Yes, it would rain very soon. Would precipitation slow her trip to her aunt? Probably so. She was almost relieved by the thought. She was enjoying her life at The Mermaid. She would be sorry to leave the old inn and her new friend, Polly Stone.

Kevin Montjoy gazed glumly at the rain streaming down the carriage window. The bleak night was as depressive as his spirits. He had sought his aunt's ward at every inn in Portsmouth, save one, and had come up empty-handed. If little Samantha was not residing at The Mermaid, he didn't know what he'd do, but he was aware of one thing. He couldn't return to Montjoy Castle without the child, or he'd best have a damn good reason for it.

The coach turned into the courtyard of the out-of-way hostelry. From what Kevin could see through the sheets of water, the inn seemed like a pleasant accommodation. Candlelight glittered from the diamond-shaped mullions. The cobblestone yard seemed clean of offal, and the walls of the building looked to be nicely whitewashed. Kevin decided to stay at The Mermaid, whether or not he found the child there. If Samantha was not at the inn, he'd go down to the docks, in the morning, and hear what was said about ships expected to arrive from the colonies . . . er . . . America.

As the carriage drew to a halt, a hostler came running from within to assist them. In moments, Kevin's drenched footman appeared at the door. Coughing and snuffling, he wrenched it open.

"M'lord, shall I make the usual inquiry?" he asked through chattering teeth.

"No, I shall do it." He reached for his hat, then thought better of it, leaving it to remain dry on the carriage seat.

The servant shivered. "Begging your pardon, sir, but you'll get a good soaking out here."

"If there is a vacancy, we'll stop for the night. We can do with a warm, dry bed, a hot meal, and a mug of ale," he told him.

"Thank God," he thought he heard the footman mutter.

Kevin stepped from the vehicle, ran across the courtyard, and darted into the inn. Ordinarily, he would have had a drink in the common room and asked about prices, but this time, he didn't bother. He peremptorily strode to the bar and commanded the tender's attention.

"I desire rooms for myself and my servants, also a private dining room for me, meals (and they'd best be good and fresh), and right now, a mug of your finest ale."

The man's eyes popped wide. "M'lord?"

"Yes," Kevin said briskly. "What is it?"

"Just wanted to know. I thought you was a lord . . . the way you come in all bossy." He sketched an awkward bow. "I'll tell Mistress Stone that yer here. She takes care of the room business. I just work in here."

"Well, be about it!" Kevin snapped, wet and irritable. "And fetch my ale before you do!"

Mumbling to himself about fancy peers, the barman shuffled to do his bidding.

Kevin impatiently waited for his drink, tapping the fingernails of one hand on the scarred bar surface. He shivered, eyeing the blazing, big fire. The inn's patrons occupied the seating nearest the hearth. He wondered if he could cause them to move, so that he could sit in the heat while he waited for the landlady. The bartender set his frothy ale in front of him, sloshing it as he did so. Frowning at the man's ineptitude, he tasted it.

"Is this your best? It has a rough, unpleasant flavor."

The bartender thrust out his lower lip in a pout. "We ain't never had no complaints before, m'lord."

"Well obviously, your clientele does not possess a discerning palate," he stated.

"I dunno what that is. What d'you mean in plain English?"

Kevin shook his head. "Never mind. While I am waiting for the innkeeper, I wish to sit by the fire. Will you arrange it?"

The bartender looked. "There ain't no more empty chairs."

"I know, but I am chilly and wet. You will see to it," Kevin ordered.

"Goddam," the man grumbled quietly and sauntered from behind the bar and over to the fireside. He spoke briefly to his customers, then dragged an empty chair from across the room to the hearth. He plodded back to Kevin.

"There's your seat, m'lord. The others don't mind if you sit with 'em. S'pose everybody's cold tonight."

Kevin made a mouth of disgust. "I'll take care of the matter. You fetch the innkeeper."

"Yes, m'lord." He ambled away.

The earl glared at the patrons by the fire. They gazed back with benign curiosity. The vacant chair stood out in sharp relief. Kevin turned away and sipped his objectionable ale. It just wasn't worth his effort. Those men were too inquisitive about him to move. And apparently, they thought they could socialize with a real peer.

His coachman and footman entered, shaking with cold. "A rainy, cool spell in the spring feels as nippy as winter," the coachman declared.

"Indeed." Kevin nodded. "Go behind the bar and draw your own ale. The tender is occupied elsewhere."

They obeyed, filling their mugs, draining them dry, and replenishing them. Drinking more slowly this time, they drifted to the group at the fireside and began to warm themselves, chatting freely with the other men. They seemed to be right at home.

Kevin gritted his teeth. Where was that innkeeper? He wasn't as wet or as cold as his servants, but he was damned uncomfortable. No matter that he had little money. He was a peer of the realm, and he deserved better than this. But nobody seemed to care.

Samantha and Polly were surprised when Old Gus shuffled into the room. They had been talking amiably, enjoying their sherry, and thinking that Gus and his barmaid were running things smoothly, but they'd seemingly hit a snag. With a frown of concern, Polly set aside her drink.

"What is it, Gus? Please don't tell me that an inebriated patron is tearing up the place. I'm too tired to carry my rolling pin into a fight."

"No, not that, ma'am." He grinned. "We got a real, live lord in the taproom, Mrs. Stone, and I will say that he's the biggest smarty-bum I ever seen."

"A lord?" Sam perked up her ears. "A real, living and breathing, English lord?"

"The same," Gus told her.

"What kind of lord is he?" she asked, fascinated.

"A snotty-nose arse," he expostulated. "A bossy, briggety son of a—"

"She means to ask about his title," Polly broke in.

"I don't know. He's just a mouthy nob." He directed his further conversation to Polly alone. "He wants a room for hisself and his servants, a meal for 'em all, and a private dining room just for hisself. I told 'im I'd go get you."

"Thank you, Gus." She finished her last sip of sherry. "I'll come right away. Sam, I'm afraid we'll have to cut short our comfortable coze. This is my only private salon."

"This excitement is worth the interruption," Sam twinkled. "I'm going with you. I want to see what he looks like."

Her friend hesitated. "Oh, my dear, I don't know. The taproom is sometimes ribald, and after all, you are a gentle young lady."

"Nonsense!" she retorted. "I refuse to miss this just because I might hear a naughty word or two. Polly, I insist!"

"Pshaw! Very well," she relented. "I suppose our haughty aristocrat appeals to a foreigner's interest, just like the Tower of London and Canterbury Cathedral. Come along then, Sam, but do not say that I didn't warn you."

Excitement coursing through her body, Samantha trailed behind Polly and Gus as they proceeded to the common room. She was curious about the taproom as well, never having passed through its doors at all. Her friend had almost been *too* protective of her.

Polly caught Nancy, the tavern wench, as they entered the room. "Neaten my salon, Nancy. His lordship will use it."

"Lordship!" she cried, nearly dropping her tray.

"You haven't heard?"

The girl shook her head. "Been at the necessary. When I came back, Gus was gone, so I was called on to fetch more ale for the men at the tables."

"Well, evidently we have a peer as a patron tonight."

"Laks!" she shrilled. "I'll hurry and serve these lads, then clean the salon, and I'll serve him, too. Is that the man at the bar?"

"Yes, it is." Polly continued on.

Guilt swept over Samantha. She could have straightened the room, but she had been too inquisitive to think of that. Ah, well, it was too late now. She glanced around the taproom. There were many candles, and the fire danced brightly, but the room was dim, the light being absorbed by the dark, burnished oak walls. A cluster of men were gathered near the hearth, quaffing tankards of ale and talking and laughing together. When Nancy went past, one of them reached out and pinched her derriere. Sam stifled a gasp and looked quickly at Polly to see if she'd noticed, but the widow walked on toward the solitary gentleman at the bar.

"Polly!" Sam hissed. "One of those men intimately touched Nancy!"

The landlady paused. "I warned you, my dear. Pinches and

groping is part of the job. Nancy understood it before she was hired. She accepted the working conditions."

Sam frowned. "You shouldn't put up with behavior like that. I wouldn't! I'd toss that man out!"

"Then you wouldn't last long in business," Polly said, somewhat impatiently. "If you ever go into business, remember that the customer is the most important facet of your life."

Embarrassed, Sam bent her head. She shouldn't have questioned her friend's way of doing things. Polly was aware of good business practice. She'd had years of experience. Later, Sam determined, she'd apologize.

"My lord?" Polly said in her low, mellow voice. "I am Mrs. Stone, innkeeper of The Mermaid. I understand that you wish rooms, a meal, and a private salon."

He turned, nodding shortly. "It seems to be taking a terribly long time for such a simple request."

While Polly framed a soothing answer, Sam couldn't help staring boldly at him. Even though she saw him by dim candlelight, she could see that he was brutally handsome, with dark hair, high cheekbones, a firm chin, and a distinguished, aristocratic nose which he carried with a marked haughtiness. His eyes were dark-lashed and seemed to sparkle in the soft illumination, but it was too shadowy, and she was too far away, to note their color. He was physically fit with nicely straight shoulders and a trim waist. He might be a fine man to look at, but she doubted that he would be pleasant to know. He fairly reeked with arrogance and selfish pride. All in all, however, he did not fit her prototype of an English peer. The lord in her imagination was effete and sisterly. This nobleman boasted such blunt manliness that it made her feel slightly uncomfortable. Rendered rather breathless, she sat down at a nearby table in the shadows.

"Instead of the usual tough, stringy meat, I would like a tender, well-marbled beefsteak," he was telling Polly in beautifully cultured tones.

Sam's anger flared in sympathy for her friend. Everything

the widow served was wholesome, hearty, and delicious. How dare he prejudge his meal!

"I am sorry, my lord," the landlady said, "but this time of night, I have only roast beef. I will assure you, however, that it is quite tasty."

He lifted a shoulder. "I suppose nothing can be done about it, but bear this in mind. I refuse to pay full price for leftovers."

"Of course not," Polly said tightly.

"Neither will I pay a high price for this ale. It is bitter," he proclaimed, draining the last of the brew and setting down the tankard with a jarring rap. "I'll have some more."

Old Gus moved to obey.

"Hurry up," said the fine peer.

Sam's irritation increased. "Fancy this," she said loudly. "He complains about the ale, yet he can hardly wait for more. Such a paradox!"

The nobleman turned around and contemptuously studied her from head to toe. Sam squirmed. No man had ever looked at her like this. He seemed to be both undressing her and consigning her to a lowly place in the scheme of life. She wished she hadn't drawn his attention.

He opened his mouth as if to address her, but old Gus served him his ale at that moment and drew his fire. "Old man, I see you're a bit speedier when your employer is present."

Gus stuck out his lip and moved to the far end of the bar.

"Your private salon must be ready by now, sir," Polly put in. "I can escort you there, or to your chamber first, if you prefer to freshen up."

"The salon," he chose. "When I go to my chamber, I'll retire for the night. Make sure that a good fire is burning by then."

"Very well," she replied. "May I have your name for the accounting?"

"Montjoy," he told her.

Polly looked blank. "My lord, I am not well acquainted with the peerage. Few noblemen come to Portsmouth, and those who do usually stay at the more accessible inns."

He sighed vexatiously. "I am the Earl of Montjoy. Do you wish to learn my pedigree as well?"

Samantha missed Polly's reply to that salvo. Frankly, she was awed by the man's high elevation. Although she wasn't entirely familiar with the hierarchy of the peerage, she knew enough to realize that the ordinary person did not meet up with an earl everyday.

Mrs. Stone was so bowled over that Sam wondered if she'd even answered his high-handed question. Her friend might be British through and through, but she doubted that Polly had ever exchanged words with a person as distinguished as an earl. She probably didn't even care that he was rude.

Sam blinked, as if that gesture would set the scene in motion. Everything seemed to stand so still, as if caught in a time warp. The widow and the earl stared at each other, then at last he broke the silence, this time in more friendly tones.

"I have come to Portsmouth to seek a traveler," he explained. "Perhaps you know something of the person."

"I doubt it," Polly replied. "The Mermaid is rather off the beaten track for most travelers. But I will help you if I can."

"I am looking for a child," he said. "She is surely traveling with a nurse or companion. She is my aunt's ward, coming from America."

Mrs. Stone shook her head. "I've seen no little girl, but I'll be happy to send someone around to the other inns to make inquiry."

"I've already asked. Damn!" He struck his fist on the bar. "What will I do? I cannot go home without little Samantha, or my aunt will worry herself into an early grave."

Eyes widening, Sam caught her breath. Polly's mouth dropped open, and she made a gagging sound. Old Gus staggered backwards against the wall.

"Who did you say she was?" Polly gasped.

"A child named Samantha Edwards. She's traveling from America. Have you seen her?"

"Oh, yes . . . yes . . . Yes, I have," the widow choked out.

"Excellent! Where is she?" he asked excitedly.

Too shaken to speak, Polly pointed.

"H-here I am." Sam got to her feet, but her knees had turned to water. She tightly gripped the table. "I . . . I'm Samantha Edwards."

He swiveled and gaped at her. "You're Samantha? You're not a child! You cannot be the female I seek."

She teetered precariously. "Mrs. Winifred Stiles is my aunt."

"She also is mine. Then . . ." His gape suddenly became a glare. "If you are my aunt's ward, just what the hell are you doing in an uncouth taproom?"

Three

Kevin knew that his mouth was hanging wide open, making him look like a total dolt, but he couldn't recapture his cool savoir faire. *This* was Samantha? The room was dim, but it wasn't dark enough to prevent him from seeing that she was a grown woman, with a grown woman's interesting attributes, and definitely not a little girl.

She was taken aback, too. First, she tried to cling to the table's edge. Then she transferred her grasp to the back of a chair. All the while, she stared at him as if he were a player in a raree show.

The landlady came to the rescue of everyone's sanity. "Let us go to the salon," she suggested, and without waiting for anyone's agreement, shooed them from the taproom like a flock of biddies.

The Mermaid's private dining room was much brighter than the other. It was illuminated by fewer candles, but with white plaster walls, their flicker was used to greater advantage. As soon as he set foot inside, Kevin began to evaluate his Aunt Winifred's ward.

Ward? She was almost too old to be anyone's charge. He had wondered immediately if she had left her home in America because she had the impression that her aunt was wealthy. If so, he would scotch that belief in a trice. If not, well, he didn't know what he would do.

He followed her toward the wing chairs by the hearth, sizing her up from the rear. She had a pleasing, upright carriage and a graceful walk, which accented her intriguing derriere. Her lush, brown hair was twisted into a soft knot at the nape of her neck. Before he had finished assuaging his curiosity, she turned and sat down. Kevin was forced to do likewise.

She looked at him with some irritation. "Such ill manners, my lord! Would you sit before all the ladies are seated?"

He lifted an eyebrow.

The innkeeper bent to her ear. "You must accustom yourself to the ways of our aristocracy, Sam," Kevin overheard her whisper. "I am naught but a glorified servant to him."

"You are my friend, my *only* friend in England," she responded loudly and firmly.

"Please, my dear, don't rock the boat," the elder woman murmured, then raised her voice. "My lord, perhaps you would prefer port or brandy to the ale. And, Sam, I shall fetch you another glass of sherry. I believe you could use it."

"Brandy would be most welcome," Kevin informed her, "but I am also starving. Do bring my meal at once."

"Please," Samantha directed.

He set his jaw. He was probably paying well for this questionable service, and he was being ill-used. He fixed the innkeeper with a lordly expression, which she understood even if Samantha did not.

"Please," repeated the obtuse American.

The ghost of a smile flitted across Mrs. Stone's face.

"Please!" Kevin ground out. "Please! I am cold, and wet, and hungry, and I wish someone would *please* bring me something to eat!"

The landlady was already on her way from the room.

Kevin openly faced Samantha. "You had best learn the social laws of this country, my daft, little American gel, or someone, someday will be sure to make mice feet out of you."

She defiantly lifted her chin. "Good etiquette is not amiss in any society. Long ago, I was taught to mind my manners. Apparently, such lessons were overlooked in your rearing, my lord, or you would not exhibit such a blatant disregard for the dignity of others."

"Fustian," Kevin muttered and withdrew from the verbal field of battle.

When he first saw her, he should have realized that the girl would be a total aggravation, even though she was attractive in a pert sort of way. She had lots of silky, rich brown hair and expressive green eyes that mirrored her mood at the moment. Her cheekbones were delicately sculpted and her chin was resolute, almost to the point of being brazenly stubborn. Her lips were as eloquent as her eyes, and right now they were set in a fine line of annoyance. Her body . . . Well, for such an ingenue, she had been nicely endowed by her Creator. In summary, she was a fetching little minx, who appeared to be quite a handful if she was crossed. She certainly wasn't the homesick brat he'd expected. He wondered what the hell Aunt Winifred would do with her. He wondered what *he* would do. Miss Samantha Edwards was of marriageable age. He couldn't afford a London Season!

"Just what are you ogling?" she demanded.

"You," he fired back. "You aren't what I came for."

"What a pity," she said with a voice full of sarcasm. "What did you expect?"

"A puling, babyish, little girl," he returned. "Aunt Winifred believes you to be a child."

She cocked her head like a saucy vixen. "She is *your* aunt, too?"

He nodded.

"Well, then, I suppose we are relatives." She looked as if she wasn't thrilled with the idea.

"You'll be happy to know that we are kinsmen only by marriage," he clarified. "We are not blood relations."

"I see." She shrugged and shifted her gaze to the flaming fireplace. "So Aunt Winifred sent you to meet me. Do you live near her?"

The question briefly stunned him. "Aunt Winifred lives with me. Did you not address her at Montjoy Castle?"

"No." She shook her head. "She used only the name of the village . . . Moorfield, I believe it was."

"Aunt Winifred lives at Montjoy Castle, near the village of Moorfield," he explained.

Her eyes sparkled. She seemed to lose a bit of her impertinence. "Is it a real castle, or only a copy of one?"

His answer was interrupted by the arrival of a serving wench, who was bringing his brandy and Samantha's sherry, but when she left, his cousin anxiously repeated her question.

"Montjoy Castle is very real, a medieval stronghold," he told her. "The keep and the gatehouse are all that remain intact. The rest lies in ruins."

"How fascinating!"

Was she a fortune hunter? Kevin decided that it was time, early on in their conversation, to let her know that finances were troubled at Montjoy. He doubted she'd like what she heard.

"I fear I must warn you that pickings are slim at Montjoy," he said wryly. "My father, a rather high flyer, left me penniless. As head of the family, I am responsible for the care of my grandmother, my great-aunt, and our Aunt Winifred. We pool our resources and manage to eke out an existence for ourselves and our staff."

"Are you asking me to return to America?" she asserted.

"Certainly not!" he exclaimed. "Aunt Winifred would have my head if I came home without you! I am only warning you not to expect to dwell in the lap of luxury."

"You mentioned staff, didn't you? Anyone who can afford to have servants seems to me to be far above *eking out an existence!*"

He frowned. "I owe a particular standard of living to my rank."

"Ridiculous," she scoffed. "If you're so penniless, you should trim your expenses and seek employment."

"What?" he gasped.

"You heard me," she lectured. "Get a job, my lord!"

If the innkeeper and her serving girl had not, at that moment, entered the room, Kevin did not know what he would have said or done. But by the time they had laid out his supper, he had thought through Samantha's words. She was an American. She had no knowledge of the English social system. She did not realize that it would be scandalous for him to be employed in anything other than the management of his estate.

Rising from the chair, he went to the dining table, where his hostess had assembled a variety of dishes. The selection was small, but the aromas rising forth were mouth-watering. When he sat down, Mrs. Stone bent close to his ear.

"Please be kind and patient with her, my lord. She is a sweet child, who means well, even if she seems misguided at times. She will quickly learn our ways."

Kevin listened, but did not reply. Who did she think she was, having the gall to advise him? He helped himself to beef, roasted potatoes, carrots, and a large slab of bread and butter.

Mrs. Stone hovered over him and Samantha, too. After pouring his dinner wine, she served his cousin a glass of sherry. Filling a glass for herself, she sat down in the chair he had vacated.

"Madam, I do not recall asking you for your company," he protested. "I prefer to speak alone with the young lady."

The innkeeper, flaming scarlet, half-rose, pausing when Samantha said, "Stay. *I* wish you to be here."

"I was merely serving as a chaperon," Mrs. Stone offered.

"It is not necessary," Kevin declared. "Samantha and I are related. We are cousins."

"Please stay," his cousin objected again. "I don't know what to say to him."

The landlady continued to rise. She looked from one to the other as if deciding which one to obey. Her English blood overcame her compassion. She laid a hand on Samantha's shoulder.

"I shall return awhile later," she promised, bowed to Kevin, and left the room.

"That was so rude," Samantha pronounced. "She is my friend."

"She knows her place," Kevin countered.

His cousin did not rise to the bait, but she stuck out her lower lip in disagreement.

He sighed. His newly met cousin was naive, and belligerent, and had everything to learn. She just didn't understand her transformation. Only a short time ago, she was a plain American girl who could be friends with an innkeeper. Now, suddenly, she was an earl's kin and could not. It was probably a difficult concept to grasp. He determined to be more patient, as Mrs. Stone herself had suggested.

He took a bite of meat and found it to be very good.

"Are you surprised?" Samantha asked, closely observing his reaction. "The food here is tasty. You shouldn't complain about anything until you have tried it."

He forgot his avowal of tolerance. "You know, I could say the same about you. You seem to have come to England with a gigantic chip on your shoulder and social reform in your heart. You are a foreigner here, due to your country's ill-bred rebellion. Since you are a guest, perhaps you should adapt to us, instead of attempting to force us to adapt to you."

She rose. "I don't agree with you. Good manners are universal and classless."

"I believe we should put a period to this topic. It is obvious that we will continue to differ." He cut another bite of beef. "Tell me about your life before you came here."

She sauntered to the table and sat opposite him. "There isn't much to relate. We lived along the river in the Ohio country. My father had a small trading outpost. Frankly, we were poor. My father's business was the only one for miles around, but the area is very sparsely settled, so there were few customers. As the country is developed, it will probably become quite a profitable enterprise."

"You sold the store?" he asked.

"Yes. That's how I got the money for passage." She folded her hands, thoughtfully studying them. "I kept some of the land, however . . . the part that our cabin is on. I believe it will be very valuable someday. The man to whom I sold the store is looking after it for me."

"Interesting." He pensively chewed a portion of carrot. "I seem to remember reading that you call this western land a frontier."

Samantha nodded.

"What does it look like?"

She smiled somewhat sadly. "The Ohio River is wide and beautiful. It provides our main means of transportation. There are sandy beaches and spits along the shore. Beyond that is the forest. It's dark, and shady, and thick with huge trees. There are wild animals . . . You should hear the scream of a painter. It would frighten you out of your boots."

"A painter?" he queried.

"That's Ohio dialect for *panther,* an immense tawny cat. There are bears and bobcats . . ." She smiled secretively as if she were remembering a fine joke. "We often see Indians. Ohio is hard to describe! But I doubt that you'd like it."

"Why not?" he quizzed between mouthfuls.

"It's too untamed. A man accustomed to being cared for by servants could not cope."

Although highly insulted by her view of him, Kevin remembered his vow to be patient, and he held his tongue. He finished his meal in silence. Happily, he noticed that the lack of conversation seemed to make her a bit nervous.

Finally, she spoke. "May I ask you a few questions?"

He wiped his mouth on a napkin. "Please do, though I hope your inquiries are not antagonistic."

"They aren't. I'd like to learn something about Aunt Winifred."

He grinned. "She is a lovely, charming old lady. You'll love her, if you overlook the fact that she is planning to treat you like the child she never had. I hope you'll understand and won't hurt her."

She looked him straight in the eye. "I want to love her, but

I cannot be someone I'm not, sir . . . er . . . what am I supposed to call you? My lord?"

"Since we are related, you may call me Montjoy or Kevin, whichever you please."

She considered. "Kevin. That seems more friendly. Will you tell me more about Aunt Winifred, and the castle, and your way of life?"

"Of course." He laughed lightly. "Aunt Winifred is one third of what I call The Connection. It's composed of our aunt, my grandmother, and my great-aunt. They are delightful ladies. All three have fluffy, white hair and sparkling blue eyes. They can be outrageous and perfectly exasperating, but they're also very sensible. One would think that a home with three mistresses would be topsy-turvy, but each has her own area of expertise. Aunt Winifred oversees the cleaning. My grandmother excels in food. My Great-aunt Daphne is talented with needle and thread."

"And what do you do?" she inquired in a tone of voice that sounded as if she believed him to be a useless drone in a hive of busy bees.

"I manage the estate," he said tersely. "I am attempting to make it pay, but its original purpose is long gone. No one needs such a fortress these days, and the land is rather poor for farming."

"Why waste your time on a nonprofitable proposition?"

A flash of anger burned through Kevin's veins. He gritted his teeth. "I believe that our evening has come to an end. I intend to seek my bed, for we have a long day of traveling tomorrow. I would advise you to do the same."

Before she had time to utter a single word, he strode from the room, leaving her to stew in her own juices. His new cousin was going to be a problem. Yes, Aunt Winifred would have a nonconforming, cheeky miss on her hands. He hoped she could tame the vixen. He himself would avoid Miss Samantha Edwards like the plague.

* * *

Samantha rose early, despite a night of tossing and turning which kept her awake into the wee hours. She didn't look forward to leaving the secure familiar Mermaid and Polly, and forging into the unknown with the arrogant Kevin Montjoy. The three elderly ladies sounded pleasant, but that was the earl's point of view. He was so terribly snobbish that he might approve of only those who were like himself. She still seethed at the high-handed manner in which he had treated Polly. What if her aunt behaved in a similar manner? Her mother had loved her Aunt Winifred, though, so that was a better reference. People could change, however. Her mother's recollections were set in Aunt Winifred's own home. Living with the earl and the two other women could have affected the lady's personality. Whatever would she do if she couldn't get along with her aunt?

Nerves on edge, Sam dressed and began packing her trunk. With all her heart, she wished she had never come to England. She should have remained in Ohio, in her cabin by the river, and kept up her father's store. By doing that, however, she would have been ignoring her mother's last request. She sighed. If she only had enough money to return to her home! But she didn't, not at the present.

There was a soft knock on the door. "Sam?" Polly called.

Bob, lying on the bed, lifted his lips and growled.

"Hush," she commanded. "It is Polly, and she is my friend." The cat ceased his warning, but sat up alertly.

"That's better," Sam approved, "but you truly do need to become a bit less suspicious."

Bob yawned and stretched, but he kept a wary eye on his mistress.

She hurriedly opened the door. "Oh, Polly, I am so glad to see you."

"What is wrong?" the innkeeper asked, entering the chamber and making sure that Samantha stood between herself and the lynx.

"I . . . my nerves are getting the better of me," she confessed with a trembling smile.

"You fear the earl?"

Sam bit her lip. "No . . . not really. Oh, I truly don't know! I don't fear him physically. I suppose I am frightened of being placed in a situation of which I have no control!"

"Set your fears at rest," Polly soothed. "You can always come to me."

"No." She firmly shook her head. "I could not presume upon our friendship."

"You wouldn't. I could use an assistant. As it is, I must be available twenty-four hours a day. I'm not growing any younger! I'd appreciate the help." She smiled kindly. "But you are a member of an important family. You must make an attempt to take your place in Society. While I would like to have you here, and to treat you as if your were my own daughter, I will not agree to it, until you convince me that you have given your family a chance."

Sam embraced her. "You are the best friend I ever had. What a fine day it was when Captain Greene brought me here."

The landlady hugged her in return. "I, too, am thankful. Now let us hope for the best. Are you packed and ready? The earl is already at breakfast and seems anxious to leave."

"I am almost ready. First, I must take Bob for his morning outing, then I'll go to breakfast." She moved away and closed the lid of her trunk. "Has Lord Montjoy asked for me?"

"He did. I told him that you must finish your packing and take out your cat. He seemed somewhat impatient, but accepted the news."

"Well, I'd best hurry. There is no point incurring his wrath." She picked up her reticule. "Polly, I would like to settle my bill."

The innkeeper smiled fondly. "You owe nothing."

"Yes, I do!" she protested. "Remember? Business is business, and friends are friends. I *will* compensate you."

Polly chuckled, shaking her head in wonderment. "We could charge the earl."

"I won't do that either." She rolled her eyes. "He already laments his lack of fortune. Ha! I don't believe that! Nevertheless, I do not wish to be beholden to him. What did you say I owed?"

"I didn't." Her friend held up her hands as if to ward off a blow. "I vow, Sam, that you are the most stubborn person I ever met. But very well! I'll prepare a statement of fees, a'd you can settle up later."

"Thank you." Sam picked up Bob's collar and leash. "Bob and I will take one last turn in your lovely garden. Won't you accompany us?"

Polly glanced at the bobcat, who lifted one side of his upper lip. "I must oversee the kitchen. I'll save my farewells for a later time."

Sam's eyes sparkled. "I do believe that Bob is beginning to accept you."

"Good heavens! I can hardly agree with that!" Polly whooped and laughingly departed.

The cat seemed to grin as Samantha put on his equipment. "Let us go, Bob. I hope Montjoy Castle has as pleasant a place to take our walks."

Bob leapt gracefully from the bed and padded toward the door. He and Sam left the room, descended the back stairs, and went outside into the garden. Morning mists still swirled, laying a light layer of moisture on Sam's face. The heavy, sweet scent of lily of the valley perfumed the air. Sam breathed deeply and wished she were in Ohio, smelling the rich, awakening earth, seeing the bursting blooms of the redbud, dogwood, and honey locust, and hearing the song of spring peepers. But alas, this was England, and the signs of spring in Polly's garden were much tamer.

She would have loved to spend more time there, but the sun had already burned away much of the fog. Kevin Montjoy would be chafing to leave. Reluctantly, she returned to the inn. Taking Bob to her chamber, she saw that her trunk had already been taken away. It was almost time to begin her final journey. Spirits sagging, she went down to the salon.

"Good morning." The earl half-rose, bowing.

"The same to you." She seated herself at the table and took a sweet bun from a large tray of breakfast pastries.

"Tea?" he asked.

"Yes." She watched as he filled her cup.

"Americans always have cream and sugar," he stated. "Is that not true?"

"This American doesn't." She sipped the warm brew and took a bite from the mouth-watering bun, chewing thoughtfully. "You know, I can scarcely believe how you arbitrarily assign national traits to us. You are a bigot, Lord Montjoy."

"That is not true," he protested. "But I don't intend to debate the issue. Are you ready to travel?"

"I am." She finished the bun and drained her cup. "I must go up to my room to fetch my bonnet and my cat."

"I did not intend to rush you," he said, eyeing her plate. "You haven't had much breakfast."

"It is all I want."

"Have it your way, but do not blame any mid-morning hunger spells on me."

"I wouldn't dream of it." Before he could stand to hold her chair, she hopped up and departed.

"Obstinate girl," she heard him say.

"Arrogant boy," she said loudly in retaliation and hastened through the door.

Polly was waiting at the bottom of the stairs to make her farewell. She threw her arms around Sam in a fierce hug. "I thought it best to do this when Bob is not present."

Samantha clung to her. "Think often of me. Do not forget me."

"I could never forget you, my dear." She stepped back and brushed a wisp of hair from Sam's brow. "I have a feeling that all will be well."

"I hope so. Now won't you tell me how much I owe?" she begged.

"Lord Montjoy paid."

"No!" Samantha wailed. "I will not allow it!"

"Then you had best settle the matter with him," she declared. "American girls may not pay heed to an earl's requests, but I assure you that we Englishwomen do."

Sam snorted. "We'll see about that!"

She climbed the steps to her room, collected Bob, and made her way back down again, the leash coiled around her hand for maximum control. The bobcat was restless, sensing a change in routine. When he saw Lord Montjoy, he lifted his lips and snarled viciously.

"What the hell is that?" the earl shouted.

Bob let forth a hideous growl, especially designed to startle prey into revealing their hiding places.

"Shh," Samantha hushed. "This is our new cousin, Bob. We must be polite."

"I repeat, what the—"

"I heard it the first time, Kevin," Sam informed him. "This is Bob, my pet."

"Pet?" he clamored. "That's a wild animal!"

"No, he is not. I have tamed him," she insisted. "I found him beside his dead mother when he was a kitten. His eyes were not even open! His litter mates were dead, too, and he was all alone. How could I walk away and leave him to his fate?"

"How indeed?" her cousin said dryly. "It must have been a tremendously difficult decision."

"You are teasing me." She laughed lightly. "Of course, it wasn't hard at all!"

"So you're bringing this beast to Montjoy Castle?"

"Certainly. What else could I do?" She smiled down at her bristling cat. "The two of us are inseparable."

"Charming, I'm sure." He frowned at Bob. "Do you intend to put him in the carriage with us?"

"Yes." She curiously cocked her head. "You aren't afraid of him, are you?"

"Of course not!" he snapped. "Who'd be afraid of a scrawny little cat?"

Sam beamed. "Excellent! I am sure you and Bob will get along quite well together."

"Oh, yes." He offered her his arm. "Shall we?"

It was time. Samantha turned to give Polly a final hug. "I shall write to you."

"Strive to be happy." The innkeeper patted her cheek.

"Let us go," commanded the earl. "We are already running late."

Sam moved to take his arm, but Bob gnashed his teeth so horribly that she was forced to decline the social nicety. She walked between Kevin and Bob, and tried to ignore Montjoy's disparaging glances and the cat's throaty growls. She hoped the two would settle down, once the journey commenced.

Her cousin's carriage, a shiny, black-lacquered one with the Montjoy crest emblazoned on the door, was awaiting them, its matching team of gray horses stamping and mouthing their bits.

The coachman touched the brim of his hat. "Morning, m'lord, and miss. The beasties are in fine fettle today."

"They're lovely," Sam admired, but again she was shocked by her cousin's spendthrift ways. The fine-blooded team had not come cheaply. How could Montjoy claim poverty, when he traversed the roads in this superb rig?

Wrapped in her thoughts, Sam did not notice that the horses were suddenly showing the whites of their eyes. In unison, the team leapt sideways, rocking the carriage. Bob yowled piercingly.

Kevin startled, too, jumping away from Samantha's side. Bob tried to run around her toward him, came to the end of his leash, flipped into the air, and fell on his back. The coachman dashed to the horses, waving his arms and frightening them further. It was only sheer luck that he and the groom were able to keep the animals from bolting.

"Enough!" Kevin shouted and pointed at Bob, who responded by cheerfully lifting his lips. "You, too, you beast from Hades!"

"Settle down," Sam declared. "The excitement has ended."

"I ought to shoot that animal," he threatened.

"You will be a sorry man if you do," she parried. "I will make you pay. Oh, yes, I will!"

"And just what are you going to do?" he scoffed. "You haven't the power to beat your way through a pasture of tall grass."

"You had better not try me, Kevin Montjoy," she warned. "If you lay a hand on me, this bobcat will tear you apart!"

"If I had the money," he ground out, "I'd turn right around and send you back to America."

"That certainly makes me feel welcome!" she shrilled.

They glared at each other, while Bob nonchalantly sat on his haunches and licked a paw.

"Look at him," Kevin said tightly. "Acting innocent as hell, after all that trouble he caused! Would you mind telling me how we're going to transport him in the coach? With terrified horses?"

"The horses will probably be more sprightly," Sam observed.

"Indeed. They will be *sprightly*. They'll be so damned sprightly that they'll run away, overturn the carriage, and kill us all."

"Please, Kevin, heed what I say," she implored, reaching down to scratch the cat's tufted ears. "Once we commence the journey, he will quiet. Shall I take him to the coach now?"

Kevin drew a deep breath and exhaled loudly and slowly. "All right, but if he misbehaves or creates trouble in any way, we'll have to put him in a crate or shoot him."

She narrowed her eyes. "You are being just awful about this."

"I thought I was being quite understanding." He signaled the coachman. "Hold on tightly to the horses, Clark! We're going to load him."

The servant stood agape. "We're takin' 'im?"

"Apparently so." Kevin shrugged.

"You'll see. He'll probably nap all the way," Sam assured, leading Bob toward the carriage.

The horses rolled their eyes and fidgeted, but did not shy. Sam boosted the cat up the step and into the vehicle. After briefly sniffing his surroundings, Bob leapt upon the rearward facing seat, circled, and lay down. Breathing a sigh of relief, Samantha followed, sitting opposite him. She leaned forward to look out.

"All is well now, Kevin!"

"Are you sure I can ride in there?" he asked.

She smiled mischievously. "Unless you are afraid."

"I am not!" he retorted. "I simply wish to keep the beast calm."

"I wonder," she mused. "Come right in, cousin."

Rather reluctantly, the earl softly entered his carriage. Bob stirred, baring his teeth and twitching his ears. He glowered suspiciously at the intruder.

"Shut up," Kevin ordered, seating himself. "If you will not bother me, I'll leave you alone. Just mind your own business, you miserable feline."

Bob merely stared fixedly at him.

"He is beginning to become accustomed to you," Sam pronounced.

"How happy I am to hear that!" he retorted. "How on earth did you bring him this far?"

"At times, I was required to give him a drink of rum and put him in a crate," Sam admitted, smiling. "He loves rum, but it quickly intoxicates him."

"Then why in the hell didn't you give him some this morning?" he demanded.

Her mirth faded. "I do not tolerate drunkenness in man or beast. Besides, I doubt if it's good for his system."

Kevin leaned out the coach window and called to his footman. "Go into the inn and procure a bottle of rum!"

The servant gaped at him, but hastened to follow the order. He returned shortly and handed the requisite spirits to Kevin. He held it out to Samantha.

"Give him enough to intoxicate him."

"I will not!" she exclaimed. "It isn't good for him!"

"Then I will, by God!" He pulled the cork and carefully

extended the bottle to the corner of Bob's mouth. The cat coughed, then swallowed and licked his lips.

"Now we'll have peace," Kevin chuckled. "That will knock him out."

It did.

Four

Bob was no trouble whatsoever, during the entire trip. The lynx began to stir around mid-morning, and over Samantha's protests, Kevin administered another dose of rum. His cousin was right in one respect. Bob truly loved his rum. The cat was vastly intelligent, too. When he woke up for the third time, yawning, stretching, and preening, just like a domestic cat, he looked squarely at Kevin and licked his lips. The earl picked up the bottle and uncorked it.

"Please do not do that," Samantha begged. "He has already had so much. It cannot be good for him."

"It will not be good for me, if I don't," he stated, eyeing the cat who seemed to grin conspiratorially at him.

"I don't know why you're worried about that," she countered. "He has obviously accepted your presence."

"Only because he's foxed," Kevin dryly observed.

"Foxed?" she asked. "What does that mean?"

"Drunk. Totally drunk!" He chuckled. "That wildcat has a rotten personality which can only be improved when he's tipsy."

"This is disgusting!" she snapped.

Ignoring her, Kevin extended the bottle to Bob, who grasped it in his mouth like a nursing kitten. Tilting it gently, so as not to choke him, Kevin dosed the animal with another large shot.

"That's enough!" Samantha pushed the bottle away from Bob's lips, earning a feline glare and a baring of teeth. "Now you see what you've done? He is angry with me."

"My dear cousin, there are some pleasures of life, which are best shared man-to-man."

"Ridiculous!" She pressed her lips together in a thin, fine line. "Aren't we going to stop for luncheon?"

"Certainly. There is an inn just ahead." He firmly recapped the bottle and pressed it into the squabs in the corner. "Are you hungry?"

"Not particularly. I was merely wondering about Bob's meal. How can he go in, if he is so terribly foxed? How can he manifest any appetite?"

Kevin regarded her with dread. "You can't mean to take him inside!"

She lifted a shoulder and gazed candidly at him. "I don't know how else to serve him. Besides, he should have exercise and the opportunity to answer nature's call."

His mind raced. He definitely did not want to take Bob into the inn and probably be forced to pay the landlord an extra sum for the privilege of it. He didn't even want to explain about the exotic creature. The cat made him look like a fool. What if someone he knew saw him catering to the beast as if it were a human child?

Thankfully, a marvelous idea came to mind. "I thought we could have our meal and ask the innkeeper to pack a portion for Bob. Then we could find a nice, pastoral place alongside the road for him to eat and stretch his legs in peace and quiet. He wouldn't be disturbed by the comings and goings of strangers. I'm sure he would be much happier and certainly more comfortable."

Samantha considered. "You're right, Kevin. That's an excellent plan!"

He exhaled in relief. "Then that is what we will do."

She nodded. "In fact, why don't we order a basket for ourselves as well? We can eat along the road, too."

Kevin disliked dining al fresco, even with tables set with the finest china, linens, and cutlery, and with a host of servants to assist. There were always flies, ants, and bees who attempted to partake along with the humans. The whole experience was fraught with shooing, brushing, and smacking.

"That would be so much fun," Samantha enthused.

He shrugged, "We would be more comfortable eating inside."

"I don't think so! And we'll save time by eating together." Her green eyes sparkled. "Please, Kevin, I would like it so very much."

"Very well," he groaned, "but I dislike eating outdoors. I can think of better things to do than to share my food with insects."

She glanced at him with disenchantment. "Then we shall do as you please."

He had the notion to do just that, but when they reached the inn, he experienced second thoughts. Ever since he had met his new cousin, he continually felt that he had to defend his masculinity. Perhaps it was because she was a product of the wild American frontier and had likely dealt with threats and hardships that he could scarcely imagine. Maybe it was because she was purely American and possessed the brassiness exhibited by the former colonists. It could stem from England's suffering military defeat at the hands of those upstarts. It could have been one of these, all of them, or even more. Nevertheless, he ordered a picnic hamper for himself and Samantha, the servants, and the bobcat.

Samantha was pleased by his decision, but she still seemed to look upon him with amusement, so he felt that he'd hardly impressed her. Why did that matter, anyway? Unfortunately for Aunt Winifred, she was not a little girl whom she could dress up and play with, like a living doll. Instead, she was a belligerent, opinionated wench, who would probably never be accepted by gentle society. She might have lived on the frontier, or in the country, whatever the barbaric Americans termed it, but she behaved like the rawest, most obnoxious Cit. Pondering those dark thoughts, he helped her into the carriage and placed the baskets on the seat by the slumbering Bob.

"You may look for a pleasant place to stop," he told her, entering the coach.

It wasn't long before she found one, a grassy spot on the banks of a babbling brook. "This is a pretty place! Get out and take the luncheon, Kevin, while I attempt to wake Bob. I wish you hadn't given him that rum. Now I shall have a difficult time."

"That's too bad, Samantha, but I don't like that cat. He is wild and dangerous; he has a rotten personality; and he'd be much happier if you'd turned him loose in the deep woods, before coming to England. A beast like that isn't meant to be a pet." With that, he exited from the coach, before she could speak out in rebuttal.

While Samantha was occupied, Kevin's servants assisted him in setting up for the picnic, bringing carriage robes from the coach and spreading them on the ground. Kevin opened the baskets and gave them their share of food and drink, and set the rest out for himself, Samantha, and Bob. Eventually, Samantha emerged half-dragging, half-carrying a yawning, stretching Bob.

"This is your fault, Kevin," she grumbled, huffing for breath.

"I wouldn't have worried about it. He looks fat enough to me, Samantha. Missing a meal or two shouldn't harm him," he said mildly.

Hearing the earl's voice, the cat pricked his tufted ears, licked his lips, and glided toward him.

"He associates you with a bottle of spirits," Samantha remarked irritably. "I forbid you to give him any more rum. *Ever.*"

"I would hope he was licking his lips in anticipation of a drink, and not a bite of my flesh," Kevin retorted. "You may be certain that, whenever I must deal with him in close quarters, I will ply him with liquor. I won't risk my neck to those teeth and claws."

She mumbled what might have been shocking expletives and sat down on a robe. Bob tippled over beside her, flopping his head in her lap. He looked like the perfect feline imitation of a man who'd been out on a spree. His fur was unkempt; his eyes were fixed and dull; his mouth was curved in a silly smile. Kevin laughed.

"I could just smack your face!" Samantha cried. "There is nothing funny about this! It's shameful."

"My dear cousin, can you not find any portion of amusement in this? I cannot believe that your sense of humor is so jaded."

"It is not *your* pet who is the butt of this ill attempt of a joke!" she snapped. "Now where is Bob's lunch?"

He proffered a package done up in butcher's wrap.

She opened it, wrinkling her pert nose. "It's a stinking old fish, and it's only half-cooked!"

Bob had a more positive attitude. He roused from his drunken stupor and tore into the big salmon. In his boisterous enthusiasm, he spewed flakes of meat onto Samantha's skirt and nearly knocked her backwards onto the ground.

"Help me!" she yelped, trying to push him away.

Kevin was not about to interfere with the beast's luncheon. Whoever did that would probably become a part of it. He poured himself a glass of mediocre wine and averted his gaze from the slovenly view.

To give Bob credit, he did try to clean up his mess, licking and pawing his mistress's skirt and tearing it in the process.

"Now see what he has done! Thank you, Kevin, for your assistance!"

"As you stated, he is not my pet." He began to nibble on a large, juicy chicken leg. "Are you certain you want me to look?"

"Oh, what shall I do?" she wailed. "My dress is ruined!"

Even the most ethical, moral gentleman could not have abstained from looking at her. From the corner of his eye, Kevin noted her dishevelment. She appeared as though she'd been dreadfully pummeled, and there was a long slit in her skirt which extended from just below her waist to her knees.

"You'd best change clothes," he suggested.

"Here?" she shrilled. "In the open air and broad daylight?"

"In the coach, you ninny. Tie that monster to a tree, go into the coach, and pull down the shades."

"But my clothes are in my trunk, which is tied onto the boot of the carriage!" She quickly gathered the folds of her gown to hide the rend.

"That is why we have servants, dear cousin," he said lightly, finishing the piece of chicken and reaching for another. "They'll fetch down your trunk."

"I wouldn't dream of putting them to all that trouble!" she gasped.

"Why not? That's what I'm paying them for."

She lifted her chin and stuck out her lower lip. "I won't do it."

"Suit yourself, Samantha. By the way, I would appreciate it if you would remove that animal from the vicinity of our lunch. I do not care to have him snatch my food away, or to eat cat hair."

"All right! I shall take him to the carriage," she spit out, "and I shall stay there, too!"

"As you wish. I will say, however, that if you had not intended to dine al fresco, I believe it would only have been polite if you would have told me, especially when I informed you that I did not like the outdoor dining environment."

"I did plan to eat," she declared, rising, "but you have ruined it for me."

"Madam, your cat did that," he countered. "I am not to blame. I did everything you requested."

She made a sound akin to her feline's growl. Holding her skirt together with one hand and Bob's leash in the other, she tried to stalk away without a reply, but the cat prevented it. Having awakened from his lassitude, he decided it might be nice to take a walk. Ignoring Samantha's desires, he set off toward the stream, pulling his mistress behind him.

Chuckling to himself, Kevin watched her go, pretending that a stroll was her wish as well. Poor Samantha was having a difficult time. At the moment, he guessed that she was greatly cast down, but he had no doubt that she would regain her spirit and return to being as frustrating as ever. His new cousin was challenging. It was most entertaining to match wits with her. He only hoped that he could always come out on top. This upstart American girl could not get the best of him!

He watched her meander along the stream, following after her wild beast. A new thought bludgeoned his mind. Samantha was rather attractive. What if a friend of his saw the aggravating miss and fell for her? Then he'd be stuck with encountering her for the rest of his or her life! He wanted her to go back to America. She belonged among those thankless, rebellious expatriates, and not in his mannerly, sophisticated country.

Frowning, he brushed away an encroaching ant and waved a fly away from his luncheon. No matter what the future held, he was stuck with her for what would probably be a lengthy time. He would just have to make the best of it.

Chin resting on her hand, and the other hand holding her skirt together, Sam stared out at the passing scenery. England was a beautiful country. It was so very green. That was what she noticed the most. America and her land on the Ohio were green, too, of course, but they didn't come close to the special, rich color of this country. Perhaps it was because it was spring, a time when England seemed to be engulfed in morning mist and frequent drizzles. Well, she would learn as the season progressed. She would not ask Kevin because, frankly, she had cut off her nose to spite her face, where he was concerned. She should have changed clothes when he'd advised her to. Now, she must greet her Aunt Winifred, for the very first time, in shocking dishabille. Or did she?

She cast her gaze sideways and perused her cousin through her lashes. So far, she'd enjoyed remarkable luck in getting her way with him. She might be able to do it once more.

"Kevin?" she asked. "How far away are we from Montjoy Castle?"

"We will arrive in time for a late supper." He looked her up and down, then grinned. "Are you waiting in breathless anticipation?"

She favored him with what she hoped was a hideously sour expression.

"Are you hungry?" he asked with a gloat.

Sam swiftly decided it might be best to play upon his sympathy, and allow him the privilege of being correct. She smiled prettily. "Yes, Kevin, I feel rather empty. I should have partaken of lunch."

He gestured toward the baskets. "There you are. Plenty is left. Just help yourself!"

To Hades with him! She eyed him pitifully. "I fear the food might be spoiled by now."

"Oh, I doubt it. It hasn't been so very long."

She bit her lip. "I have to stop at an inn to change my dress. You are right, Kevin. I should have changed earlier in the coach."

He considered.

Sam's temper flared, but she succeeded in keeping it hidden. Her newfound cousin absolutely infuriated her. He was rubbing in whatever he felt was necessary to rub in, and there was nothing she could do about it, but play along with it until his abominable masculinity was assuaged. She clenched her teeth. She disliked using feminine wiles, but she'd discovered, quite by accident, that they worked on American men. Would they work on an English lord? He might be an earl, but he was also a man.

She batted her eyelashes and laid a hand on his forearm. "Please, Kevin."

He looked rather surprised.

"Please," she repeated urgently.

"Really, Samantha," he said at last. "It seems ridiculous to pay for a room in order for you to perform an act which could well be accomplished in this carriage."

"It will not be an easy task," she murmured. "Neither will I have a mirror."

He smiled. "I shall be your mirror, Samantha. I'll judge your appearance."

She caught the flesh of her inner lip between her teeth and pinched it, to keep from erupting. He was being vengeful. He was trying to subordinate her. Never once did she believe that his true reason for flaunting her request was a lack of money. No matter what he claimed, no one in such circumstances lived as well as he seemed to do. He was merely finding enjoyment in scorning her pleasant appeal. For this reason, stopping at an inn grew into a matter of gigantic proportion. She cast her gaze downward and delivered her greatest volley.

"Cousin, I must use the *facilities* of an inn."

He looked rather frantic for a moment. Sam wished she could allow her glee to burst forth. She had provided him with a first-time experience. The earl must have never been in control of a lady's opportunity to perform bodily functions. He was totally nonplused.

"Very well," he said soberly, his cheeks somewhat flushed. "You should have told me that, in the beginning."

"It is not a suitable topic for discussion," she airily chided.

"But I am your cousin."

"It doesn't matter. You are still an adult member of the opposite gender." She bent her head and primly folded her hands, hoping she looked demure. "Besides, even though you are my relative, I am not well acquainted with you. Also, you are only my cousin by marriage, not by blood."

"Does that make a great deal of difference?" he queried, and something in his voice told Sam that he just might be inwardly laughing at her.

"Yes, it does," she said archly.

If he was amused, he did not slip and expose it. He opened the window between the coach's interior and the box, and solemnly gave the order to stop. He sat back against the squabs.

"I am unaccustomed to traveling with ladies."

"You live with ladies. Don't you ever take them anywhere?" she asked.

"No." He shook his head. "There isn't money for travel."

There it was again! He certainly was adamant about his financial standing. Did he think she had come to England to avail herself of his fortune?

"Kevin, I do not wish to take a shilling of your money," she avowed. "I will get a job and support myself, while saving money for my return trip to America. I shall even do better. I'll provide for Aunt Winifred's keep!"

"Don't be ridiculous," he bit back. "What could you do? Nothing!"

"Well, it seems to me that someone in this family must seek employment. Apparently, you won't do it!"

"It isn't done! It isn't done! It isn't done!" he shouted. "How many times must I tell you? When am I going to get it through your thick American head that this family has a position to uphold?"

She lifted her chin and pursed her lips. "If all you say is true, this family has already gone downhill. There is, no longer, a *position!*"

He leaned back his head and rolled his eyes, looking upward toward the roof of the carriage. "Lord, give me patience."

"I doubt that the Lord is interested in helping anyone who refuses to help himself . . . or someone who is not telling the whole truth," she stated.

"Samantha, I am telling the truth, and for your information, I am trying to do something about this foul situation."

She raised an eyebrow. "And just what is that?"

"I am trying to make the estate more productive."

She nodded. That was reasonable. She was no stranger to improving the land. In addition to operating the little store, her parents had worked on their large piece of acreage. Especially in late years, Sam had helped them fell the big trees, burn out the stumps, and till the soil. But England had been settled for centuries. There wouldn't be work of that kind. Perhaps the ground was worn out.

"And," he continued, "more importantly, I am attempting to wed an heiress."

Sam eyed him with horror. It was her turn to send aloft a prayer. "Oh, God," she groaned.

Kevin's lips curved in a half-smile. "That is the customary way of repairing one's fortune. Many men proceed to run through their wife's money, but I would make careful investments, so that it would continue to grow."

"You mean you would marry just *anybody,* so long as she had wealth?" she gasped. "You are serious about this?"

"Yes, I owe it to the title and to our august family history."

"I have never heard anything so outlandish!" she cried. "No title is worth that! You are mad, Kevin."

"Now see here, Samantha," he said severely. "I am telling you the facts, and you'd best believe them. Furthermore, I'll wager that the same thing is done in America."

"Not to my knowledge!"

He lifted a shoulder and let it fall. "Well, I won't argue about it. Suffice it to say that I am going to do it, and currently, that's the only thing that matters."

She gaped at him. If this was what he intended, he should have no difficulty procuring his heiress. Kevin was handsome. Breathtakingly so! Heiresses must be absolutely fighting for his hand. The whole idea made her rather ill. He would go to the highest bidder, no matter what kind of person she was, or what she looked like. It was perfectly awful, which made her wonder, once more, if he was actually telling the truth.

He continued to smile ruefully. "I am already paying serious court to one such lady. I believe she'll have me."

"Who wouldn't?" she blurted.

"Goodness, Samantha, are you actually complimenting me?" He laughed.

"I am merely stating fact," she proclaimed. "You are a marvelously handsome man, Kevin, a fact I'm sure you know. Therefore, who wouldn't want to marry you?"

"Many wouldn't, I'm sorry to say," he told her. "The beautiful, desirable heiresses go to handsome, wealthy, titled gentlemen."

She frowned. "Are you telling me that you must accept second-best?"

He shrugged. "Yes, I suppose I am. Lady Frances has been on the Marriage Mart for several years. She isn't the best to look at. She has a rather difficult personality and manner. *But* she has a dowry of thousands, and every year she remains a spinster, her father ups the ante."

"I hate her," Sam flatly announced.

"You don't even know her."

"I don't care. I despise her anyway! We must think of a better solution." She nodded emphatically. "I will think of something."

"Samantha," he warned, "don't you dare do a thing to spoil this match. I've practically jumped through hoops for that woman, and I do not intend for it to have gone for naught."

"There must be a better answer," she mused, as if she had not heeded his warning.

"Samantha! Stay out of this!"

"Do you want to marry her?" she asked.

"It isn't a question of want," he stressed. "It's a matter of *need*. I won't have you meddling in my life. Do you understand me?"

She sighed. "Yes, Kevin, but if you could find a preferable solution, wouldn't you try it?"

"Yes, but there isn't. Also, my attentions to Lady Frances have become marked. As a gentleman, it is my duty to follow through," he explained. "It is a point of honor."

"It seems to me that Englishmen must be too overly concerned with some self-imposed, absurd chivalry, and not enough committed to their own well-being." She smiled smugly. "Perhaps that is why you English lost your war with us. Your soldiers were too occupied with being gentlemen."

"Cousin Samantha," he growled. "I have heard enough. You will cease making proclamations about concerns you do not understand, else I'll put you up on the box to ride with the coachman and bring down the footman to ride with me."

"No, you wouldn't," she couldn't keep from gouging one final time. "It wouldn't be *gentlemanly*."

* * *

At last accepting that Kevin told the truth about his finances, although suspicious that he spent money needlessly, Sam came up with a way to save the earl's coin and still have a room in which to change her gown and refresh herself without being forced to undertake it in the carriage alongside the road. She kept on the alert for a likely farmhouse, and when her cousin dozed, she ordered the coachman to stop at one such place. By the time Kevin woke up, she was out of the coach and had been welcomed by the farmer's wife, who was greatly impressed and more than enthused to be the hostess of an earl and his cousin. Sam had the feeling that Kevin was furious, but it was too late for him to do anything about it. The good woman had already taken Samantha under her wing and had sent to the fields for the farmer, so that he might act as host to the earl. Wisely, Sam left Bob full of rum and sleeping soundly in the carriage.

The stop took only a bit more time than if they had stopped at an inn. Armed with a chess pie and a bottle of the farmer's best home-brewed ale, they were on their way in the midst of waving and well-wishes. Sam felt rather proud of her ingenuity. She had saved money and still attained a goal. The farm family seemed to have had the experience of a lifetime.

Kevin had other ideas. "Don't you ever do that to me again, Samantha."

"I see nothing wrong with it. In Ohio—"

"This is not some damned wild frontier, Samantha. Until you are thoroughly grounded on the proper social ramifications and the duties of a young lady of your station, you had best ask before you act," he chided. "But even with an American democratic mind, you should be aware that an earl and his family do not seek the company of farmers."

"You have a country estate. You are a farmer," she challenged.

"Oh, for God's sake!"

"Kevin, you are a great snob," she informed him, smoothing her clean skirt. "I thought the Lees were very pleasant people. And did I not hear you and Mr. Lee avidly discussing topics of agriculture? I thought you might be learning something."

"That is beside the point."

"And they refused to be paid for our use of their facilities. Indeed, they (especially Mrs. Lee) seemed terribly in awe of you. They will tell of our visit for years. It will go down in their family annals." She sighed and shook her head in wonderment. "I can scarcely believe that people can be so worshipful of a title. In America—"

"I wish you would leave off comparisons," he interrupted. "This is England, not America, and sure as hell not that damned wilderness you call Ohio! We are civilized here!"

Sam sniffed. "Is that what you call it? I have a few names of my own for it. *Pretentious* comes to mind, as well as *arrogant* and *vain.*"

The earl exhaled loudly. "Samantha, I am not responsible for instituting this country's social system. I am what I am, and I attempt to conduct myself as expected. If my countrymen choose to stand in awe of my title, and therefore, of me, I cannot help it, and I am weary of your blaming me. Now, that is enough."

She fell silent, not because she was thoroughly digesting the practice of English protocol. Mainly, she was still amazed at the deference with which the Lees had treated the earl. It was beyond all belief.

She lay her head against the squabs and watched the passing scenery. England was bursting with the promise of spring. Fields were tilled, brown now, but soon to be green with seedlings. Fruit trees were heavily flowered. Blossoms cheered the lawns.

A wave of homesickness sloshed over her. She could practically smell the rich earth of Ohio, and see its bounty of wildflowers such as spring beauties, bloodroot, mayapple. Would Montjoy Castle be as charming? She somehow doubted it. The very word castle conjured up a vision of cold, bleak stone. Built for war, it would be a very masculine place. She dozed off, thinking of formidable fortresses, unsoftened by flowers and shrubbery, and of her future way of life in such a fearful abode.

Five

"Samantha?"

"No, Kevin," she murmured semiconsciously, pushing herself more deeply into the carriage's squabs and attempting to recover and continue the dream she'd been having, a vivid fantasy of handsome, muscular frontiersmen descending upon her father's store.

"Samantha!" This time Kevin nudged her, not too gently, in the ribs. "Wake up. We're almost home."

The stalwart frontiersmen disappeared. Sam yawned, and straightened, and yawned again. "How far?"

"Just up ahead."

She blinked the sleep from her eyes and snapped to the alert, her mind banishing the attractive fur traders and fastening on the moment almost at hand. Soon, she would meet her Aunt Winifred and the rest of the elderly ladies, and the thought of it was rather unsettling. Encountering Kevin had not posed such a challenge. He had come along unexpectedly, so she hadn't the time to become nervous. Now, she did, and her heart began pounding swiftly, in anticipation. Would her aunt be happy to see her . . . or disappointed? According to Kevin, her relative thought she was a little girl, and certainly not a grown woman. Aunt Winifred probably had other plans for her, such as playing with dolls and the like. Ah, it wouldn't be long until she learned the lady's reaction. She saw high stone walls looming ahead.

"Is that Montjoy Castle?" she asked, somewhat breathlessly.

Kevin nodded. "Yes, but I don't think you'd actually consider it a true castle, now. When its purpose as a fortress became obsolete, my ancestors cut larger windows, filled the moat, partitioned a number of overly large rooms, and lowered ceilings, making it into more of a comfortable country house. Of course, it still retains some of its medieval ambiance."

Sam gazed out the window as they drew ever closer. Montjoy Castle was a huge place, the biggest house she'd ever seen, but it didn't look cold or unwelcoming. The walls were warmly bathed in the setting sun, the window panes sparkling like thousands of diamonds. On a pool in front, a marble swan rose up and stretched its wings. She could never say that the place was homey, but she couldn't call it intimidating either.

"What do you think?" her cousin asked, as if he truly cared about her opinion.

"It's fascinating," she pronounced. "I hope you will allow me to explore its every nook and cranny."

"You may do whatever you wish."

"Thank you!" she enthused. With such a marvelous place to live, perhaps Kevin had some slight reason to be arrogant. She might be able to forgive him a bit.

She glanced at him and caught him staring at her instead of his castle. A sense of panic dashed through her mind. "Do I look rumpled and . . . and awful?"

He shook his head. "You'll do, but you seem terribly nervous."

"I so badly want Aunt Winifred to like me," she confessed. "And first impressions are so important."

"Aunt Winifred is easy to know. You shouldn't have any difficulties, unless you decide to pick an argument, which seems to be a favorite sport of yours." He lifted one corner of his mouth in a cynical smile. "In short, don't be so opinionated, and don't continually compare England to America. It's vastly irritating."

Sam tossed her head. "Perhaps you bring that about by being so opinionated yourself."

"Nonsense," he proclaimed. "You deliberately draw my fire."

"Oh, you are so very frustrating, Cousin." She leaned forward, picked up her hat from the seat where Bob lay, and settled it on her head.

"You are hell-bent on having the last word," he accused. "You seem to delight in being at odds with me. Now there's an end to it! Period. No more. Enough."

"Hm!" she snapped. "I wonder who exactly demands the last word."

The earl ignored her and reached for the bottle of rum. Bob, somehow sensing that a treat was in store, opened his eyes and stretched. A silly smile seemed to turn up his lips.

"No!" Sam cried. "That isn't necessary!"

"You want to make a good impression on Aunt Winifred, don't you?"

"Of course I do, but . . ."

"She won't think much of a snarling, growling wildcat," he gloated, uncorking the bottle. "You had best keep him docile. No one could mistake him for a domestic cat, but if he does not make himself troublesome, he should be accepted."

Bob stood on the seat, reaching his head toward the earl and actually purring.

"This is outside of enough! That liquor cannot be good for him." Helplessly furious, Sam watched her pet down a large gulp of rum. This drink, on top of all the others he'd guzzled today, would be sure to make him exceedingly tipsy. He'd probably stagger into the castle like a dedicated, feline sot. It was totally embarrassing.

Kevin lifted an expressive shoulder. "The rum may not be good for him, but it is for me. It seems as though he is developing a tolerance for me in exchange for a belt of spirits. That, indeed, is very healthy for me. I don't relish becoming a part of his meal."

"That is ridiculous," Sam retorted.

Kevin considered. "You are correct. I'm too big for the size of his stomach. It would take him several days to polish me off."

Bob reached for more, but Kevin stoppered the bottle. The cat narrowed his eyes into burning slits and glared. He extended his paw and batted at the rum. The earl chuckled, reopened the bottle, and gave him one final, small sip, then put the drink away.

Samantha eyed him disparagingly and turned back to the window. They were fast approaching the castle, and it seemed to loom larger and larger. She knew she was gaping like a perfect bumpkin, but she just couldn't help it. She, Samantha Edwards, would live in a home such as this? It was beyond her wildest dreams.

She glanced from the corner of her eye at the earl. He, too, was staring fixedly at Montjoy Castle. He was seemingly entranced by his own home. He truly did love it, she suddenly realized, and that made him much more human.

She smiled faintly, studying his profile. Her cousin was a very handsome man. It was a terrible shame that he'd go to an unchosen, undesirable heiress. He should wed a beautiful, vibrant woman, who could match the splendor of his magnificent castle and whose wit was as razor-sharp as his own.

As if he could physically feel her perusal of him, he turned. "What do you think?"

"Breathtaking," she replied, almost giggling at the fact that it was his face she spoke of and not the castle. Rather awkwardly, she put the collar and leash on Bob. Her tête à tête with Kevin had ended. She was somewhat sorry that she'd spent so much time of it in argument. She should have asked him more about The Connection and the daily life at Montjoy.

The carriage swept through the arched gate house with its threatening lions rampant and passed into a lush, green courtyard. Once again, Sam found herself in awe of the place. "Oh, Kevin, it is glorious, to say the least. There are simply no words to express what I feel."

He smiled proudly. "I'm glad you like it, Samantha."

"I cannot believe that any place in England could match it," she waxed on. "It must be very unique."

"It is considered to be remarkable, primarily for the way my forebears remodeled it into a comfortable country seat. But I wish . . ." His proud smile changed to a rueful one. "I wish I had the money to refurbish it. You will find that it looks a bit down at the heels."

Sam truly decided that Kevin's financial position was probably as dismal as he had said. Her cousin thought too much of Montjoy Castle to leave it wanting. She laid her hand on his forearm.

"Perhaps something can be done to improve matters," she ventured thoughtfully.

"Something will be done," he said bitterly. "I'll marry Lady Frances."

"No-o-o-o, something *else.* There must be another way."

"Samantha, you had best stay out of this," he warned, casting her a suspicious scowl. "You do not understand the situation."

"I realize that there is usually more than one way to solve a problem." She patted his arm and prepared to depart as the carriage drew closer to the castle.

"I'm telling you," he said worriedly. "Stay out of it!"

"I hear you." She shifted her gaze to the front of the castle and saw three elderly ladies, along with a number of servants, anxiously awaiting their arrival. "Is that The Connection?"

He grinned fondly. "Indeed so, and they are the three most wonderful ladies you'd ever expect to meet."

She briefly and covertly studied the scene through her lashes. The formidable castle, the very proper English ladies, the body of servants . . . It all seemed suddenly so very unreal. Her pulse hammered in her ears. Could she ever hope to fit in?

The carriage drew to a halt. A footman let down the steps and opened the door. The moment of arrival had come.

"I'm nervous," Sam burst out, voice trembling.

"You'll be fine." Kevin got out and reached for her hand. The hand she extended, however, was the one holding Bob's leash. He backed up. "No, thank you, Samantha."

"Oh, dear, I suppose I'd best leave him here until introductions are made." She tossed the leash aside, took his hand, and stepped down.

The ladies stared wide-eyed at her.

"This is Samantha?" gasped the tall, slender, white-haired one.

Sam's heart pounded uncomfortably as she remembered that they'd expected a little girl. They were disappointed! There was no pretty, dainty child, whom they could cuddle and read stories to. There was only a great, grown woman, who would be no fun at all. She wished that a large crevice would open in the ground and swallow her up forever.

"This is Samantha," Kevin assured them. "Isn't she lovely?"

She could have kissed him. Despite their tiffs, he was trying to make her welcome, and he wasn't being arrogant at all. She positively owed it to him to help his financial situation, so that he wouldn't have to marry that awful Lady Frances. Surely, she could think of something!

"You will find Samantha to be most charming," he rattled on. "I've quite enjoyed the time we've spent together."

"I . . . I, too. Kevin told me you were expecting someone younger," she managed. Suddenly realizing that she still clasped the earl's hand, she let it go, flushing.

"I was a fool!" the tall woman suddenly exclaimed. "Of course you would be a young lady! This just goes to show how time flies by so quickly for one of my age. Samantha, my dear, I am your Aunt Winifred."

Sam stepped into her embrace. "I hope I am truly not disappointing."

"No, no, how could you be? You are my dearest Elizabeth's daughter." She patted her back. "I am so happy that you are here."

"Don't be so one-sided, Winifred," the striking, silver-haired woman declared. "You told us we could share your little girl."

Laughing, Sam's Aunt Winifred stood back. "Samantha, this is my sister-in-law and Kevin's grandmother, Margaret, Lady Montjoy."

"How do you do?" Sam said politely.

"Curtsy," said Aunt Winifred.

"What?" she asked.

"Do not forget to curtsy. Margaret is a countess."

"Oh." Sam swiftly pondered the correct way to execute the maneuver.

"It is not necessary." Lady Montjoy laughed. "Samantha, I welcome you and hope you will come to love Montjoy Castle as much as we do."

"She will not be here long." The third lady moved forward for an introduction. "We must find her a handsome young man to wed! Samantha, I am Margaret's sister, Daphne, and you need not curtsy!"

Sam smiled at them. "I am so happy to know you, and I'm glad I needn't curtsy, for truthfully, I don't know how. And frankly, I'm not anxious to marry."

"But every young lady your age must find a husband," Aunt Winifred insisted. "It is your duty."

Once again, Kevin came to her rescue. "Samantha has just come to our country. I'm sure she wishes to learn a great deal more about it, before she takes such a serious step."

"Yes," Sam echoed. "I am rather overwhelmed by it all. I must become accustomed, before making important decisions."

"But we will make the decision," Aunt Winifred pronounced. "We shall decide whom you will marry, my dear, just as our families chose for us."

Sam's heart leapt to her throat, and she knew that her facial expression must reflect her horror. "My mother wed whom she wished."

"Yes, well . . ." Aunt Winifred looked uncomfortable. "It was the greatest good fortune that she remained happily in love. Seldom is there such a felicitous result. So it is best to abide by the old way."

Sam could scarcely believe that she was faced by such a dilemma before she even became well acquainted with the residents of Montjoy Castle. She was tempted to change the subject. That would be the easiest way to avoid the issue, but it also could lead to false hopes or awkward situations.

"I shall choose my own husband," she emphasized firmly, "if indeed I decide to wed."

"But that is not the best way—" Aunt Winifred murmured.

"Times have changed. Many marriages aren't arranged today," Kevin broke in. "Samantha, it might be well to exercise your cat. He's been cooped up so long."

"Yes, I shall." She smiled her gratitude. Returning to the carriage, she picked up Bob's leash and led him out.

When The Connection saw him, there were universal outcries.

"That isn't a normal cat," Kevin's grandmother observed. "It's not the kind of cat we have in England."

"Perhaps it's an American version," Aunt Winifred guessed.

"He is a bobcat," Sam explained. "I found him in the woods when he was an orphaned kitten."

Bob, still under the influence of alcohol, tried to lift his lips and show his teeth, but he only managed a simpering grin.

Kevin chuckled. "He's a wildcat, Grandmama."

"He doesn't look very wild to me," she proclaimed.

The earl grinned. "He's intoxicated."

"What?" she cried.

"I got him drunk on rum. It improves his personality."

"Kevin, for shame!" she scolded merrily.

"Indeed," Sam darkly agreed. "If you will excuse me, I shall attempt to drag him along to the grass."

Lady Montjoy tittered.

Sam hurried Bob across the courtyard, tears suddenly prickling her eyes. Her introduction to the denizens of Montjoy Castle hadn't gone well. No matter how much they had tried to conceal it, Aunt Winifred and the other ladies had been disappointed that she was all grown up. Then, they hadn't been happy about her independent attitude where marriage was concerned. In short, she wasn't at all what they'd hoped for.

A tear slid down her cheek. She hadn't enough money to go home, and apparently, no one here could lend it to her. Even if they did, she had no real means to pay them back. She must brazen it out here in England. Perhaps she could find a way to earn money to pay for her passage to America, along with a small amount to live on, until she was established in . . . what?

Bob pulled on the leash, forcing her to cease her march. Turning, she stared at Montjoy Castle. Only a short while ago, it had seemed like a beautiful place to be, an exciting adventure. Now it was like a prison. It looked stark, cold, and forbidding.

"Come, Bob." She jerked on the line. "Let us go outside this confined compound."

Bob, now a bit more alert, trotted along beside her as Samantha hastened toward the gate house.

"I don't know what to think," Aunt Winifred murmured unhappily, watching her niece and the overgrown cat half-run to the greensward beyond the castle precincts.

"I fear we didn't properly welcome her," Kevin's grandmother mused.

"You're right, Margaret," his quiet Great-aunt Daphne ventured. "We were not hospitable."

"I'm ashamed of you!" Kevin heard himself burst out. "Samantha feels alone, and strange, and vulnerable. She was nervous about this meeting, and now you've shown her that she was right in feeling that way. That talk of marriage! I'm sure she is certain that you cannot wait to get rid of her."

"Oh, dear," Aunt Winifred moaned. "What shall we do to make up for it? Shall I go after her?"

In the first place, Kevin couldn't see the elderly Winifred going after the lithe Samantha and her bobcat, let alone catching up with her. Secondly, he doubted that Sam would be very pleased to encounter her aunt, and he knew that Bob definitely wouldn't. The cat was probably sobering up just now.

"I believe it's best to leave her alone for a while," he advised.

"Yes, well, let us see to her baggage," she said. "My, we must change her room, too. We'd assigned her to the nursery."

"Let us give her the Rose Room," Lady Montjoy suggested.

"It's quite suitable for a young lady, and it's not so terribly raggle-taggle."

"Yes, let's," Daphne seconded, "and we'll add a bouquet to cheer her."

"That will be fine." Samantha's great-aunt smiled at Kevin. "Where is her abigail, dear boy?"

"She doesn't have one."

"Doesn't have an abigail!" she shrilled with shock. "Did she travel all the way from America without a chaperon?"

"Apparently." He shrugged. "At least, she had none when I made her acquaintance. I didn't think to inquire."

"I can scarcely believe it! How can she be so naive?" Winifred slowly shook her head and looked speakingly at the other women. "Goodness, but we have so much to teach her."

"I would go easy on that," Kevin said, watching Samantha in the distance as she meandered around the pond, with Bob sniffing the foliage. "This is all so very new to her. Allow her the freedom to adjust at her own speed."

"You speak as if you know her quite well." His grandmother keenly eyed him, watching as well as listening for his response.

"There was a great deal of time for conversation . . . all the way from Portsmouth, and of course, the evening before." He looked at The Connection, who were gazing at him with eyes full of speculation. "What are you thinking?"

The three smiled mischievously.

"Oh, no, you don't." He lifted his hands as if to ward off a blow. "Don't try to matchmake. You know I have to wed Lady Frances. I have to wed money, and Samantha is as poor as a church mouse. She's also opinionated and totally exasperating."

When their naughty smiles did not fade, he turned away. "I am going to the library to check over my mail before dressing for dinner. If you don't wish to wait for Samantha, you should post a footman to do so, in order that she might be shown to her room and apprised of our mealtime hour."

Without waiting for a response, Kevin went inside and sought his private domain. The Connection seldom bothered him here.

He was free to engage in such masculine activities as drinking spirits or smoking a cigar. This time, he did neither, however, sitting down at his desk to sort through his mail. Right on top was a letter from Lady Frances. Surprised that she had the nerve to be terribly forward and challenge propriety, he picked up a letter opener and broke the seal, pulling out a rather overwhelmingly perfumed sheet of stationery. With a feeling akin to distaste, he perused the missive.

Lady Frances was having a delightful time at a house party in Derbyshire. He doubted that. She was not the type of young lady who enjoyed such an informal gathering as he knew the Craycrofts would host.

Lady Frances missed the honor of his company. That was probably true. No one else would dance attendance on her.

Lady Frances hoped to see him very soon. He imagined she did, but he doubted she'd get her wish. He had too much work to do on the estate to go larking about, socializing. She might not understand his reason, but her father would, and that was of more importance. He could easily make up with the lady. Aside from other, less promising, fortune hunters, there was no competition for her hand.

Fortune hunter. He disliked the term, but it exactly described him. The practice had gone on for centuries. He wished he could be more selective, like other more fortunate men, but he had no choice. Lady Frances must repair his finances.

He put down the letter and glanced out the diamond-paned window. Dusk was falling. He should freshen up for dinner. He wondered if Samantha had returned to the castle. Perhaps he should find out.

Outside the front door, he discovered a footman yet waiting. "She hasn't come back?"

"No, my lord. The lady is still sitting by the pond."

"You may go back to your duties. I shall tend to the matter."

"Yes, my lord." He bowed and went inside.

Striding vigorously, Kevin crossed the courtyard and passed through the arched gate. Bob saw him before Samantha did and watched his approach, sniffing the air and twitching his tufted ears. Samantha looked up.

"Hello, Kevin. I suppose I am late."

He stopped a safe distance from the cat. "If you are, then so am I, and at Montjoy Castle, the earl is never tardy."

"Such feudal majesty," she commented in a vestige of her former pert tongue, but she did not appear very saucy. "You may come closer. He is growing accustomed to you."

He edged around on the other side of the bobcat and sat next to her on the bench. "Are you all right?"

"I don't know if I am or not," she candidly replied. "It didn't go well, did it?"

"I've seen better welcomings."

"It's my fault." She bleakly fingered the leash and stared into the water. "It's all my fault, and now I've started off on the wrong foot."

"I don't think that the blame should be fixed on you," he soothed. "It isn't your fault that you are a young lady instead of a child. Those darling old hens are of the age when they speak before thinking. Furthermore, Aunt Winifred should have known your age. She must be growing senile."

"Perhaps," she said, her voice dull with gloom, "but I should have held my tongue concerning that husband business."

He chuckled.

"It isn't funny, Kevin!" She irritably tucked back a loose strand of hair, exposing a tear track on her cheek. "I suppose I was rude."

He shook his head. "You were correct in expressing your opinion. It was best not to allow them to embark upon plans that could not be carried out."

"Maybe." She sighed. "But oh, Kevin, what am I to do? They are probably very aggravated with me."

"Not at you, Samantha. At themselves. When I got through with them, they were greatly cast down."

"You stood up for me?" She took his hand and squeezed it.

"Thank you, especially since I have caused you so much torment."

He laughed and impulsively planted a kiss on her knuckles. "I hope you will continue to do so. Your plaguing is greatly preferable than your dejection."

She managed a fleeting smile. "It is kind of you to say so."

"No, it isn't. It's selfish. I rather enjoy bandying words with you." Keeping her hand, he rose. "Come now. Let us return to the castle. We've just enough time to ready ourselves for dinner. I may never officially be late, but at the present, I happen to be starving."

She stood. "Far be it from me to cause your death from malnutrition. Bob? Let us go and see what a real castle looks like."

"It isn't . . ." he began, with an apology for the condition of the interior uppermost in his mind. "Frankly, its decor is shabby. I believe I already know you well enough, however, to trust that you have the imagination to see what it could be, if one had access to enough money."

"I am sure it will be marvelous. I've never seen a castle, much less lived in one, so I will positively be thrilled." She smiled up at him. "Thank you for coming out after me. Going in alone would have taken a great deal of nerve, of which I currently seem to be in short supply."

"A footman was waiting to guide you," he assured her.

"Still, this was best. And you cheered me up, too."

She continued to clasp his hand as they strolled across the greensward. Kevin wondered if they should engage in this contact. It was rather romantical, and he was not available for romance. Well, officially he was unattached, but essentially he was not. Yet, he was not giving Samantha false expectations. She was fully aware of his need to marry wealth. Besides, they were cousins, even if their actual relationship was only by marriage. Moreover, she had been through so much difficulty. He couldn't help giving her hand a swift squeeze.

Again, she smilingly looked up. "Kevin, you are being so sweet to me. I truly do appreciate it."

He grinned. "Remember that when you regain your confidence and decide to cut up stiff."

She innocently batted her eyes. "Do I do that?"

"Vixen! You know you do."

"Vixen," she mused. "I wonder if a fox would be a good pet."

"No!" he cried. "Bob is enough! Another pet would make him jealous."

"I suppose you are right," she agreed, but her eyes danced merrily.

"Would you look at this!" Winifred said in awe, gaping out the window.

Daphne glanced up from her embroidery. "What is it?"

"Kevin and Samantha are walking along, hand in hand and gazing at each other."

"What?" Margaret leapt to her feet and hastened to spy.

"They look like lovers," Sam's aunt observed.

"Well, they can't be," her sister-in-law groaned. "Kevin is as good as promised to Frances. He should not be dallying with Samantha."

"I must warn her," Winifred said darkly. "Even the best of men are tempted to take advantage of such an innocent girl."

Margaret took umbrage at that remark. "Kevin isn't the *best* of men. He is my grandson!"

Daphne tittered.

"What, pray, is so amusing?" Lady Montjoy demanded.

"You just said that Kevin isn't the best of men," she twinkled. "What do you consider him to be? A lout?"

"Daphne, your brains always were lodged in your bottom," her sister said severely. "My grandson is the finest gentleman in all England. I do not know what has come over you . . . calling him a lout!"

"Oh, Margaret, for heaven's sake!" Daphne made a moue of disgust. "As usual, you have gotten everything wrong."

The dowager countess pulled her lips into a very taut line.

"You may contribute somewhat to your keep, but I do not know what you would do, if it weren't for Kevin. You would be indignant."

"Indigent," Daphne corrected.

"Whatever." Margaret waved a negligent arm and turned again to the window. "They've come in. Kevin must be showing her to her room."

"That isn't proper!" Winifred wailed.

"Fustian!" said her sister-in-law. "They're cousins."

"Not really. Not by blood, only by marriage." Winifred started toward the door. "I'm going to find them and act as chaperon."

"I'm going, too," Lady Montjoy announced, darting after her. "Samantha is my niece, too."

"No, she isn't." Winifred swung her elbows, commanding the lead.

"She shall call me Aunt Margaret."

"That is incorrect!" Winifred stopped and swiveled to face her.

Margaret tossed her head. "I am the chatelaine of this castle, and Samantha's hostess. She will call me whatever I wish, and I *wish* her to call me Aunt Margaret. Now there's an end to it! Shall we stand here bickering, or shall we go to welcome the gel properly?"

"We'll go," Winifred responded, "but it is my right to be the first. If it hadn't been for me, she would not be here."

"Oh, very well!" She called over her shoulder to her sister, "Daphne, are you coming?"

There was no reply.

"Daphne?" She pivoted. "Where is Daphne? Merciful heavens! While we were standing here quibbling, that sly wench slipped away. She will be the first to arrive at Samantha's side!"

"Come on! Let us hasten!" Winifred cried breathlessly. "She won't steal a march on us!"

Both ladies dashed through the door and fled posthaste toward the Rose Room.

Six

"Hello, my dear."

Samantha turned to the doorway and smiled at the petite, slender, white-haired lady. "How do you do?"

She nodded pleasantly. "Quite well, considering my age. You may call me Aunt Daphne."

"I shall be happy to." She touched the earl's forearm. "Kevin has been showing me my rooms."

"This suite is one of Montjoy's prettiest," the elderly lady proclaimed. "I hope you will like it."

"I know I shall." Sam gazed around the chamber which would be hers, she supposed, for as long as she wished. The Rose Room was named for its balcony view of a rather weedy, walled, medieval knot garden. Profusely planted with roses which had yet to bloom, the garden's bright daffodils and Poet's narcissus competed with the weeds, making up for the roses' lack of blossom.

The room's decor echoed the garden's spirit. The wallpaper was covered with roses of all colors. The window and bed hangings were of spring green. A floral carpet graced the floor. The wallpaper was a bit dingy and the fabrics worn, but it looked lovely to Sam. Kevin might call it threadbare and shabby, but it was much finer than she had ever had before.

"You should have seen my bedroom in Ohio," she said. "It was in the loft. I had to climb up a ladder to get to it. The walls were chinked logs, and there were only two pieces of furniture, a small dresser and a narrow rope bed with a corn husk mattress. On the floor was a braided rug that we made from scraps of fabric."

"It sounds awfully primitive," Kevin mused.

"It was." She smiled in reminiscence. "It was small, but so very cozy in the winter."

"Well, we are glad that you are here with us, and not living in that uncivilized place, surrounded by wild animals and red savages," Daphne declared. "I shudder to think of what fate could befall a young lady in such a vast wilderness. Yes, it is well that you are here."

"Why, Aunt," Kevin stated, "that is one of the longest statements I've ever heard you make."

"My goodness, so it was!" She smiled sweetly.

"Aunt Daphne is usually taciturn," her cousin explained.

Sam laughed lightly. "Sometimes listening is better than talking."

There was a commotion in the hall as Sam's aunt and Kevin's grandmother arrived on the scene.

"Some people are best off being silent," Kevin remarked.

"If you are referring to us, you are right." Winifred wrung her hands and gazed with remorse at Sam. "I fear our welcome left much to be desired. I hope you'll forgive us, Samantha."

"Of course." She nodded. "I only hope I am not too big a disappointment."

"You have not been disappointing," Lady Montjoy assured her. "In fact, we'll enjoy you more than we would have delighted in a child running about and making noise. We are entirely too old for antics like that."

While she was engaged in conversation with Kevin's grandmother, Sam noticed Aunt Winifred staring anxiously around the room. Curious, she questioned her. "Aunt Winifred, are you looking for something?"

"Someone, actually," the lady replied. "Child, have you seen a young servant girl here?"

Sam shook her head. "No, ma'am."

"Well, one is supposed to be present. Young Patsy is to be your abigail."

"I haven't seen her." She cocked her head sideways. "What is an abigail? And what do they do?"

"My dear!" Winifred gasped. "You do not know?"

Sam shrugged, shaking her head. Servants were one of the mysteries of the British class system. She had seen several now, and they all seemed to have particular duties and designations.

"An abigail . . ." Winifred mulled. "Let us see . . ."

"Goodness gracious!" Lady Montjoy cried. "Can you not explain to the gel, Winifred? An abigail takes care of one's clothes and helps one dress. She will do your hair and assist you with your bath, and . . . hm . . ."

"An abigail helps one shop," Winifred put in, "and fetches things. Sometimes she serves as one's chaperon."

"Briefly," Kevin interrupted, "an abigail is a lady's personal servant."

Sam frowned and wrinkled her nose. "I don't need anyone like that."

"Of course you do," her aunt said briskly. "Everyone does. Daphne and I share a girl, but Margaret has one of her own."

"As befits my station," Kevin's grandmother pronounced.

Sam considered. "Servants cost money, which Kevin told me was in short supply. But even if there was wealth aplenty, I wouldn't need an abigail. I can do for myself. In fact, I prefer it."

Her Aunt Winifred gasped. "But one must keep up appearances!"

"That's right," Margaret joined in. "You must have a maid."

Sam looked to Kevin for assistance. "I really don't want one. I cannot imagine having someone performing such private tasks. No, I shall do well enough, without."

He merely smiled, leaving her to the mercy of The Connection.

"You have never had one, Samantha, so you do not know the comforts of having one's own maid," his grandmother counseled.

"Patsy, however, is untrained. Since you are unaware of an abigail's duties, it will be best if you have a gel who knows what she's doing. Yes, that is how it will be. You may have Effie. She is Winifred's and Daphne's maid. They can take Patsy and train her."

"No!" Winifred objected. "Why can't she have your Martha? With Daphne and I sharing a maid, it will not be easy to train her."

"Martha is mine," Lady Montjoy commanded in a voice that would quell dissension. "I am the mistress of this house, and I will decide what is done. Samantha will have Effie."

Winifred rolled her eyes. "That is not efficient. Since I am in charge of the housekeeping, I should know what is best."

Margaret set her jaw. "I am the ultimate mistress."

Kevin quickly edged to the door. "If all of you will excuse me, I must dress for dinner."

Traitor, Sam thought. He could have controlled the quarreling ladies with one word. Instead, he had retreated. English noblemen were weak-kneed, spineless, and effeminate.

His blue eyes sparkled. "I shall see you at table, Samantha."

She glared. "Maybe you will, and maybe you won't."

The Connection had been too busy with their verbal tussle to know that he had gone.

"Kevin, will you decide this matter?" his grandmother queried and glanced at the place he'd been standing. "Kevin?"

"He's gone to dress for dinner," Sam told her. "Let us settle this matter later, or we'll be late, too."

"No, you may have Martha," Margaret offered magnanimously.

"You may have Effie," Winifred echoed simultaneously.

"I offered first," Kevin's grandmother insisted.

"No, first you said that she could have Effie."

Bob settled the controversy. Having lain down on the bed for a nap, he decided that the ladies' chattering was entirely too disturbing. Standing, he growled ferociously and exhibited his teeth.

The Connection startled.

Sam laughed inwardly as each took one look at the aggra-vated bobcat and hustled to the door, where they briefly jostled each other for position and hastened away.

"Lady Montjoy!" she shouted after them.

Kevin's grandmother opened the door only far enough to stick her head in. "Call me Aunt Margaret, my dear."

"Very well. Aunt Margaret, please inform the servants not to enter my room unless I am present. My pet does not like visitors."

"I will certainly do so. My, that is a fierce beast!"

"He will soon grow accustomed," she explained. "Then, though he will not be friendly, he will tolerate those whom he knows."

"I shall breathlessly await that day." She disappeared, firmly closing the door.

"Well, Bob," Sam giggled, "because of you, I shall have my way around here. And I do not intend to have an abigail! Good gracious, how embarrassing it would be to have someone help with my bath! That is one English custom I do not intend to embrace."

The cat seemed to grin.

Sam thoughtfully eyed him. "I suppose it isn't entirely an English custom, however. Wealthy Americans have servants, too. This service matter is something I don't understand at all. If Kevin is poor, why does he harbor so many employees?"

Slowly shaking her head, she went into her dressing room and opened her trunk. She wished she had thought to ask what was worn for dinner. At a loss for advice, and with a limited number of dresses to choose from, she pulled out her unadorned, green muslin gown. She had worn it to dinner at the inn, and Kevin had not objected. It must be fine for the evening meal at Montjoy Castle, too. Besides, it was only slightly wrinkled. Washing up in a bowl of tepid water, she put it on and tidied her hair. Satisfied, she patted Bob's head.

"I'll see to your dinner after mine. Tomorrow. I'll find out where the kitchen is, and I'll fix your food earlier," she promised and left the room, carefully retracing her steps down the hall and the worn stone stairway to the entrance hall where a footman stood at attention.

"Can you tell me where the dining room is?" she asked.

"Yes, miss, I can, but the family assembles in the drawing room before going in to dinner."

"Will you kindly direct me?"

He was already leading the way. Just a few paces beyond where he stood, he opened a door and bowed. "The drawing room, miss."

"Thank you . . . uh . . . I don't know your name."

" 'Tis Simpson, miss."

She nodded. "I will remember. But you needn't have gone to the trouble to show me the way. I'm very good at following directions."

"I am only doing my duty, miss." He stiffly bowed again.

Seeing that none of the family had arrived yet, she decided to question him. "May I ask you some more things, Mr. Simpson?"

He gaped at her. "It's just Simpson, miss."

She frowned quizzically. "Why just that?"

"I don't know, miss. That's just the way things are done."

"It's ridiculous, especially since the English seem to be such sticklers for manners." She shrugged. "Ah, well, far be it from me to criticize! Is it all right that I ask you some questions?"

"Certainly, miss."

"Let us go in here." She entered the drawing room and chose a chair in the conversational group by the hearth. "Please sit down, Mr. Simpson."

He looked totally aghast. "I cannot do that, miss!"

"Why not?"

"If someone saw me, I'd be fired!"

Again, Sam frowned. "You would?"

"Yes, miss! It would be unforgivable!" he said with horror. "It would ruin my career and any chance I had to be a butler, someday."

"It seems like an odd rule to me," she declared and stood.

"Having someone standing over me makes me nervous, but I don't want you to be fired. What are your duties? I've never been around servants before, so I don't know what a footman does."

"We assist the butler, miss. We serve the meals, open the doors, polish metals, and lay fires. We deliver messages." He paused. "We do lots of things."

"I see." She was prepared to ask him more, but the earl entered the room.

Simpson bowed deeply. "My lord."

"I was just asking him to explain what a footman does," Sam explained.

"One thing he does is to serve us a glass of sherry," Kevin told her. "See to it, Simpson."

"Yes, my lord."

Sam expected the servant to leave the room to fetch the drinks, but he merely walked a few paces away and extracted a bottle and glasses from a cabinet.

"Now, that's absurd," she remarked. "Why would you ask him to do that, when we ourselves could easily do it?"

"It's part of his job, Samantha."

"It doesn't make sense," she decreed. "You may be too lazy to do it, Kevin, but I assure you that I am not."

Kevin sighed patiently. "Very well, my dear cousin. You may perform Simpson's duties, and I will terminate his employment."

The footman's eyes nearly popped from their sockets. "Sir, please . . . I beg you! Mistress Samantha does not realize how necessary I am!"

"You cannot fire him!" Sam shrieked.

A smile played at the corners of Kevin's mouth. "Rest assured that I have no intention of doing so."

Simpson breathed a sigh of relief. "Thank you, my lord." Serving the drinks, he rushed from the room.

"That was cruel," Sam scolded.

He chuckled. "It served to get you down from your high horse."

"You did it at his expense," she ground out. "You frightened him unnecessarily. Besides, I am still on my high horse, as you like to call it. If you are so hard-pressed financially, why do you have all these people working for you?"

He gleefully clapped his hands. "By Jove, you're right! Just pick out which ones I'm to fire, and I shall do it immediately!"

"I cannot do that!" she cried, then sobered. "They are already hired. To toss them out now would be heartless. You shouldn't have taken them on in the first place. Kevin, I don't think you know a jot about matters of business."

"And you do?" he chortled.

"Yes," she stated. "I assisted my papa with his store."

"What did you do?" he jeered. "Dust the inventory?"

"I kept his records!" she hotly proclaimed. "I excelled at mathematics. With my skill at figures, I was able to advise him on what items to stock."

"That's rare! You are a woman of business!" Kevin laughed so hard, he began to cough and was forced to take a large gulp of his sherry.

Samantha felt her jaw begin to grow tighter and tighter. "I know more than you!" she snapped.

"What on earth is so amusing?" Margaret asked, leading The Connection into the room.

Kevin tried to catch his breath. "Samantha . . . thinks . . . she knows more about business . . ." He reeled with laughter, and it was a full five minutes before he was able to control himself.

"Samantha thinks she knows more about business than I do!"

Sam clenched her teeth. "That's true. I do!"

Kevin removed his handkerchief. Still shaking with merriment, he wiped his eyes. "I have never heard such a batch of foolishness!"

Sam pursed her lips. "You are perfectly obnoxious, Kevin Montjoy. You act just like a man!"

"Well, fancy that!" he howled. "I cannot imagine how that could be."

Shaking their heads, The Connection retreated to the liquor cabinet, where Simpson was pouring glasses of sherry for them.

"Ever since I met you, Kevin, I have seen nothing but waste. You even decried the condition of Montjoy Castle, which in all truth, is far better than the places most people live! You cry poverty, and live in luxury."

"What a spiel!" he roared. "Samantha, you are so dramatic that I'm surprised you are not on the stage."

"Lord, but you are exasperating," she hissed. "I am better at business than you. If you would allow me to take charge, I could make you a rich man," she recklessly vowed.

He sailed off on gales of more laughter. The Connection gaped at her. Simpson fled from the room.

Sam lifted her chin and narrowed her eyes. "I dare you!"

It took a long while for him to compose himself. The butler entered the room, announced dinner, stared, and departed. The Connection remained in their tight little knot. At last, Kevin managed to speak.

"Done," he said, blue eyes glittering. "Make me a rich man, Samantha, but it must be through your vast financial experience. No marrying heiresses."

"All right." She tossed her head. "Just watch me!"

Lady Montjoy ventured forth. "Dinner has been called."

Winifred followed her. "Yes, and, Samantha, you are not even dressed yet."

Sam looked down at her plain green gown and then at The Connection's stylish evening fashions. Compared to them, she looked like a farmer's daughter. She exhaled loudly and irritably.

Kevin chuckled. "She thought she was clad in the first stare of fashion."

Sam flushed, pain stabbing the pit of her stomach. She was, however, too irritated to shatter into humiliated pieces. "Well, I tell you I don't give a damn!"

"Samantha!" Aunt Winifred wailed. "Such language from the lips of a young lady!"

"That's more like it!" Kevin applauded. "You've regained your spirit. I was beginning to worry about you."

"Worry about yourself," she said. "Worry about how you will spend those thousands you will soon possess."

"Come on, brat." He tucked her hand through his arm. "Let us lead the way to the dining room."

The Connection followed, looking both unsettled and amused.

Sam could scarcely eat her dinner, even though it was the most delicious food she'd ever tasted. She was just too worried about how she'd make Kevin a rich man. Why had she shot off her mouth and made such a proclamation?

Barely listening to the mundane dinner conversation, she glanced around the dining room. Kevin had said that the room was what remained of the medieval great hall, and in keeping with that designation, the lords of Montjoy had decorated the walls with tapestries and knightly weapons of war. At one end was an immense fireplace, big enough to sit in. At the other was a huge, carved walnut screen, with two doors to allow access for footmen bearing food. At the top was a musicians' gallery. Crowning the whole of the room was a lofty, vaulted ceiling. Sam felt dwarfed and rather intimidated by the magnitude of the place.

"Can you believe?" Aunt Margaret's voice cut through Sam's reverie. "He is nothing but a rich cit! Those people will pay any amount of money to rub shoulders with a peer. And their numbers are growing! They are composing a social class unto themselves."

"What is a *cit?*" Sam asked.

"It is a term we use for wealthy merchant townsmen and their families," she explained. "They, particularly their wives, will go to any expense to climb the social ladder. It is quite vexatious."

Sam quizzically inclined her head. "Are there a lot of them?"

"Oh, my dear! Their number is growing by leaps and bounds!" She shuddered. "One of them has bought the estate next to ours. I know he has done it only in hopes of dining with us or partaking in some sort of mutual entertainment. But he is wrong! He will never set foot in this house, and if his wife has the audacity to come calling, she will be turned away."

Sam narrowed her eyes in thought. "You mean that these . . . cits . . . would pay huge sums of money just to associate with the nobility?"

"Goodness, yes." This time Aunt Winifred took up the subject. "It is their fondest ambition, except, of course, actually wedding one of their daughters to a peer. Unbelievably, it really has happened. Lords who are in desperate need of money have married cits' daughters."

Sam smiled. Cits . . . money . . . ambition. There must be a way to extract riches from a cit's pockets and place it into Kevin's.

"Oh, no," Kevin interjected. "No, no, no! I can see the wheels turning in your head, Samantha. Marriage is not a part of our agreement, remember? Besides, I don't need a cit's girl. I have Lady Frances."

"I'm not thinking of that," she scoffed, "but it would be good to get hold of some of their wealth."

"You cannot do that without associating with cits," Lady Montjoy moaned, "and that would never do."

Sam concentrated. There were fragments of thoughts peppering through her mind, but she couldn't seem to put them together. She took scant notice when the butler and his minions removed the dinner plates and replaced them with their desserts. Unconsciously, she took a bite of her profiterole. The flaky pastry and creamy filling almost melted in her mouth.

"This is marvelous," she enthused, "and so was the whole meal. I thought that the food in the inn at Portsmouth was excellent, but . . . that's *it!*"

"What?" asked Aunt Winifred.

An inn . . . an earl . . . and cits . . . rubbing shoulders . . .

"We will all be rich!" Samantha cried.

Motion arrested, they stared at her.

"Montjoy Castle will become an inn," she announced, "but not just any inn. Our prices will be high as the sky, for we will deal in luxury only. *And* we will have an earl as the host at meals and entertainments. In short, ladies and lord, we will cater to rich, social-climbing cits!"

Eagerly, Sam surveyed her audience.

Lady Montjoy's mouth was agape. "I have never been so shocked!"

Aunt Winifred clasped her hands together as if she were petitioning the Almighty. "Oh Lord, please. My ears must be hearing falsely. It sounds as if a cit has penetrated our boundaries."

Kevin sat speechlessly, frozen as still as a pillar of ice, eyeing Samantha warily.

Of all, only Daphne appeared enthused. The usually taciturn lady surprised them all by fairly bouncing in her chair. "I believe it might work! We could advertise in all the large towns where cits congregate. Why, I think they will flock to our establishment!"

"Our Samantha could not know the social ramifications, but, Daphne, you do. It would cast us beyond the pale," Kevin's grandmother moaned. "We would never again be able to show our faces in proper society."

"We don't, anyway," Daphne said tartly.

"Margaret is right," Winifred seconded. "We would never again be received by the *ton.*"

"Do you want to be rich and comfortable, or go to a party?" Sam ruthlessly queried.

"Lady Frances would probably refuse to wed Kevin," Margaret predicted.

Sam smiled victoriously. "He won't need that antidote. He'll be wealthy. What do you think, Kevin? You've been conspicuous by your silence."

All eyes turned toward the earl.

He sat motionless, a forkful of profiterole halfway to his mouth. "Let us discuss it after dinner."

Conversation ground to a halt. Each family member was silent with his or her thoughts, but Sam's were practically bubbling over. It would work. She was sure of it! Now, if Kevin could only be convinced.

* * *

Kevin did not linger for his port. All food and drink had lost its appeal. He could hardly believe what he had heard. Montjoy Castle? A stopping place for cits? Impossible!

As soon as they were seated and tea had been served, Samantha started on him.

"You said I could do what I wished, short of arranging an engagement," she reminded.

"Yes, my dear gel," broke in Aunt Winifred, "but you wouldn't wish to ruin our good name. You just don't understand the ways of the *ton*."

"What is the *ton?*" she asked.

"It is a group composed of the wellborn and well-bred. People like us," she explained. "But to be accepted, one still must display exemplary behavior. Your idea, well meaning though we know it is, would be looked upon with derision. Lady Frances's parents would never allow her to marry Kevin, if such a thing took place. Nor would we be able to arrange a suitable match for you."

He would not have to wed Lady Frances if Samantha's idea worked. Kevin thought of Frances's sharp pointed nose, her prominent teeth, her whiny voice, and most of all, that cloying scent of roses that accompanied her wherever she went. That odor alone was enough to make one's stomach recoil and threaten to cast up one's accounts.

But his grandmother and Aunt Winifred were right. Going into such a business would put him beyond the pale. If it worked, however, would that matter? What was most important? Montjoy Castle or the *ton's* acceptance? He wouldn't have to carry on business forever. He could make his pot of gold and quit. Then he could insinuate himself back into the *ton*. The social lions just might decide that he was an eccentric and forget all about it. There were many bizarre members of the *ton*.

"Kevin?" Samantha prompted.

"I'm seriously thinking about it," he mumbled.

His grandmother moaned. Aunt Winifred looked as if she'd

introduced an ogre into their midst. Aunt Daphne was avidly
consuming her tea with a gusto he'd never before witnessed. And
Samantha? Samantha was rather entrancing with her sparkling
animation. The infuriating minx could be alluring when she
wanted to be.

No Lady Frances. Oh, he was so tempted to try it, but still he
held back. What if he absolutely could not bear playing host to
cits? What if the plan didn't work? He be ruined *and* have pockets
to let.

It seemed like Samantha was reading his mind. "I know what
we can do. We should be able to gauge our success on responses
to our very first advertisements. If it appears that we will fail,
you can blame it all on me. Everyone will feel sorry for you,
victimized by your horrible, ignorant American cousin."

"All right," Kevin said abruptly, "but I won't hide behind
your skirts, Samantha."

"O-o-o-h! Kevin, I can scarcely believe it's really you!"
shrieked his grandmother. "Don't expect me to entertain cits!
I shall remain in my chamber and not come out!"

"I won't," Aunt Daphne vowed. "It will liven things up
around here."

Aunt Winifred rode the fence. "I just don't know what to do."

Samantha was wreathed in smiles. "We'll be successful! I
just know we will!"

Kevin grinned back at her. "I hope you are right. Remember,
we have a great deal at stake."

"We shall not fail!" she cried valiantly. "Now, let us make
plans. We must commence our business as quickly as we can."

Samantha spent the rest of the evening making lists of things
to be done, in order to make Montjoy Castle ready to welcome
its first paying guests. Kevin's brain was soon swimming with
endless housekeeping details. By bedtime, things seemed so
complicated that he wished he had put a period to the scheme
when first it was mentioned, but Samantha, a regular whirlwind
of energy, was not deterred. Kevin, with a brilliant headache,
was.

Seven

If anyone thought that there would be hesitation for further discussion, procrastination, or even a change of mind, concerning the scheme to turn Montjoy Castle into an inn, they were sadly disappointed. With Sam's determination and skill at organization, the preparations to receive guests were commenced immediately. Sam was astonished that her idea was actually being carried out. Of course, she found it necessary to swap favors. In short, she accepted Martha as her personal maid until another could be trained. Although she liked the woman and knew that the servant only meant well for her, she despised the intimacy of the whole arrangement. She did not need help in dressing or undressing. She was quite capable of getting up in the morning and performing her ablutions. She definitely did not need someone to assist her in bathing! Modest by nature, she found the whole arrangement to be perfectly horrible.

There was also the matter of Bob. Before she had an abigail, Sam had told the other servants to rap smartly before entering her chamber so that she might take control of the cat, but Martha needed to enter the suite at will. Sam decided to keep Bob in her sitting room, whenever she was not present. The provision seemed to work, although Martha continued to be a bit timid about the situation. But in time, Sam believed, the abigail would grow accustomed to the lynx, and Bob would become tolerant of Martha. Sam wished that moment would arrive very speedily. She had her hands full in launching the Montjoy Enterprise, as she called it, much to the dismay of Aunt Margaret, who thought such a title was vulgar and smacked of cits.

Indeed, everyone at Montjoy Castle was busy, working long hours to ensure that the residence was well prepared for what, hopefully, would be a huge onslaught of guests. Winifred, whose bailiwick was house cleaning, joined the housekeeper and butler in overseeing the footmen and maids to make certain that every inch of the castle was clean and sparkling. With the assistance of the chef, Margaret prepared toothsome menus and coordinated food purchasing, preparation, and service. Daphne, skilled in the finest needlework, combed each room in search of fabric which needed mending. Kevin helped the butler in the inventory and restocking of the wine cellar, the coachman and the head groom in readying the stables for guests' horses and carriages, and the groundskeeper in making sure that the lawns, gardens, and miscellaneous plantings were trimmed, weeded, and immaculate. Samantha commanded the entire endeavor, lending a hand whenever or wherever it was required. Bob did nothing but eat, sleep, and frighten slackers when he accompanied Sam on her rounds.

The bobcat was developing a great partiality to Kevin, which Sam was at a loss to explain. Whenever Bob was in the earl's vicinity, he made a beeline for the man. Sam suspected alcohol, but she couldn't prove it. The cat was always within her control when he and Kevin met. Besides, he never seemed tipsy. She could only put it down to the drinks Bob had received during the trip from Portsmouth to Montjoy Castle. Even so, Bob's preference seemed outlandishly strange, but she was just too busy to seek an explanation.

She had a list that was almost book length, with large and minute tasks in all areas of responsibility. Each evening after dinner, she, Kevin, and The Connection gathered in the drawing room to tick off the day's accomplishments. She, and everyone else for that matter, had never realized, when they began the project, that there would be so much work to do in order to open the castle to paying guests. Sometimes one job led to another that no one had thought of. So there was cheering for work marked off, and groans when something had to be added. As the target date for opening approached, however, it seemed as if they would meet their self-imposed deadline. At last, their meeting commenced with designing their advertisement.

"I have toyed with several ideas," Sam announced. "Has anyone else done the same?"

There was universal head-shaking.

"Very well. Glance over these." She passed the scraps of paper to the group.

Lady Montjoy frowned her disapproval at each one. "They all have Kevin's name on them. Can we not maintain some small measure of anonymity?"

"Kevin is our greatest attraction," Sam said flatly. "The earl and his castle are what make us different from any other inn."

"Luxurious accommodations," Aunt Winifred read. "I have a problem with that, and Daphne will back me up. Many of the chambers have furniture which, in earlier times, was quite fine, but now is scuffed and needs refinishing. So many of the fabrics are threadbare, and, frankly, dry-rotted."

Aunt Daphne nodded. "They fall to pieces just by handling. I mend one place, then have to repair several new ones."

Sam sighed. "We haven't the time, nor the money, I assume, to replace anything. Instead of luxurious, could we say 'fascinating, historically accurate accommodations'?"

All agreed.

"At least the food will be luxurious," Margaret stated. "Luckily, we have a fine chef. It is too bad that I will have to take my meals from a tray."

"You could resume your position at the foot of the table," Sam told her.

"Not I! I will not dine with vulgar, jumped-up cits!"

Kevin smiled charmingly at her. "Grandmama, you would help make things easier for me, if you would dine with us."

"No," she declared. "You will have to look to Samantha for support."

"I will not be seated at the table," Sam told them. "I will be acting as manager; therefore, I perform the role of a glorified servant."

"You will dine with me," Kevin insisted. "No one will consider you a servant."

"Nevertheless, the guests would not welcome my company."

"I think they would," Aunt Winifred claimed. "They will find you fascinating. Just regale them with stories of red savages and wild beasts."

"I will not do that," Sam refused. "In the first place, our American Indians aren't red, they're brown, and moreover, they aren't savage. I found the Indians who visited my father's store to be rather dignified. Secondly, I cannot attend because I haven't the wardrobe."

Kevin turned to Daphne. "Can you make her some dinner gowns?"

His aunt nodded with certainty.

"Excellent!" His blue eyes twinkled merrily. "You will join me for meals, Samantha, or I will not attend, either. I'll go right up to the last minute, and then renege."

She stuck out her lower lip. "That's blackmail."

He shrugged nonchalantly.

His grandmother chimed in. "This was your idea, Samantha. It is your duty to assist Kevin. I don't know what on earth he can find to discuss with cits. You must support him."

"I do not think Samantha should be exposed to cits any longer than she must," said Winifred. "She is a young unmarried lady and should be protected from such a situation."

Kevin glanced at his Aunt Daphne. "We haven't heard your opinion, ma'am. Grandmother and I say Samantha should be at the table. She and her aunt claim that she should not. Your opinion could break this deadlock."

"Oh, dear," whispered Daphne. "I haven't a clue as to what should be done. I know nothing of cits. Can they be as crude as everyone thinks?"

"I don't understand why everyone has such a dim view of cits," Sam put in.

"They are vulgar and rude," denounced Lady Montjoy.

"Are they?" Sam queried. "How many of them have you known?"

"That is beside the point," she said archly.

"No, it isn't. How many?"

Margaret's nostrils fluttered as if she'd detected a bad odor. "If you must know . . . none."

Sam nodded emphatically. "How many have you known, Kevin?"

He smiled grimly. "I suppose you could consider my man of business a cit."

"Is he rude and vulgar?" she demanded.

"Well, no, but . . ."

"And you, Aunt Winifred, have you ever had dealings with a cit?" Sam asked.

"Shopkeepers," she readily replied, "but they are on their good behavior because they wish to sell one something."

"From that I assume that they know how to conduct themselves properly," she mulled. "Why wouldn't they do so here?"

"Because they wouldn't be in their shops." Winifred lifted her chin and looked down her slender, patrician nose. "They wouldn't be engaged in *making money.*"

"No," Sam agreed. "I suppose that *we* would be the ones doing that. Does that make us rude and vulgar?"

"Leave off, Samantha," Kevin advised.

"No! Once and for all, I want to get to the bottom of this! Does everyone consider my father a cit? He owned a store!"

"He was a landowner," Winifred stated.

Sam began to laugh. "I wish you had seen that land! I wish you could see where we lived! It was a one-room log cabin with a loft. I slept in the loft. The one room was used for cooking, dining, and sitting. It was also my parents' bedroom. The whole building could be set down in this drawing room. And you think cits are bad?"

Her aunt had covered her ears with her hands and was rocking back and forth. "My poor Elizabeth! I cannot bear to hear more!"

"Enough, Samantha," Kevin ordered. "Your American style of living does not apply here. You must adapt to our standards."

"I find it difficult to be so arrogant," she fired back. "I cannot condone this class discrimination. How can you believe that you are so much better than many others, Kevin? If you had earned your lofty position, I could understand, but because of birth? No."

He set his jaw. "I did not invent England's class system."

She lifted an eyebrow. "But you perpetuate it."

He glared at her. "What do you expect me to do? Give up my title and become plain Mr. Montjoy?"

She pursed her lips. "What, pray tell, is wrong with that?"

He rolled his eyes heavenward as if he were dealing with a complete dolt. "Who would be so monumentally stupid as to prefer not to possess a title?"

"Apparently, the majority of Americans are quite well satisfied by not being titled." She smiled smugly. "That was one reason why we were so perfectly successful when we soundly defeated you British in our war for independence."

"Frankly, I doubt that Americans gave much of a thought to titles." He narrowed his eyes. "The colonials behaved like children, rebelling and revolting against their parents. And like most children, they will live to regret it."

"I wouldn't place a wager on that if I were you." She tossed her head. "Americans are not children. Our women are strong, not like helpless English ladies. Our men are brave and manly, not like dandified, parasitic English lords!"

Her Aunt Winifred, who had abandoned her posturing when the conversation had become fascinating, shuddered. "Samantha, you should not speak so about Kevin."

"Indeed," Lady Montjoy sniffed. "That was just awful."

Daphne simply looked pained.

Realizing that her tongue had run away with her, Sam swiftly leapt in to correct the blunder. "I was not particularly speaking of Kevin," she explained. "Obviously, one cannot make generalities about such a thing. I thought you would understand that."

"Then why didn't you explain in your statement?" Kevin accused.

"My phraseology was incorrect," she told him. "I did not set out to insult you, Kevin."

"I think you did," he pressed.

"Well, think what you will!" she snapped. "Moreover, if the shoe fits, wear it! I'm beginning to believe that you see yourself in my description. That is why you—and everyone—is taking such exception to it. You're guilty, Kevin!"

"Lord, but you are an aggravating wench!" he declared.

"That is not a nice word to use when referring to me," she pointed out and put a cupped hand to her ear, like one who has difficulty hearing. "I don't hear anyone speaking up in my behalf. Perhaps it's because I don't have a cursed title!"

As soon as the words left her mouth, she was ashamed of them. She was like a child in a temper tantrum, yammering to have her own way. No wonder no one supported her.

"Samantha, dear," Aunt Winifred began, and then was interrupted by a sudden din in the hall.

"Here he comes!" someone shouted.

"Run for it!" yelped another.

Sam and Kevin exchanged quick glances.

"It's that damned cat!" cried the earl.

"It's Bob!" Sam said simultaneously, and leapt up from her chair, hastening to the door with Kevin hard on her heels.

The sight she beheld was one of chaos. The butler and his footmen stood on tables and chairs. Two maids peeked out from behind doors, their eyes wide with horror. Kevin's valet was perched on the stair railing, holding tightly with one hand, while helplessly gesticulating with the other. The center of attention was Bob.

The cat appeared to be having a perfectly marvelous time. In his mouth was a bit of white fabric, which he tossed in the air, adroitly catching it on its way down. Quickly tiring of that game, he stepped on the cloth and pulled upwards, making a loud, ripping noise. He lay down to chew in earnest.

Sam started forward. "How did he escape?"

"I thought the door between your sitting room, where you keep that cat, and your chamber was always closed," Martha called from above. "I entered your dressing room through the little door in the hall. I could see right away that that cat's door was cracked open. I didn't see the cat, so I rushed to close it and forgot to close the hall door. That Bob, he must've been hidin' somewhere and sneaked out in the hall when my back was turned."

Kevin's valet continued the saga. "I was putting away my lord's laundry, when I felt someone . . . something . . . staring at me. I turned around and saw that damned cat. Pardon my language, miss, but it's been a most trying time! Naturally, I jumped and yelled. That beast turned a bad face to me and showed his teeth. Then he grabbed one of his lordship's neck-cloths and ran off with it. There's what's left of it!"

Sam watched in dismay as Bob held the item between his paws and jerked on it, violently shaking his head. She walked up to him. "Bob, this is truly bad of you."

"Why did he have to pick on my clothes?" Kevin complained. "He should have torn up yours, Samantha."

She shrugged helplessly. "He has done nothing like this since he was very young. It is probably a sign that he is upset by our move."

"I've been overset before, and I haven't ripped things apart," he growled.

"Really, Kevin," she said crossly, kneeling to try to remove the cloth from the bobcat's mouth. "Are you likening yourself to an animal?"

Bob decided to engage Samantha in a game of tug-of-war. When she tried to extricate the cravat from his mouth, he grimly held on. The moment she relaxed, he yanked sharply.

"Bob!" she cried. "You must give Kevin his neckcloth!"

"What the hell for?" the earl exploded. "He's already torn it up!"

"Yes, I suppose you are right." She grasped her pet by the scruff of his neck. "Come, Bob, let us go upstairs."

The cat refused to cooperate, lying heavily upon the center design of the Turkey carpet.

"Please, Bob." Sam tried to pick him up, but he loosened all his muscles and became a dead weight. "Kevin, when he is like this, he weighs too much for me. Will you carry him up?"

"Are you daft!" he cried. "He'd bite the hell out of me!"

"Not with your neckcloth in his mouth."

"He can drop that very quickly and latch onto my arm! No, Samantha, I won't do it, and I doubt that any of your *brave, masculine American men* would do so, unless they're complete idiots."

She stuck out her tongue at him and called upstairs to her abigail. "Will you bring down Bob's collar and leash, please?"

"I won't bring it," Martha vowed with determination. "I'll drop it down."

"The servants are certainly afraid of Bob," Kevin remarked.

"Just what do you expect me to do? Shoot him?" Sam said furiously.

He sniffed. "Perhaps you'd best care for your own room, clothes, and person."

"You think that would bother me? It would not! Unlike some of us, who are probably unable to button their own shirts, I am accustomed to caring for myself." She looked up as the lady's maid tossed down Bob's equipment. "Martha, in the future, I shan't be needing your services. Please resume tending to Lady Montjoy."

"That was stupid," the earl muttered, then raised his voice. "Martha, you will continue to tend Miss Edwards!"

Samantha ignored him and fastened Bob's collar and leash. Either because the cat respected the restraint, or because he was ready to go up, he stood obediently. With the neckcloth remaining in his mouth, he accompanied his mistress upstairs.

"What if he escapes when there are guests in this pseudo hotel?" Kevin shouted after her.

She held her tongue. She was thinking of the very same thing herself. They would have to be very, very cautious.

Sighing, she crossed the gallery toward her room. At least it was easier to think about Bob than it was to dwell upon what she'd said about English lords. La, why did her tongue run away with her? She must guard her speech as stringently as she must regulate Bob's whereabouts. Also, in the heat of the moment, she'd behaved ridiculously. She would hide out in her rooms until tempers had eased, then she must apologize to her cousin and The Connection. And *that* would be a bitter pill to swallow.

Still smarting from Samantha's opinion of English lords, Kevin returned to the drawing room with The Connection, picked up his cousin's samplings of advertisements, and perused them carefully. There was no doubt about it. He was, indeed, the leading man in what seemed to be a veritable Covent Gardens extravaganza. Damn, but it was embarrassing! Did he really need to stoop so low? He must have been totally mad to have gone along with this nonsense. Oh, yes, he did have a chance to gain, but he also had everything to lose. Cits wouldn't be the only ones to see the ad. The *ton* would, too, and they would never forget it. It would certainly cast him beyond the pale. Also, he'd be sealing his fate with Lady Frances. After this lunacy, her parents would never sanction a match. If the scheme failed, he'd have to marry a cit's daughter.

With a deep sigh, he held up the least offensive ad. "This looks like the best one," he told The Connection, passing it around.

They nodded unhappy approval.

"Kevin," his grandmother murmured. "It is not too late to back out."

Although sorely tempted, he shook his head. "No, I agreed to it. I gave my word."

"Honor need not be binding when cits are involved," she decreed.

Despite his misery, he smiled. "It is for me. Don't ask me to shed what self-esteem I have left. No, I'll wholeheartedly try this. We may be surprised . . . by success, maybe by the cits, too. Maybe it won't be as bad as it seems."

"Well, I shall not associate with cits. Not I!" She proudly lifted her chin. "I have *my* honor, too!"

"I wonder what it will be like," Aunt Winifred mused. "Strangers at Montjoy Castle!"

Kevin lifted a shoulder. "If it works, it will be much more profitable than agriculture. It can go on year round."

"If and when the coffers are filled with money, we shall cease this business," Lady Montjoy stressed.

"We shall hope that is soon," Winifred waxed fervently. "In the meantime, I shall be glad to do everything I can to help make the project successful."

"So will I," whispered Daphne. "I shall work far into the night to create a lovely wardrobe for Samantha. She is such a pretty young lady. She will be attractive in most everything."

"Pretty is as pretty does," denounced Margaret. "Her actions and especially her tongue are not very handsome."

"Do not judge her prematurely," begged Winifred. "She must grow accustomed to our ways."

"Balderdash!" cried Lady Montjoy. "She is an impertinent piece of baggage. She is opinionated and disrespectful. You should box her ears, Winifred, and wash out her mouth with soap."

"Me?" Samantha's aunt asked pitifully.

"Leave off," Kevin put in. "Let us not quarrel amongst ourselves. We must be united in this endeavor."

"If you insist." His grandmother took the ads, sorted through them, and handed him one. "There. That is the least appalling."

Kevin stared at the slip of paper which spelled his social downfall. In the morning, he'd have it delivered to the country's best newspapers. Soon, his reputation would be ruined.

"Ladies, if you will excuse me, I believe I'll take a walk before bed." Bowing to them as they gave their assent, he quickly exited the room and the castle.

After the warm atmosphere of the drawing room, the cool, invigorating spring air condensed into refreshing, light dew on Kevin's face, as he sauntered toward the restored rose garden. The grounds of the castle looked better than he'd ever seen before. Of course, it had cost money. He'd had to hire assistants to help the elderly gardener. Money! It was never far from his mind. Some might say that they'd readied the castle at very little expense, but to Kevin's purse, it was costly. If the venture failed, or had only moderate success, he would be forced to wed some wealthy female as swiftly as he could. Otherwise, the residents of Montjoy Castle would not have a comfortable winter.

Clasping his hands behind his back, he passed through the quaint, ancient arch in the wall that enclosed the bower. Even in the moonlight, he could see how beautiful the garden was, now that it was cleared of its wild growth and the brick walkway weeded. If it could only be that easy to uproot his problems.

Pausing, he looked up at the dark gray walls of the castle. "I wish I knew what the hell to do," he muttered aloud.

In response, there was a soft growl.

"Oh, no," Kevin groaned. "I know that voice all too well!"

"I'm sorry," Samantha said, emerging from behind a lichen-stained statue of Venus. "You looked as if you wanted to be alone, so I tried to hide until I could silently make my escape, but . . ."

"But unfortunately you were discovered," he finished.

"Yes, I suppose you could say that." She bent her head, fixing her gaze on the ground. "Kevin . . . I know you must be very annoyed by my previous behavior this evening. Sometimes, my tongue runs away with me."

He waited for her to expand the apology, assuring him that she did not truly think that English lords, which must include him, were weak and parasitic. Nothing more, however, seemed to be forthcoming. He set his jaw, determining to treat her to a chilly contempt. If he was an unmanly Englishman, then she was a vulgar American. But he didn't believe in cliches, especially when the moonlight was bathing her beguiling features in its soft, lustrous light. Samantha Edwards, his vexatious, colonial cousin, was the most beautiful woman he'd ever seen. Mesmerized, he took a step forward.

Bob, who had been sitting on his haunches, rose onto all fours and lifted a lip in warning. Entranced as he was, Kevin paid little heed. He took another short stride.

"Samantha?"

She looked up, green eyes shining like expertly chiseled emeralds. Kevin watched as surprise, then disbelief, and finally longing registered in those expressive orbs. She quizzically tilted her chin.

"Kevin?" This time, she stepped toward him.

It had been a long time—not since his salad days, in fact—that he had made an advance on a woman for reasons other than pure lust, which was directed toward a demi-rep, or the financial necessity aimed at an heiress. Neither motive had touched his heart, as this seemed to do. For Samantha, he felt . . . tenderness. It was a strange, alien emotion.

"Kevin, I . . ."

"Hush." He lifted her chin with his forefinger.

Bob growled loudly and positioned himself between the two of them. This time, Kevin did notice and cursed lightly. Dropping his hand to his side, he backed away.

"No," Samantha said ardently.

Kevin took several deep breaths, willing his body to ease its desire. "The bobcat is smarter than we are."

"I don't understand," she murmured. "Were you . . . Were you going to kiss me?"

"Yes," he managed.

"I've never been kissed before." Her voice quivered. "Won't you continue? So that I will know what it's like?"

Regaining control of himself, Kevin adamantly shook his head. "We're cousins."

"Not really."

"Samantha, nothing can come of it. It was a mistake. Thank God the cat put an end to it. Now we both shall forget it ever happened." Abruptly, he turned on his heel and marched toward the castle.

"But it did happen. Kevin!" she called wanly after him.

He did not turn, and he did not retrace his steps. He had not truly been attracted to her. It was merely a trick of the moonlight, and a selfish desire to prove to her that he was very much a man, in all senses of the word.

Eight

The advertisement for Lord Montjoy's country inn appeared in all of England's largest newspapers. It even captured the favorable attention of their editors. These newsmen were genuinely impressed by the venture. A top-lofty earl was actually lifting a hand to earn his daily bread! Unlike his fellows, he wasn't afraid or contemptuous of honest labor. They saluted Lord Montjoy in editorials, thus aiding the earl with free, glowing publicity.

The editors were not the only ones to take note. Wealthy, social climbing businessmen and their wives saw it, too, and put pen to paper to request reservations. Rubbing shoulders with a real, live earl was not their only goal. They soon discovered that Lord Montjoy was a bachelor, and of just the right age to be seeking a wife. Many of these hopeful guests had daughters of marriageable age.

Of course, the *ton* inevitably saw the notice and was appalled. It was no secret that Lord Montjoy was almost penniless, but he had been following the usual, expected method of repairing his finances by courting an heiress. No one could fault him on that. So why had he committed the hideous sin of entering business? It was simply beyond all belief.

A certain female in Portsmouth saw the announcement, and laughed and laughed. Polly was delighted to find that Sam had not been swayed by the hoity-toity ways of the aristocracy. She'd a notion, when business grew slow in the winter, to book a reservation for herself!

While the whole British world rocked with scandal, Sam excitedly began booking the flood of reservation requests and felt very smug about the success of her idea. For some time to come, Montjoy Castle would be bursting at the seams with paying guests. If the trend continued, Kevin would become a very wealthy man. It almost seemed too good to be true. Sam wanted to celebrate the triumph with a festive dinner, but The Connection thought that would be premature. Also, of late, Kevin was not the most pleasant company.

Ever since their meeting that evening in the rose garden, the earl was being most obvious in his care to avoid Sam. She was sure that The Connection had noticed and were curious, but she wasn't going to satiate their hunger for information. The accidental tryst kept threatening to be uppermost in her mind and was very difficult to banish. She *must* keep her thoughts on the inn and not on personal matters. Telling the aunts would only make things worse.

Bob was no help either. He had decided to tolerate Kevin. In fact, he actually appeared to wish he could be with the man. Whenever Sam took him out, he tried to pull her in the direction of the earl's bedchamber. When they descended the stairs, he attempted to go to the library. Something this odd had never happened before. She could only conclude that Bob genuinely liked Kevin.

So a myriad of emotions were baking under the surface normality of the denizens of Montjoy Castle, when the day of the Grand Opening finally dawned. Sam, nervously putting the final touches to an enormous bouquet of flowers on the hall table, heard the crunch of hooves and wheels on the carriageway. Dashing to the window to look out, she saw a shiny, black-lacquered coach with a matching, high-stepping, ebony team draw to a halt. With a cry of glee, she ran to the library to fetch Kevin.

He didn't look very happy to hear the news. "So it begins,"

he mused. "Perhaps I'd best stay out of sight. If I'm present too often, the excitement will wear off."

She clenched her jaw. "Kevin Montjoy, you are the master of this house, and therefore the host. It is proper etiquette to greet these guests and make them welcome."

"You do it," he suggested. "You are the mistress."

"I most certainly am not!" she cried. "I am nothing but the business manager! Your grandmother should be your feminine counterpart, but as you know, she has vowed to keep to her room. Now, these people have taken three rooms for a very hefty sum. They must get their money's worth. You'd better come with me!"

"All right." His voice dripped with stately sulkiness. "But I don't like it."

"I don't care whether you like it or not," she lectured. "You agreed to it, and I will hold you to your word. That is, of course, if you are an honorable gentleman."

"Vixen! Leave off the prattle, Samantha. I'm going, am I not?" He strode irritably into the hall and toward the door.

"My God, no one can be as perfectly sullen and spoiled as an English peer," she muttered, following in his wake and wondering if he was going to be awkward and arrogant with the guests.

"Shut up, Samantha," he commanded, as the brass lion's head on the door clanged. "You haven't met any others, so you do not know how charming I am. Greeting cits! Damme!"

With a sour grimace of disapproval, the butler opened the huge door. Instead of a footman, the family of four stood on the stoop. When the two women saw Kevin, their faces lit up like a thousand candles.

"This is a fascinating place!" the elder woman effused, before Samantha or Kevin had time to greet her. "I'm sure we will have a *fascinating* adventure here!"

Accustomed to soft, pure tones, her nasal accent grated on Sam's ears.

"Welcome to Montjoy Castle," Kevin said, looking down his finely chiseled, aristocratic nose. "I am Montjoy, and—"

The woman curtsied so low that Sam thought she might fall over. "Thank you, my lord, for making possible such a *fascinating* experience."

". . . and this is my American cousin, Miss Samantha Edwards," Kevin finished.

The woman's husband eyed his spouse with disgust and extended his hand to shake Kevin's. "Name's Milton, m'lord. This'd better be good. It's cost me a pretty pence, and worst of all, I had to leave my business in the hands of others, while I'm gone. Don't like that one whit!"

Sam surveyed his corpulent figure. "I don't think I'd be wrong in saying that the food and wine at Montjoy Castle are worth every shilling you're spending."

He brightened. "It is, huh?"

"Oh, yes. It is both plentiful and mouth-watering." She smiled graciously. "May I offer you a light repast now, or would you rather be shown to your rooms?"

"We'll eat." He frowned at his wife. "Get up off the floor, Flossy. We're going to have a bite."

"Will you give me a chance?" she hissed. "Introductions have not yet been made."

"Sure we have! That's the Montjoys, and we're the Miltons. Now what are we waiting for?" he complained.

"Just a minute," she said and scorchingly eyed Sam. "Are you Lady Montjoy?"

Sam shook her head. "I am Samantha Edwards, Lord Montjoy's cousin."

"Thank heavens!" she cried. "I thought he might have up and got married on us."

Kevin winced.

Sam's heart went out to him, but there was nothing she could do, except to say a silent prayer that he would be forbearing.

Mrs. Milton took the girl's arm and edged her forward. "This is our Delphinia. As you can see, she's a diamond of the first water! And she's just as talented as she is beautiful." She gestured toward the lad standing behind her. "And this is our son, Fennimore."

Flushing prettily, the young lady curtsied. "How do you do, my lord, ma'am?"

Behind his mama, Fennimore screwed his face into an ugly expression and stuck out his tongue.

Mr. Milton chuckled. "Our Fennimore's one hell of a regular brat. His mam won't discipline him, and I'm too busy with my enterprise to do it. Reckon we'll have to send him to one of them schools what whip the sauce outta boys. That'll teach him to mind his manners!"

"Go to hell," said Fennimore. Turning, he went back outside, a slingshot visible in his back pocket.

A frown quickly crossed Kevin's face, lasting only seconds before he concealed it. Delphinia, however, noticed and nodded appreciatively. "He is a horrible, little urchin, Lord Montjoy. He must be a changeling."

Through the open door, Sam saw the child grasp his slingshot, fit a pebble into it draw back, and fire. The stone hit a footman in the backside. The servant jumped, then rubbed his derriere. Fennimore danced with glee.

"I sure stung his ass!" the boy shrieked. "That'll hurry him up!"

"Oh, Fennimore?" his mother shrilled. "Do watch your language, love."

"Listen here," Kevin warned. "If you can't control that little makebait, you will have to leave."

Delphinia wailed. "Why must that brigand be continually permitted to ruin my life?"

"You'd best punish your son," Mrs. Milton begged her husband.

"I s'pose he deserves a whoop on the butt," Mr. Milton declared.

"Then do it!" she screeched. "You know I'm incapable of it!"

"Please, Papa," his daughter whined. "I don't want to leave. Why must everyone be afraid of him?"

"Well, I ain't. Not me!" Mr. Milton stalked toward the door. "I'll mend that imp's manners!"

As he stepped outside, Fennimore aimed and fired, striking his father in the stomach.

"You little bastard!" Mr. Milton shouted and ran after his son, moving astonishingly fast for a man of his age and size. Fennimore tried to run, but his effort came too late. His papa caught him by the collar and yanked him up short, holding him with one hand, and with the other, he broke a branch from a nearby bush. Soon the slap of the switch and Fennimore's hideous squeals filled the air. Mr. Milton returned with the slingshot and without his son.

"He's hid in the bushes to cry," he explained. "He'll be in when he's good and ready. Let's eat! All that exercise has given me one hell of an appetite!"

"Papa," Delphinia moaned. "Can't you cease cursing? It oversets me more than I can bear."

"I ain't gonna try to be something I'm not," he said jovially. "There's the earl I paid for. He can do the pretty."

From the corner of her eye, Sam saw Kevin wince again. Without looking further, she was certain that his expression was cold as an iceberg. Oh, why did the Miltons have to be the first guests to arrive?

"Come along, young woman," Mr. Milton prompted her. "Lead the way to food and drink!"

"Be sure to take Mrs. Milton's arm," Sam whispered to Kevin.

"I will not." Before Sam could protest, he took her arm and tucked it through his, escorting her to the drawing room, with the Miltons trailing behind.

Sam's nerves seemed raw and jangling. She could feel the tension in Kevin's arm and feared for the worst. Mr. Milton had rented *three* rooms, plus accommodations for the family servants. He was spending a great deal of money. Surely, Kevin would remember that and, at least, be civil.

Upon further reflection, however, her worry abated. English lords might be arrogant, conceited, and dandified, but they never failed to be gentlemen, or so she'd been told by Aunt Winifred. If this was so, she could trust Kevin to do the pretty, as Mr. Milton had said, even though he had escorted *her*, instead of Mrs. Milton, to the drawing room.

Encouragingly squeezing his arm, she beckoned to the butler. "Please bring a refreshment tray . . . a large one, and send in a footman to serve drinks. I prefer you to remain at the front door."

"Yes, Miss Samantha." He bowed and departed.

"Do you care for a glass of brandy?" Kevin asked Mr. Milton.

"Certainly, m'lord!" he enthused. "What a question to ask!"

"A footman will do that," Sam reminded Kevin as he left her side and walked toward the liquor cabinet, followed by his portly guest.

He ignored her, pouring the drinks himself as the manservant entered the room.

"Thank you, Lord Montjoy," Mr. Milton acknowledged. "That's right nice of you . . . doing the brandy yourself. I can have a servant set me up, anytime. This's an honor."

By that, Sam decided that Kevin knew what he was doing. He had impressed Mr. Milton, the man with the money, and he continued to do so. "Tell me about your enterprises," she overheard him say. That was the best thing he could have done. Mr. Milton launched into a lecture on his favorite subject, making money.

The footman served sherry to Sam and Mrs. Milton, and ratafia to Delphinia. Sipping her wine, Sam opened conversation with the cit's wife. "You have a lovely daughter, Mrs. Milton."

The woman beamed. "I'm proud of her, even if I do say so myself! She's gone to the best female school that'd have her. I

had the best dressmaker in London to make her wardrobe. Now
she's ready to be fired off to snag a husband."

Sam glanced at Delphinia, who had drifted across the room
to gaze out the window. Speaking about the young lady, in such
a matronly manner, made her feel rather odd. After all, she
couldn't be much older than the girl. She could see that she
pleased Mrs. Milton, though, just as Kevin had pleased her
spouse. She smiled.

"I'm sure that your daughter will be quite successful," she
commented.

A shadow crossed Mrs. Milton's face. "Yes, if she is invited
to the right parties. Will you be attending the next Season?"

Sam was rather stymied. She'd heard the London Season
mentioned, but she wasn't truly sure of what it was, other than
a place one went in order to find a spouse. She didn't want Mrs.
Milton to know how ignorant she was, though, so she used the
inn as an excuse. If they were as busy as she hoped they'd be,
no one would be going anywhere.

"I don't know, Mrs. Milton," she replied. "We have our hands
full here."

"Of course," the woman said sympathetically, then brightened. "But if you do, you'll make sure that Delphinia is invited
to your parties, won't you? And maybe she can go with you to
other events, too?"

"I seriously doubt that we'll be there," she vacillated.

"Well, if you are, will you help us?" She smiled fondly at
her daughter, who was walking back from the window toward
them. "I'll make it worth your while."

"What?" Sam wondered if she was hearing right.

"I'll pay handsome." Mrs. Milton pulled a diamond ring from
the many on her hands. "Take this as a pledge."

"I can't do that!" she gasped.

"I want you to have it. It will seal our bargain," the cit's wife
pressed.

"I will not take it." Sam backed up a pace. "Especially when
I am unsure as to whether I can help."

"Then just remember it, and remember that there's lots more where this came from. If Delphinia had the sponsorship of the Montjoy family . . ." The woman sighed, a silly simper on her face.

Wheels turned in Sam's head. One might do a brisk business in introducing wealthy cits' daughters to the *ton*. How intriguing!

Delphinia drifted up to them, sipping her ratafia. "Are you talking about me? I've seen you looking."

"Yes, my darling. We were admiring your beauty," her mother gushed, then returned her attention to Sam. "My husband was all set to make a match for Delphinia with a son of one of his business associates, but I refused. Our daughter is lovely enough to look higher. Personally, I think she can land a title. She only needs to be shown off in the right places."

"Are titles so important?" Sam mused. "What about love?"

Delphinia giggled. "We'd love any man with a title. Papa's working on it, even though he'd rather wed me to a businessman." She openly gazed at Kevin. "I hope there are lots of titled, impoverished gentlemen who'll be willing to marry for money alone."

Sam stared aghast. "You don't even care that a man would marry you only for money?"

The girl and her mother laughed. "No!" they said in unison.

"It would be nice if the man is handsome," Delphinia added. "Your cousin is awfully good-looking, Lady Samantha."

Sam started to correct the form of address and to state that Kevin was all but engaged, but decided that it would be better for business if she did not. These people were bowled over by titles. That was just what she wanted them to be, although she didn't care for the unmarried girls and their matchmaking mamas to chase after Kevin. That would aggravate him immensely. He might just blow up and ruin everything.

The butler arrived with the tray and the information that a carriage had been sighted, coming toward the castle. Evidently, the next party of guests was arriving. Sam was grateful for the diversion. Making polite excuses, she collected Kevin and departed to the front door to welcome the newcomers.

Lady Montjoy peered through the window of the second floor sitting room, utterly astonished by the scene below. She shook her head in wonderment. "There really are people paying to come here. I know we've had lots of mail, but I didn't really believe that anyone would actually come, especially with those hideously high prices Samantha was charging."

"How could you doubt my niece's idea?" Winifred queried.

"It seemed so farfetched, but then, I've never had a head for business. Why should I?"

"Why, indeed?" her sister-in-law agreed.

Margaret eloquently lifted a shoulder. "If this will truly help Kevin, I'm all for it."

"Then why won't you help him by lending your consequence?" Winifred retorted.

Daphne laid aside her embroidery. "Well, I intend to do so. If so many people are arriving, our children must need assistance. I shall go welcome guests and set them at ease."

"You?" Lady Montjoy snorted. "You are too shy in public to put a sentence together. I can just see you greeting strangers. You hardly speak to the people we've known for years!"

"I shall contrive."

"Fiddlesticks!" Her sister peeped out the window again. "Here comes another coach! The entrance hall will be filled with people you don't know, Daphne."

"I do not care." She rose rather unsteadily, her nerves apparently threatening to give her a case of the quakes. "I'm going to help Samantha and Kevin."

Winifred also stood. "I shall accompany you, Daphne. I wouldn't miss seeing you in action for all the tea in China!"

Margaret dithered, looking back and forth from the window to the other members of The Connection. "I vowed I wouldn't be a party to this!"

"No one is asking you," Winifred said smugly. "Daphne and I will attempt to remember all that takes place, so that we may report to you later."

"Yes," Daphne seconded. "We wouldn't want you to miss out on any of the excitement. Let us hurry, Winifred. I'm certain that the children must desperately need our help. My, but they'll be ever so grateful!"

"The two of you are ridiculous," Margaret spat out, "participating in such a nodcock scheme."

"No," Winifred differed, firmly shaking her head. "I will help Kevin in any way I can, if it will free him from his financial distress."

Lady Montjoy sprang to her feet, hands belligerently on her hips. "Are you insinuating that I refuse to aid my grandson?"

"Of course not," Winifred said, ever so sweetly.

"We would never do such a thing," Daphne added. "We are well aware of your dislike of cits."

"Farewell, Margaret." Winifred opened the door. The hum of voices, interspersed by laughter, could be heard echoing from the ground-floor hall.

"Let us hasten!" Daphne cried. "Just think how happy Samantha and Kevin will be to see us coming. It thrills me just to imagine it."

"Oh, yes," agreed her cohort. "Even though the crowd may consist of cits, there hasn't been such excitement at Montjoy Castle for many a year!"

Margaret frantically nibbled her lower lip. "Oh, very well!" she snapped. "Wait for me. I'm coming, too!"

Kevin was already growing weary of doing business, and there still were guests to greet. It was the unfamiliar strain, he supposed, of having such a swarm of strangers making free with his ancestral abode and expecting him to dance attendance on them. He felt that the smile he had fixed on his face was so brittle it would crack like glass.

Samantha, however, seemed to be in her element, welcoming people with warm hospitality, and thus, making money. He didn't know how she could bear up so well. The business was just beginning, but he wanted this crowd to leave and for Montjoy Castle to be his again, with only Samantha and The Connection to keep him company.

"Kevin?" his hostess called. "I wish you to meet these two ladies."

It was their private cue for him to exchange a few words with the guests, and then shunt them off to the ministrations of the butler and footmen in the drawing room, or to the housekeeper to show them to their rooms.

He detached himself from the couple with whom he'd been chatting, walked over to where Samantha stood, and bowed to the two elderly women. "Ladies, welcome to the Castle. I am Montjoy."

They performed two rickety curtsies.

"This is Miss Pixley and her sister, Miss Julia Pixley," Samantha introduced. "They are former schoolteachers."

He breathed a pleasant sigh. Educated ladies came only from genteel families. They would know how to conduct themselves.

"You no longer teach?" he asked.

"Good heavens, no, my lord!" the elder Miss Pixley responded. "Children today behave so atrociously. We could not bear another minute in the classroom."

"At our age, we were unable to cope," explained Miss Julia. "So with our savings and a small inheritance, we bought a little cottage in Hampshire. Our needs are simple, so we have enough money to keep us comfortable when the wind whistles, and still have a bit left over for travel."

"We also write children's books," said her sister. "We're currently working on one about castles. That is why we have come here."

Kevin was relieved to hear that they'd come to see Montjoy Castle instead of him. "Ladies, I hope you will make yourselves at home. When you have rested, and we are not so busy, I will be happy to take you on a tour of my home."

"Thank you, Lord Montjoy. You are so very kind," Miss Julia replied.

"Indeed," Miss Pixley politely agreed.

The Pixleys opted to go to their rooms. As Kevin watched them climb the stairs, he saw a sight he could scarcely believe. His grandmama was descending, along with the other two members of The Connection! Catching Samantha's attention, he nodded pointedly toward the stairway. He saw her eyes widen.

The Montjoy ladies immediately joined in to greet the horde. Although people continued to wish to meet him, the extra hostesses took away much of the burden. They had almost finished "processing the guests," as Sam called the procedure, when Kevin caught a movement from the corner of his eye.

The Miltons' brat, Fennimore, had entered the castle and somehow regained possession of his sling shot. The boy glided around the perimeter of the crowd and suddenly halted. With a wicked grin, he sighted in on Lady Montjoy's derriere. Before Kevin could leap to prevent it, Fennimore let fly a stone.

Nine

"No!" shouted Kevin simultaneously as his grandmother reacted, stiffening and reaching back to grasp her derriere in a most uncountesslike manner.

"That odious brat!" cried the man with whom she'd been speaking. Face crimson with anger, he charged toward Fennimore.

Pushing through the crowd, Kevin arrived at the scene of the crime, just as the gentleman grabbed the astonished lad and began to shake him until his teeth audibly rattled.

"Let me go!" Fennimore yelped in between his teeth clacking. "You ain't got no right!"

"I most certainly do!" claimed the nicely dressed, silvery gray-haired man. "I am defending the lady's honor. I just ought to call you out, you miserable urchin!"

The lad spied Kevin. "Help me, m'lord! He's gonna kill me!"

The earl's arrival distracted the gentleman. Taking advantage of his inattention, Fennimore ducked free and dashed toward the drawing room, jumping, yodeling, and flailing his arms.

"I'll catch you, you briggety, spoiled, little brat!" The man sprinted after him, nearly knocking down the earl in his blind haste.

"Capture him!" urged Lady Montjoy. "Make him pay!"

The crowd surged after them, trapping Kevin within its confines. Samantha was literally forced to shove her way to his side. "What are we going to do?" she wailed.

"At the present time, there's nothing much we can do," he observed.

"This will ruin everything," she complained. "Guests will be irritated, and your grandmother will be absolutely furious. Just when she was making an effort to be supportive! Fiddlesticks!"

"I could think of a more apt phrase, but I daresay you wouldn't like it." He managed a weak grin.

"Kevin, you could say *damn,* or *hell,* or both, and I would not take umbrage!"

"Actually, I had something much stronger in mind."

The crowd pressed into the drawing room, sweeping Kevin and Sam along with it. The scene within was not a pleasant one. Fennimore was hiding behind his mother, while his papa and Lady Montjoy's champion stood toe to toe, brangling.

The dowager countess had never before had such a diligent protector. Her life had been rather uneventful in matters of physical attack. She was terribly flattered that Mr. Courtney, an Egyptologist, had stood to defend her, but she decided that she could do a better job of it. She stepped regally into the fray.

"Mr. Milton," she declared in a high-pitched, authoritarian voice. "Your son has committed the unpardonable sin of shooting me in . . . well, in a location modesty forbids me to disclose."

"Oh? And just who are you?" the businessman demanded, jutting out his jaw and looking rather like a bulldog.

She drew herself up, straightened her shoulders, and looked down her aristocratic nose as if she were observing the lowest form of life on the earth. "I," she stressed with a lengthy pause, "am Lady Montjoy."

"Oh, God," he muttered.

Every drop of blood seeming to have drained from her countenance, Mrs. Milton jerked Fennimore from behind her skirts. "Here is the imp. Do accept my most heartfelt apologies, my lady." She curtsied so low that she became off balance and was compelled to grab her husband's arm to stagger upright.

Several members of the crowd tittered, but Kevin's grandmother remained grandly stone-faced.

"Please forgive us." Mrs. Milton visibly trembled. "Fennimore is at that awkward stage in which children, particularly boys, are almost uncontrollable in their deviltry."

"Indeed?" Lady Montjoy's voice dripped with icicles. "The present earl's mother died when he was but a babe. I reared him myself, and never once did I encounter misbehavior so blatant as I have witnessed today."

Mrs. Milton hung her head. "I have never been so mortified."

"Papa, why don't you take Fennimore home?" Delphinia suggested angrily. "Twice he has acted up, and we haven't been here above an hour! He's a bad boy, and I hate him!"

"Come on, Fennimore." Mr. Milton grasped his son by the scruff of his neck. "I'll teach the lad a lesson. Never you fear, Lady Montjoy! He won't be sittin' down for a while."

"He'd best mend his ways," she threatened, "or we shall be forced to evict him from this house. There is a long waiting list of people who know how to conduct themselves."

"Yes, ma'am," he said humbly.

Kevin chuckled. "Grandmama is magnificently intimidating."

Sam watched Mr. Milton lead his son by the ear to the hall. She sighed. "This occupation is going to be very wearying."

"Perk up, dear cousin," he challenged. "You must be ready for the next misadventure."

"Surely there will be none," she said in a voice almost prayerful.

Delphinia approached them. "I am so horridly embarrassed that I could swoon! I cannot understand why my parents brought Fennimore in the first place! He is naughty beyond all belief. And why do they allow him to have that sling shot? O-o-o-oh!"

"Many boys are mischievous," Kevin remarked.

"But not you, Lord Montjoy." She gazed worshipfully up at him.

Samantha snorted. "What a tale."

"I was a charming child," he said, grinning broadly.

"I'm sure you were," Delphinia purred.

Sam groaned. With each sentence, the Milton chit had moved further and further in front of her until she totally blocked her from Kevin's sight. *Baggage,* she thought. Delphinia was attempting to set up a flirtation with the earl! Sam was infuriated. She'd known that Kevin would attract customers, but she hadn't envisioned it in just this way.

The girl moved slightly and Sam caught a glimpse of her cousin's profile. He was handsome enough to take one's breath away. He would probably entrance all the young ladies who visited, and they would fall in love with him. The thought of it rankled, but there was nothing at all she could do about it. She could, however, caution him to watch his step, so that none of the females could maneuver him into a compromising situation. Alas, she couldn't do it now. That odious Delphinia had drawn him away from her.

Aggravated, Sam returned to the hall to make certain that there were enough servants posted near the stairs to show the guests to their rooms. Happily, everyone was in his place. She nodded approval and paused to straighten a flower in the huge arrangement. Casually looking upward, she saw Bob's haunches glide out of sight across the top of the stairs. For a split second, her heart seemed to stop, then rushed on in a fierce staccato.

"Bob is loose!" she cried to the butler and dashed up the steps in hot pursuit.

There were gasps from the servants, but no one came to help her—not that she had expected them to. Instead, the staff seemed to melt into the woodwork, leaving her alone in the hall. Their fear of Bob was obviously so great that they would risk being let go rather than possibly confronting the lynx, even with her in their midst.

With an inward groan, she started up the stairs. When she reached the next floor, the bobcat was not to be seen. Sam felt like crying. What a day! She had expected some awkward moments on opening day, but she had certainly not imagined what actually had unfolded. First, that awful little boy, now Bob on the prowl. And she mustn't forget that flirtatious Delphinia! She wished she could give in to a flood of tears, but she couldn't afford such a luxury. No one else would capture Bob. It was up to her. Slowly, she started down the hall in the direction she'd seen her pet take.

One of the footmen came out of a chamber, and seeing her, was startled. "Miss?"

"Bob is loose," she said without preamble. "Please stand here and call to me if you see him. I must check every room that has an open door."

The servant began to quake. "There's the backstairs, too, Miss Samantha, what goes down to the kitchen."

"Good heavens!" she wailed. "What if he's gone down there and ruined the meal Cook's preparing?"

The footman had no ready answer. He was too busy frantically watching and holding a chamber's doorknob, in order to beat a speedy retreat if necessary.

Walking softly on, Sam, almost at once, found that the door of Kevin's dressing room was ajar. She entered and spied the earl's valet brushing a navy blue coat. "Hello," she said.

He seemed to leap a foot off the ground. "Miss Samantha!"

"I'm sorry I frightened you," she apologized, "but I'm searching for Bob. He's loose again."

His eyes bulged. "I don't think he could have come here, miss, or I would have seen him."

"You left the door open?"

"Well yes, miss, I suppose I did. I just came up with my lord's fresh laundry. But I've been right here all the time. That cat couldn't have entered."

She nodded. "Just the same, I believe I'll have a look around."

She knew she shouldn't waste time, but seeing Kevin's private quarters was just too tempting. Passing from the dressing room into the chamber proper, she stared in awe at the faded magnificence. The bed's heavy canopy was the focal point, with its massive lions' heads on the posts and gold-fringed, scarlet trappings. She lowered her gaze and choked. In the center of all the luxury was Bob, lazily stretched out for a nap. Pricking his ears, he lifted his head and grinned, flopping down again to relax in regal splendor.

"You are a bad cat!" Sam exploded. "How did you escape again?"

He idly raised a paw and began to lick.

"You are going to have to come with me." She started forward. "What is wrong with you? You have ideal quarters in my sitting room."

He lifted a lip.

"Don't threaten me!" She smacked his rump. "You know better than that."

He grinned again.

He was too heavy for her to carry. She glanced around the room for something to act as a leash, but saw nothing. "Martin?" she called. "Please bring me one of Lord Montjoy's neckcloths."

There was no reply.

"Fiddlesticks!" She returned to the dressing room to find that Kevin's valet had fled the scene.

Making sure that the door to the hall was securely closed, Samantha began to search the premises, beginning with a large chest of drawers. Self-consciously, she opened a drawer and discovered with a blush that it contained Kevin's unmentionables. The next was neatly filled with stockings. At last, she looked inside one which boasted neckcloths and handkerchiefs. Just what she needed! She pulled out a snow white cravat.

"What the devil do you think you're doing?" a masculine voice rang out.

Sam jumped, spinning. "Kevin! There you are! How propitious!"

He frowned. "Why are you rifling my drawers, Samantha?"

Guilt burnt her cheeks. "I'm looking for something to use as a leash."

Blood drained from his face. "I'm afraid to ask why, but where is he, and how the hell did he get loose again?"

She winced. "On your bed, Kevin."

He took a deep breath, closed his eyes, and exhaled slowly. "Tell me, Lord, that this isn't true."

"But it is," Sam muttered miserably. "I don't know how he got loose or entered your rooms, but he did. I hated to take the time to return to my chamber to fetch his collar and leash. I was afraid that guests might be coming up by now, and espy me. So . . . so I was looking for something closer at hand."

"My neckcloth," he finished.

"Er . . . yes. If guests had seen him, I doubt that it would be good for business."

"Brilliant deduction, Samantha."

She cringed, lowering her gaze and looking at him through her lashes. "I didn't wish to cause harm, Kevin. I would have returned the neckcloth and explained."

"Indeed?" he asked sarcastically.

"Of course." Catching her lip between her teeth, she raised her head and received a further jolt. "Uh, Kevin, do not be alarmed, but Bob is coming toward us."

"Son-of-a—" He froze. "Samantha, if he bites me, I will shoot him dead. Do you understand? Dead!"

While his stunned mistress gritted her teeth, the cat, however, seemed to have come to the total decision that Kevin was a friend. To Sam's horror and Kevin's terror, he rubbed languor-ously against the earl's legs. They could actually hear his throaty purr.

"He has accepted, nay, *likes* you!" Sam enthused.

"How wonderful," Kevin said without expression.

"This is an honor! You should be flattered," she gushed. "He has never accepted anyone but me. I wonder if he'd let you pick him up?"

"I don't know, and I damn sure am not going to try. Take a neckcloth, Samantha, tie him up, and get him out of here! You shouldn't be here either. It's scandalous."

"It is? Why?" Perhaps he'd seen her staring at his unmentionables.

He stared at her in disbelief. "Why? Because you're a young lady, I am a bachelor, and this is my bedroom; that's why!"

"It don't see what difference it makes. We're cousins." She removed a neckcloth from the drawer and started toward him.

He adamantly shook his head. "We are cousins only by marriage. Don't you realize how compromising this situation is? If anyone saw us, we'd be forced to marry."

Her green eyes grew wide with surprise. "Really? What if we did not want to? There can be no law in England to force people to wed. If there is, this country is more ridiculous than I ever expected."

He made a mouth of disgust. "Of course, there is no actual law. But there are social edicts involved."

"You and your class system!" she jeered. "I'll never understand why the lot of you strain to obey what I imagine to be a batch of snobbish, indolent, old harpies, who have nothing to do but to sit around criticizing the conduct of others, without knowing the particular circumstances."

"Samantha?" he demanded. "Are you telling me that such societal tenets do not exist in America?"

"Well . . ." He was trapping her, and she saw no means of escape. Even on the frontier, there were rules of behavior. Perhaps it was just a bit more difficult to be caught. No matter, she wasn't going to allow him to win this battle. In a very businesslike manner, she tied one end of the neckcloth around Bob's neck.

"We shall continue this discussion at another time," she announced loftily. "Right now, I must remove Bob from your chamber, Kevin. Do look and see if the hall is vacant."

As soon as he opened the door, she heard the babble of voices.

"Fiddlesticks! Oh, this is wonderful. Is there no other way out of here?"

"There is a door to a vacant chamber," he said.

She curiously tilted her head. "Another chamber we could rent?"

"No!" he shouted. "That bedroom connects with mine! This is the suite of the master and mistress."

"We could have a secure lock installed."

"No!" he ranted. "Leave off, Samantha! I won't have guests residing in my future wife's abode."

"We could rent my rooms, and I could—"

"No!" he blared again. "There will be no further mention of it. I'm not sure why I brought up the subject. It will not facilitate escape."

Sam shrugged. "Don't you wish to become rich, Kevin?"

"The use of that room will not make or break this scheme of yours."

"Coward!" she dismissed. "How can anyone help you, if you refuse to help yourself?"

"That's all, Samantha! *That is all!* Am I not doing enough in allowing you to set me up as the main attraction in a raree show?" He jerked open the door, listened, and peeked out. "The way is clear. Now get out of here!"

"Gladly! You remind me of a cross old maid!" She wrapped the free end of the neckcloth around her hand and fairly dragged Bob to the door. "Do whatever you wanted to do when you came here, Kevin, and accomplish it quickly. I shall require another *performance* from you very soon!"

"Goodbye, Samantha." Rather ungraciously, he slammed the door behind her.

Ungrateful wretch, she said to herself and tried to hasten Bob down the hall, but the cat refused to cooperate. She tried to drag him, but he erupted in a fit of coughing, forcing her to halt altogether. It seemed like a very long and nerve-wracking time before she entered her own chamber.

Her abigail was within, wringing her hands. "Oh, Miss Samantha, thank the Lord you've found him! I heard him me-owing earlier . . . well, he doesn't really meow like a normal cat, does he? Anyway, I heard him making this pitiful noise, so

I peeked in to make sure he was all right. I must not have shut the door good. I suppose he picked it open with his claws."

Samantha hadn't the heart to scold her. "No harm has been done, but with paying guests in the castle, we must make very sure that it doesn't happen again."

"Not just the customers, miss! Everyone's afraid of that Bob. The way he looks at me with those cat eyes . . ." She shuddered. "He's a mean'un!"

Sam did not bother to explain that she thought Bob would eventually tolerate the residents of Montjoy Castle. It was best that the staff remain frightened of him. Then they would be more careful to keep the particular doors closed.

"You're right to be cautious," she agreed and led Bob into her sitting room, removing Kevin's neckcloth. The cat promptly strolled to the window seat and leapt up, stretching and preparing to nap. Sam returned to the bedchamber and firmly secured the door.

"I got a good look at the people from the top of the stairs," Martha chirped in obvious relief that the bobcat was locked away. "That one girl sure is pretty."

"Delphinia," Sam easily guessed, the name almost curdling in her mouth. "Quite a piece of baggage!"

The maid looked askance at her.

"She's attempting to set up a flirtation with my cousin," Sam volunteered. "I hope he can see through those silly wiles! It is thoroughly nauseating."

Martha smiled secretively. "So it must be! Now, Miss Samantha, won't you let me freshen you up a bit? I'd like to try a new style of hair I've been thinking of."

"If it doesn't take very long, have at it," Sam agreed, "but bear in mind that I do not intend to spend the rest of the day primping. I have business to attend."

"Very well, Miss Samantha. Shall we commence immediately? Perhaps you'd like to put on your pretty green gown." Without waiting for a reply, she took position behind Sam and began to unfasten the tapes of her dress.

* * *

Suddenly feeling very weary, Kevin shut the door behind his cousin, pulled the bell rope to summon his valet, and went to his sitting room—the connecting alcove he would share with his future countess one day. Pouring himself a glass of brandy from the liquor cabinet in the sideboard, he wandered across the room to the window and idly stared out.

His suite, like Samantha's, overlooked the rear gardens. This year, because of the intensive work, they looked more attractive than he could ever remember. With the aid of the assistant gardeners his cousin had hired, the flower beds and walkways were neatly weeded, new plantings and mulch had been added, and the topiary was trimmed. It was the sort of orderly setting that Montjoy Castle had long deserved, but attaining it, along with other venturesome projects, had been expensive. If they were not successful in this endeavor, he would be bankrupt, and then . . .

If the worst occurred, Lady Frances's dowry, if the female would still have him, might not be enough to set him to rights. He might have to wed a wealthy cit's daughter, a girl like Delphinia. His father-in-law would be a red-faced, blustering oaf, who'd control his life by making him answer for every shilling. His mother-in-law would be a gushing, boot-licking toady. His grandmama and the rest of The Connection would glare down their aristocratic noses at his wife and in-laws. Cousin Samantha . . . who could predict how she would behave? Bob . . . was Bob. And as for himself, it went without saying that he would be miserable.

Kevin heard his valet enter the room, but did not turn. "I suppose I'd best get ready for dinner, Lemaster."

"Sir, I was just met in the hall by an emissary from Lady Montjoy. The countess requests a word with you, immediately, in the ladies' private parlor."

He groaned. "Lord, it's probably about the ill treatment she received at the hands of the Milton brat."

"I wouldn't know, my lord."

"And even if you did, you wouldn't tell," Kevin said sourly. "Am I left in abandoned ignorance to meet my fate?"

"I . . . don't understand, sir," his manservant murmured cautiously.

"No, I imagine you wouldn't." Kevin turned from the window and walked back to the sideboard to refill his own glass. "Is the hall free of cits?"

"At the moment." He sniffed disparagingly. "Those people have gone to their chambers."

The earl briefly closed his eyes and put his hand to his forehead as if he had a searing headache. "Lemaster, are you and the other servants truly aware of the reason we are playing host to these guests? Please be frank."

His valet flinched. "Money, my lord."

"Yes, money, or the lack thereof." He nodded curtly. "Now, one further question. What does the staff think of Miss Samantha?"

Lemaster uncomfortably shifted from foot to foot. "Oh, sir, I hardly know what to say. We like Miss Samantha. She is like a breath of fresh air, but . . ."

"Go on," Kevin prompted.

"Well, my lord, we cannot understand why she seems to disregard the advantages of her station. This may be because she's American, but, sir, both you and I know that it isn't her place to hobnob on an equal basis with servants." He emphatically shook his head. "We don't like it when she appears backstairs. That's our dominion, and she shouldn't frequent it. So there's our opinion, my lord. You asked for it, and I hope you don't feel ill will to me for speaking out."

Kevin had never heard Lemaster offer such a blatant assessment, even on the rare occasions when he'd asked for it. Samantha must have conducted herself with so much familiarity that she had upset the stringent barrier that divided the house both physically and socially between the classes. Since his valet had been so openly critical, he supposed he'd have to do something about the situation. He sighed. Would life ever become uncomplicated?

"I'll speak with Miss Samantha about the matter," he promised, "but for now, I'd best present myself to my grandmother."

His valet bowed. "I shall be laying out your evening attire, my lord."

"Nothing too formal," Kevin advised. "Not with this company."

"As you wish, sir."

He left his chamber and strode down the hall. Montjoy Castle was silent now, with guests closeted in their chambers to prepare themselves for a social evening, and servants hastening to make certain that all was ready for them. Kevin wished that he could take to his bed and pull the covers over his head until all this was ended. But when would that be? When he was wealthy, or when he was ruined. Until the future was known, he must suffer strangers in his home. Lips twisting into a wry smile, he paused before his grandmama's door and rapped lightly.

Ten

Waiting for his grandmother's abigail to answer his rap on the door, Kevin had never felt so exposed. It was as if multiple strangers' eyes were boring into his back and staring at him as if he were an animal in a menagerie. Fidgety, he knocked again, this time more loudly.

"Be still, and give me a chance to answer!" his grandmother shouted imperiously, jerking open the door herself. Frowning severely, she motioned him in.

"Kevin," she grumbled, "I have never been so humiliated. Merely thinking about that awful incident is enough to give me the vapors!"

She looked quite robust and not at all faint, but he said nothing of his observation. "Yes, Grandmama, the Milton lad is a regular handful."

"To say the least! In my opinion, he is a horrid little urchin who should be sent to a workhouse! What a spoiled brat, and what a common family! I want you to ask them to leave." Taking his arm, she piloted him to a love seat. "In fact, I want all of them to go, but you will not do that, will you?"

"Some of the guests are not so bad," he soothed. "I believe you appreciated Mr. Courtney's intervention on your part. You haven't met everyone, remember? You may be pleasantly surprised."

"No, I will not." She sat and drew him down beside her. "From now on, I intend to remain in my rooms. You must admit that I made an effort to be gracious. No longer shall I do so! I have learned a bitter lesson today."

Kevin searched his mind to find something to say that would pacify her. "Grandmama, do you realize how much money we are making?"

She shook her head. "I venture to say that it will not repay the amount Samantha caused to be spent on this hideous arrangement."

"Well, not quite," he admitted, "but we are only beginning."

She threw up her hands in frustration. "You will probably make a few guineas until the novelty wears off! Then there will be more pain than promise. You are paying a high price, Kevin, for the loss of our good name. Your Montjoy forebears must be spinning in their graves."

"Good for them. Good for them, I say!" He wrenched to his feet and crossed the room to peruse the ladies' liquor cabinet. Finding only sherry aggravated him even more. Irritably popping the cork, he poured himself a glass. "If those disapproving ancestors had been more careful of their money, I wouldn't have had to face this dilemma. I'm staring down the throat of ruin, thanks to those old rotters!"

Lady Montjoy gasped. "You cannot be speaking that way about your father and grandfather, Kevin. I cannot believe this is really you!"

"Well, it is," he said roughly, emptying the glass and refilling it. "It's me, and I'm going to do whatever I must to avoid doing the same thing to any offspring of mine!"

"O-o-o-h . . ." She sank farther into the love seat, draping one arm exhaustedly over the pillows. "Are you telling me that money is more important than honor?"

"I believe that a man who must work for his bread can be just as honorable as a man who does not," he said hotly. "Maybe more so! What honor lies in wedding a wealthy heiress so that one may live in idle luxury? The members of the *ton* should review their tenets."

She wagged her head slowly back and forth and sighed audibly. "My dear, you cannot change our way of life. It has been proven good over the course of centuries."

"Our life can only be sweet if it has a vast amount of money to support it. Grandmama, can you not realize the fortune that a man like Milton has made? He may be vulgar, but he's as smart as they come."

"I only want you to be financially secure, Kevin." She removed a fine lace handkerchief from her nearby reticule and dabbed at her eyes. "Why can't you marry an heiress, as other men do?"

Surprised at his own rather democratic speech, he sat down on a footstool beside her and took her hands in his. "Please understand. I must try to help myself before hiding behind a woman's skirts like a frightened child."

"No one looks at it that way," she protested.

"I do . . . I think." he added.

She compressed her lips into a snit. "It's that chit, Samantha, and her money-grubbing American ways, isn't it? She is the one who came up with this invasion of cits."

He couldn't deny it. "But I agreed," he reminded her.

"America is a nation of shopkeepers," she prated on. "It is populated by the Old World's dregs and rejects."

"Oh?" He lifted an eyebrow. "Is that what you think of Samantha and her parents?"

"That case is different, although Samantha could benefit by a strong hand to guide her." She snorted. "I am speaking of the majority of Americans. They're a passel of odious, obnoxious cits!"

"My, but this household is rampant with prejudice," he observed. "You believe that all cits are repulsive and crude, and Samantha maintains that all peers are indolent, unmanly drones."

"Samantha is wrong."

"So are you, Grandmama." He squeezed her hands and rose. "We've exhausted this topic of conversation, and it's time to dress for dinner."

"I shall not attend," she vowed. "I will not be put on display like an ancient relic."

Kevin grinned. "What a thing to say!"

"I mean it," she muttered.

"Please, Grandmama," he wheedled, smiling. "You will greatly aid me if you are present."

"No! I cannot bear seeing you make yourself into—" She swiftly glanced in all directions and lowered her voice. "Into a prostitute, Kevin. This impossible farce renders you into a Jezebel, selling your body for a mess of pottage!"

His smile broadened. "I believe the Biblical reference concerned trading one's birthright."

"That, too!" she snapped.

"Well then, I'll have to do without your succor," he stated. "So I imagine that Samantha must sit in your place at the table and act as hostess."

"I will not permit that! My chair will remain empty, so that everyone may witness my displeasure."

"My, what a punishment for us all! I would think you'd prefer to assume your seat in regal splendor, casting disparaging glances and looking down your lofty nose at your social underlings. That would be a much better way of putting people in their places." He chuckled. "Just think of how Mrs. Milton would grovel!"

"I do not care what she or others may do! They are my inferiors, and therefore, I do not notice them." She flicked her hand in the air as if she were fanning smoke away from her face. "They are nothing! I do not even see them!"

"Very well, if that is how you truly feel." With a shrug, he turned to leave.

"Kevin!"

He halted, swiveling.

"You had best not put anyone in my place at the table. I might decide to join you, just for dessert," she proclaimed.

"Why just for that course?"

"Dessert, then a savory, finish the meal. The men will linger over their port, while the women adjourn to the drawing room."

"So?" he inquired.

"Winifred is a scatterbrain. Daphne is a mouse. That leaves only Samantha to act as hostess in my stead." She pursed her lips and turned down the corners of her mouth. "The gel isn't capable of doing it properly. I can just see it now! She will treat those people as if they were her social equals. They must be reminded that they still occupy stations far below us. One cannot buy noble breeding!"

"There are peers who have married cit's daughters to repair their fortunes," Kevin mused. "That strikes me as purchasing blue blood."

"Fustian!" she uttered tightly. "I shall not debate the matter. Just make sure that my chair is available, should I deign to attend."

"As you wish, Grandmama," he acceded with a bow and left the room, wishing that he could pick and choose the appearances he would make. Lady Montjoy might be top-lofty in matters of descent and decorum. In spite of his speech on equality, maybe deep down, he felt the same way, too. But he couldn't afford to express it. He must try to make the scheme work. If Samantha was right in her assessment, it could be his very salvation.

Samantha was the first in the drawing room before dinner. Glancing at the clock on the mantel, she thought of the long evening ahead and dreaded every minute of it. She could almost hear the chitter-chatter about subjects that did not interest her. Also, she could feel the deadly silences which occurred when topics were changed or conversation stalled. In addition, she visualized the embarrassing moment when someone asked her about the neighborhood, the Montjoy family, or the castle's history. If Aunt Winifred or Aunt Daphne didn't know the answer, she'd have to refer the inquiry to Kevin. She doubted that he knew much either. He'd been too busy playing the lofty earl to indulge in such study. On the other hand, Lady Montjoy probably knew all the history of the castle and family and should be present to act as hostess. It was her rightful duty. But Sam was relatively certain that the countess would not appear. Having been the victim of that odious Fennimore and being against the whole idea from the very beginning, Aunt Margaret would stay holed up in her room.

At least Sam would not be completely alone. Aunt Winifred and Aunt Daphne would be on the scene to assist, and of course there was Kevin. She peeked again at the clock. Where was her cousin? She was early, but, as host, he should be early as well. When the door opened, she smiled gratefully toward it.

"We're in the same room as before," Miss Delphinia Milton remarked plaintively, as she and her parents were shown in by a footman. "I thought we'd see more of the castle."

Sam stepped forward to greet them. "I have a tour of the castle scheduled for morning, and one of the grounds after lunch."

"Surely this huge place has more than one drawing room," the young woman went on.

Sam nodded. "Many rooms are in the midst of extensive redecoration."

"I would still like to see them," she persisted, "and I'd like to see Lord Montjoy's chamber. It must be very grand."

"Not really, Miss Milton," Samantha replied, wondering what the chit would think of Kevin's faded draperies and bed hangings. "And I'm sorry to say that the family rooms are kept private."

The girl lifted a negligent shoulder. "Perhaps I can obtain special permission."

Sam tried to ignore the comment and also Delphinia's attire, but it was rather impossible. The cit's daughter was dressed entirely too daringly for a female her age. The gown's pink hue went well with her hair and coloration, but that was all that was pleasant. Its neckline, if so it could be called, plunged so low that it exposed a shocking view of her deeply clefted, nicely shaped bosom. The skirt clung very close to her body, leaving little to be imagined of Delphinia's youthful curves. Next to her, Sam felt like a child, and a boy-child at that! Her genteel dress concealed and only hinted at what few bodily attributes she did possess. Next to Delphinia, she must look like a school-girl. It was horribly disheartening.

While a footman served glasses of sherry, Sam tried to carry on conversation with Mr. and Mrs. Milton, while Delphinia prowled about the room like a caged animal. She was relieved to hear that Fennimore would not be taking luncheon or dinner with the adults and would eat from a tray in his own room. This announcement was literally applauded by his sister.

"We should have left him at home in the first place," she pronounced. "He is obnoxious, mischievous, and repulsive. Like a dog, he should be kept in his kennel and trotted out only when he is leashed."

"Now see here, young lady," her father scolded. "Fennimore is my only son and the heir to my business enterprises. He should know something of the world."

"Hm!" she snorted. "He should be whipped black and blue for shooting Lady Montjoy in the botsy."

"He has been punished."

"Not strongly enough," she quarreled, wrinkling her nose. "If he were severely flogged, he would not be such an embarrassing little criminal."

"You'd best make up with him, girl," her father warned. "One day he will likely be controlling your share of my company."

"If the day ever comes when Fennimore takes control, I'll instruct my husband to sell my shares," she fired back. "That nauseating, hideous, ignorant nuisance will never administer one shilling on my behalf!"

"Please," Mrs. Milton begged, "can't we speak of something else?"

As if in response to her plea, Kevin entered, looking more handsome than any man had a right to be.

"My lord!" Delphinia blushed, curtsying deeply. "You will be happy to know that my atrocious brother will dine in his room. Are you not thrilled?"

Kevin bowed gallantly over her outstretched hand and treated her mother in identical fashion. He ignored Sam. "I cannot claim to be enthused or not," he said diplomatically. "I scarcely know the lad. I suppose it's a case of boys being boys."

"Thank you, Lord Montjoy," interjected Mr. Milton. "I'm getting tired of people talking ugly about Fennimore. He's merely a fine little fellow who has much to learn. He doesn't usually act in public the way he did today."

"No, he acts worse," Delphinia stated.

A footman with a tray of drinks interrupted the exchange. Before he finished serving the new arrivals, others entered. Sam lost sight of Delphinia and Kevin in the shuffle. When the crowd settled, she saw them standing together near the window. Kevin was speaking, and Delphinia was avidly hanging on every word, her pink lips formed in an appreciative O. A surge of anger rushed through Sam's veins. Kevin should play host to all. He shouldn't single out only one to entertain. She started toward them, but Aunt Winifred reached out a restraining arm.

"Don't chastise, Samantha," she advised so softly that Sam, let alone any one else, could scarcely hear. "It isn't his fault, and he will resent you for interfering."

Sam questioningly raised an eyebrow.

"Rescue him, if that is your wish, but do not criticize him." The white-haired lady smiled, eyes twinkling. "At times, you are too overbearing with him. Remember, one can catch more flies with honey than with vinegar."

Sam was flabbergasted by her aunt's advice. Did the sweet old lady think that Sam had set her cap for Kevin? Nothing could be further from the truth! Currently, the earl was putting forth a display of working for a living, but that wouldn't last. As soon as he became wealthy, he'd quickly revert to the role of a layabout lord. No, she'd never look upon Kevin, or any other English nobleman, as a potential suitor. She didn't like the dilatory breed.

Delphinia certainly was of a different opinion, she admitted as she glanced again at the couple by the window. The girl was insinuating herself as close as she could to Kevin without falling into his arms. Disliking the invasion of his space, her cousin continually took a step backward. Delphinia then took a step forward, and on and on in a disgusting, pseudo dancing routine. Sam started toward them, but was hailed by Mr. Courtney.

"Won't the countess be joining us this evening?" he queried.

Sam swiftly gazed over the room's population. "Apparently not, sir."

"Because of that ill-mannered lad, I'll wager." He frowned. "At least, he isn't here. I can well imagine what a shambles he'd make of a dinner table."

"I can visualize it, too," she dryly declared. "Perhaps I should have set an age limit on our clientele."

"By that comment, may I assume that it was your idea to make Montjoy Castle into an inn of sorts?"

She nodded.

He smiled broadly. "I thought I sensed a touch of American ingenuity in this venture. You *are* American, aren't you, Miss Edwards?"

"Yes," she replied. "How did you guess?"

"Your accent, of course, plus this business enterprise. Our peerage is not characterized by dirtying their hands in commerce." Mr. Courtney chuckled. "I would further bet that His Lordship is in murky financial waters and hasn't yet found an heiress to bail him out. Do not take that as criticism, Miss Edwards. My father was a marquess, so I am intimately familiar with the machinations of the aristocracy. Indeed, my elder brother was forced to wed for money."

Sam slowly shook her head in wonder. "You are right. Cousin Montjoy did inherit debt, but until I came up with this scheme, he thought his only salvation was to wed an heiress. He probably still does, for that matter."

The Egyptologist smiled and nodded.

"When I arrived at the castle," Samantha went on, "I immediately noted that the place was run-down, yet I saw no other signs of poverty. There was a large staff of servants; my relatives dressed well; the food was excellent. It seemed that few economies were practiced. I just don't understand it all."

"A peer must keep up appearances," Mr. Courtney explained.

"But if one hasn't the money, one cannot spend it. It's as simple as that. One cannot live above one's means."

The discussion ended abruptly as the butler announced dinner. Sam mentally crossed her fingers and hoped for the best. The protocol of the seating had been awkward. For example, no one had known that Mr. Courtney was the son of a high-ranking peer, since he had not used his courtesy address of lord. He should have taken precedence over all the guests. Luckily, he didn't seem to mind.

Also, the serving was ungraceful. With Lady Montjoy's chair empty, all order was lost. The butler evidently decided that Sam was the acting hostess and was forced to carry out his duties to her in an unaccustomed place. It was beyond bumbling and rather outrageous. Sam decided that she must confront her Aunt Margaret and beg her to cease this yes-or-no arrangement.

She was worried about the food, too. These people had spent a great deal of money to stay at Montjoy Castle, and their palates must be well satisfied. Many of them probably had French chefs at home. The Montjoy cook served sumptuous country fare. It was delicious, but it featured products of the estate's land. There was nothing cosmopolitan about this menu. Would they like it? Sam was pleased to see the gentlemen and even some of the ladies eating with gusto, enjoying the meal to the hilt.

Her further fear arose when she adjourned the ladies to the drawing room for tea, while the gentlemen lingered over their port. She was happy to find that she needn't have worried. Aunt Winifred initiated a lively conversation and called upon Delphinia to play the pianoforte. Quiet Aunt Daphne gracefully poured the tea. Sam actually ended up with a moment of relaxation. When the gentlemen joined them, she was surprised to see that the time had passed so speedily.

Although Delphinia doubled her efforts of piano playing, obviously trying to catch Kevin's attention, he made a beeline for Samantha. "I must apologize for my grandmother's absence. She led me to believe that she would join us for dessert."

Sam lifted a shoulder. "All went as well as could be expected. There were awkward moments, but we overcame them."

"I believe that she decided that her vacant chair would be a reminder of Fennimore's misbehavior."

She smiled. "If so, it worked. Mr. Courtney noticed her absence even before we entered the dining room, and speculated that it was caused by the boy."

"Oh, Lord Montjoy!" Delphinia caroled, fingers rippling over the keys. "Do sing a song with me."

"Your public is calling," Sam said sourly. "You'd best go carry on your nauseating flirtation. Overplay your role. *I* certainly do not care."

"What the devil are you talking about?" he asked.

"You should know," she retorted, casting Aunt Winifred's advice to the wind. "You are one-sided in your attentions, Kevin. Delphinia is not the only person here."

He momentarily looked puzzled, then grinned brightly. "Are you jealous, Samantha?"

"Of your regard for another woman? Don't make me laugh!" she scoffed, cheeks burning. "Why should I be envious of that?"

His blue eyes danced with glee. "You are. Oh, how rare!"

Sam had been prepared for his anger, not for this mockery and merry accusation. Kevin might as well allege that she had set her cap for him. It was vastly oversetting, and nothing could be more untrue. She could never become a snobbish, uppity countess. Instinctively, she despised the *ton*. No, she could never be the lazy, vaporish wife of a nobleman. It would be too totally boring. No, she preferred to continue to manage this unique country inn.

Suddenly, she felt a stab of fear. If Kevin became wealthy from this venture and/or married an heiress, he probably wouldn't want his house to be full of strangers. The inn would close, and she would be out of luck and unemployed.

His chuckle drew her back from her unhappy visions of the future. "That certainly must have given you pause, Samantha," he jeered. "You look as though your mind is lost in the stars."

"And you look as though your mind is lost, period!" she snapped. "You are insane, Kevin, if you believe I am jealous. I have never heard such bunk."

"Ah, Samantha, fencing with you is such a joy. I arise each day with the hope of crossing swords with you."

"Fiddlesticks, Kevin Montjoy!" she cried, flushing. "I refuse to listen to this nonsense."

Blindly flouncing away, she found herself heading in the direction of the pianoforte. Kevin followed her. When they reached the instrument, Sam dropped back to watch Delphinia's fingers as they skillfully moved over the keys. The girl was very talented. For one brief moment, Sam wondered if the young woman's parents appreciated her expertise, or if they merely considered her playing a device to assist her in snaring a husband.

Delphinia finished the piece with a light crescendo and looked up at Kevin. "There, my lord. Now would you like to sing?"

Sam interrupted. "That was absolutely beautiful, Miss Milton. I am truly in awe of your genius."

The cit's daughter smiled, somewhat surprised. "Thank you, Miss Edwards," she said carefully, as if she were waiting for a verbal trap to spring.

"You must bring great pleasure to all those who hear you," Sam waxed on.

Blushing intensely, Delphinia bent her head, fingers meandering over the keys. "Truthfully, I do not often perform for a

group. It . . . it invariably brings forth caustic criticism and biting remarks from the other females present."

"They envy you," Sam declared. "They think it garners you
too much favorable attention. You should fly in their faces and
play anyway. Your light should not be hidden under a bushel
basket. Am I not right, Kevin?"

He held up his hands as if to ward off a blow. "I make it a
practice never to advise a young lady on these certain matters."

Sam shrugged. "Well, Miss Milton, you will simply have to
rely on my suggestion."

"Mama agrees with you." Delphinia stared at her hands and
idly played a scale. "It's a difficult matter for me though. I'm
not so good at parrying their verbal thrusts."

"Have you any other hobbies, Miss Milton?" Kevin asked.

She batted her eyelashes. "I like to ride. I was hoping that I
would be able to ride through the countryside here."

"Perhaps tomorrow?" he proposed. "I shall be happy to accompany you."

"That will be wonderful!" she enthused. "I'm sure I could
also benefit by some instruction too, my lord."

Sam stifled a groan. Wasn't it just her luck? Those two knew
how to ride, and she did not. She swiftly pondered the situation.
Riding would bring forth certain humiliation, but the idea of
refraining from the sport caused a sharp pang of . . . of jealousy? Her brain was scrambled with contradictions. Which
emotion would be worse? Embarrassment or envy?

"Samantha?" Kevin prompted. "What do you say to this?
Will you go, too?"

She made her decision. Her pride was more important than
anything else. "I am not sure I'll be available tomorrow."

The earl lifted an eyebrow. "Then we will set a time when
you are free."

"No! Do not do that," she pronounced. "Set a definite hour,
and I will attempt to change my schedule."

Kevin looked at Delphinia. "Ten in the morning?"

"That will be fine."

"Samantha?" he asked.

"I shall endeavor to be present," she lied. "Let us leave it at that."

Suspicion was written all over his face. In accents of lordly command, he said, "We shall expect you."

Sam bristled. Who was he to address her in such a tone? She wasn't his servant. She frowned resentfully. "I said I will endeavor, Kevin. I am a very busy person. I have responsibilities far beyond my years."

He had the audacity to laugh.

Delphinia looked curiously from one to the other. Sam just knew that the girl was speculating on her relationship with her cousin. Well, she needn't wonder any longer.

"Our conversation seems to have come to an end," she observed. "Do enjoy yourselves at the piano. I shall delight in hearing the two of you sing. I imagine you will make a pretty melody together."

Kevin looked daggers at her. Pleased that he was irritated at being left with the cit's daughter, Sam strolled toward Aunt Daphne, who was having difficulties conversing with the strangers. But even as she did so, she was aggravated with herself for leaving the two. Did she not know her own mind?

Eleven

Kevin, still smiling broadly, watched Samantha's departure with great humor. His little cousin was above annoyed. She was positively seething. It was fine fun to prod her into such a display. He had seen her anger and irritation, but being a red-blooded, virile male—in spite of what she said—he wondered how she would respond to tender or passionate catalysts. Feigning an interest in Delphinia's piano playing, he surreptitiously eyed Samantha through his lashes. She seemed to have discarded her pique and was now bright and cheerful, chatting with the guests in sparkling animation. The young lady was a good "people" person. She had the gift of drawing out the guests and setting them at their ease.

"My lord?" Delphinia broke into his reverie. "Weren't we going to sing together?"

He despised singing. On the occasions when he was forced to perform, people complimented him on his voice, but that did not make him seek encores. He wriggled out of playing whenever he could.

"Truthfully, Miss Milton, I would rather sit back and listen to you," he smoothly informed her. "I'm sure you can sing like an angel. I'm looking forward to hearing your trills."

She flushed. "I hope I do not disappoint you."

"I seriously doubt that you could."

"You flatter me, Lord Montjoy." She shuffled through a pile of sheet music and selected a score.

"Shall I turn the pages for you?" he asked.

"I would greatly appreciate that, my lord." She rippled through several bars of the song, then launched into it.

Kevin was rather surprised at what a beautiful voice she had. So often it seemed that the young ladies of the *ton* offered up strident, off-key performances, and were unjustly applauded loud and long. Delphinia's voice was almost professional, and her piano playing was faultless. When she finished, the room rocked with applause.

"That was very good," Kevin told her, amid the congratulations. "You have an innate talent for both playing and singing."

She dimpled. "I'm sure it is not all talent, Lord Montjoy. From a very early age, I have had both piano and vocal lessons."

"Nevertheless," he effused, "the raw ability must be there in the first place. I could have lesson after lesson and still I would not be able to equal your accomplishments."

"Your praise is a grand reward for all the hours I spent in practice." She ducked her head, suddenly shy. "You would not believe how many lessons on how many varied subjects I have experienced."

"Indeed?" Kevin flipped through the music to find another selection.

"In addition to music, I have had dancing, deportment, and elocution instruction. I've learned to paint watercolors, to embroider, to ride." Her rosy lips pursed in a pout. "I won't even go into the academic studies. I vow I can name every country in the world, every flower ever grown, and every bird that flies. Shall I continue? No! I'm certain you've heard enough."

"Do I detect a note of disenchantment in your voice?" he asked quietly.

She sighed. "I feel as though I have never had five minutes in my life that I could call my own. Mama organizes everything. I suppose that I should be happy. If it had not been for her, I would not have garnered this praise tonight. But I am not pleased. I feel used. It is as if she is living her life through me.

I wish she would turn her attention to Fennimore. He could benefit by it!"

Kevin smiled kindly at her. He was well aware of why Mrs. Milton pushed her daughter so hard. She was aiming for a husband above the girl's station. She reasoned that if Delphinia was proficient in all the arts and graces, she would snag a prize catch. All she needed was *entrée* into aristocratic circles. She thought Montjoy Castle would provide that. How wrong she was!

Kevin supposed that he was Mrs. Milton's quarry. Well, she would never snare him, not unless Samantha's scheme failed and Lady Frances refused him. He suddenly felt very sorry for Delphinia. She was merely a pawn in her parents' game of social climbing. They'd marry her off to the devil himself, so long as he possessed a title. Poor girl! He could just visualize her wed to a lecherous old peer with ivory skin and yellow snaggles of teeth. Maybe he should marry Delphinia instead of Lady Frances. She might be far below him on the social ladder, but she was vastly prettier and probably would be much more malleable than his tonnish choice. It was worth further consideration.

While he'd been wrapped up in his meditation, Delphinia had played a selection from Bach. As she finished, the company burst forth in a round of applause. She closed the keyboard, rose, and curtsied.

"Surely you aren't quitting?" her mother shrilled.

The girl bit her lip and hung her head.

Kevin sprang to the rescue. "Miss Milton has consented to join my cousin and me for a stroll in the garden before bedtime."

"What?" Samantha eyed him piercingly.

"The evening walk you mentioned," he said. "I've invited Miss Milton to join us."

"Oh, you have?" she asked in a haughty voice and glanced slowly around the crowd. "Perhaps there are others who wish to come along?"

No one took up the invitation.

Kevin offered his arm to Delphinia and motioned Samantha to take his other. She refused it, but she did walk along beside him. Without being obvious, he tried to keep an eye on her. He sensed an air of volatility emanating from her. The walk may have been a drastic mistake.

"What a pleasant way to end the evening," Delphinia remarked, as they left the castle by a rear door and entered the gardens.

"Yes, isn't it?" Samantha curtly agreed, halting. "I do believe I'll fetch my cat for this outing."

"If you do, I will cheerfully kill you," Kevin warned sweetly.

"But why not?" Delphinia asked.

"Yes, I would like to hear the answer to that question," Sam stated, her expression filled with challenge. "My poor little kitty is probably weary of being cooped up in my rooms. Why shouldn't he join us, Kevin?"

He could scarcely believe that his cousin would jeopardize her business venture by bringing forth the bobcat. Surely she realized that Bob could very well scare away the customers. What was wrong with Samantha?

"We're waiting," she prodded.

"My dear girl," he said in tones heavy with caution. "You know that Bob dislikes strangers. Your *kitty,* I fear, would not enjoy our stroll."

"Most cats are not immediately warm toward those they do not know," Delphinia declared, bending to sniff a pristine white rose.

"This one magnifies all negative traits of the feline personality," Kevin smiled. "His presence would be awkward at best. Samantha, I forbid you to fetch him."

As soon as the words left his mouth, he knew he had made a horrible blunder, but there was no way that he could take them back. He watched Samantha draw a huge breath, seeming to puff up all over with righteous fury. If she had been an animal, she'd have flattened her ears, showed her teeth, and growled. Kevin inwardly cringed and waited for the storm to break.

Apparently, Delphinia sensed it, too. "You must excuse me," she murmured. "Strangely enough, I am suddenly stricken with a horrid headache." Snatching up her skirt, she fled toward the castle.

Samantha ignored her flight. Sucking in her cheeks, she exhaled slowly. "I, too, shall retire. *With your permission, my lord.*"

"Samantha . . ." he weakly began.

Favoring him with a nasty glare, she turned on her heel and departed.

The next morning, Samantha awoke still smarting from her cousin's display of lordliness the previous evening. Just who did he think he was, commanding or forbidding her to do anything? She was not the subject of any king, nor of any social hierarchy of lords and ladies! She was an American, and Americans had fought long and hard to rid themselves of this disparaging way of life.

Also, she was angered by Kevin's attempt to go walking with a female on each arm. How condescending! Did he visualize himself as a sultan with a harem?

Furthermore, she'd been forced to wait until very late to take Bob on his nightly outing. She had known this would be the case when the guests arrived, which was why she had outfitted her pet with a sand box to use for his bodily needs. But it was nice to blame Kevin, anyway.

With all these iniquities in mind, she leapt from bed when the sun was only a scarlet promise. Gritting her teeth in aggravation, she hurriedly performed her morning ablutions and began to dress herself in the quick, jerky motions of one who is irritated beyond all belief. She wasn't sure how she would do it, but she'd show Lord High and Mighty a thing or two!

Martha entered just as Sam finished her toilette. "Miss Samantha! You did not wait for me! Am I late?"

"No." She gestured toward the clock on the mantel for verification. "I arose early so that I could walk Bob and then be present in the dining room when the guests arrived for breakfast."

"Then I'll start coming to you sooner," the abigail vowed. "Shall I fetch your tray?"

"No. I'm in a rush. I'll wait for my tea." She sat down at her dressing table. "Do you know if Lord Montjoy is up and about?"

"No, miss. I didn't pay attention to his valet's activities. I can find out."

"It doesn't matter. Please help me with my hair. I shall discover my cousin's whereabouts all too soon, anyway."

Sam gazed into the mirror while Martha ministered to her hair. This was one concession to English false notions of necessity that she secretly enjoyed. She had never excelled at styling her hair. In Ohio, she had merely tied back the tresses with a riband. Since that simple fashion was unacceptable to Aunt Winifred, Martha had done up Sam's hair in a loose knot, with wispy tendrils framing her face. The Connection thought it vastly becoming. In her heart, Sam thought so, too.

Martha stepped back. "There now, Miss Samantha. Your beauty would rival any young lady's. But are you sure you want to wear that dress? The pink muslin would be pretty."

Sam looked down at her unadorned blue gown. "I see nothing wrong with it."

"There is nothing . . . not really. I just thought you might want something fancier." The abigail eyed her hopefully. "The guests will be fixed up, and Lord Montjoy . . . well, I know you'd want to be the prettiest for him."

She gaped at the older woman. "You surely don't think that I've set my cap for my cousin? Nothing could be further from the truth. I couldn't be happy wed to such an arrogant, layabout lord! Besides, I intend to return to America."

Martha opened her mouth to speak, apparently thought better of it, and closed it with a tiny snap.

Sam briefly waited in vain for her maid to comment. When nothing more was forthcoming, she rose. "I must be about my routine."

"Yes, miss, but . . ."

Again, she paused.

Martha hung her head, then brightly looked up. "Is there anything you want me to do, Miss Samantha?"

"No." Confused as to what her abigail meant by her strange behavior, Sam decided not to attempt to force her to reveal whatever it was she wished to say. Picking up Bob's leash and collar, she went to the sitting room and called the cat from his perch on the window seat. Usually he came to her, yawning. This time, however, he bounded very overenthusiastically to her, making her wonder if he had seen something in the garden that excited him. She certainly hoped not. Her mind was occupied with the guests, and she was not in the mood to deal with an overenthusiastic wildcat.

Leaving her room, Sam and Bob descended the servants' stairs and exited through the service vestibule. Turning toward the rose garden, they first passed across a corner of the boxwood maze. The cat, however, had no notion to stroll among the old-fashioned roses. With a speedy jerk, he ripped the leash from Sam's hand and dashed out of sight down a narrow path.

"Bob!" she called, recovering from speechless surprise. "Bob! Where have you gone, you mischievous beast?"

There was no sound. With his feline grace, Bob could silently make his explorations without giving a single clue as to his whereabouts. Moreover, he could escape capture for an undetermined span of time within the folds of the intricate maze.

"Bob!" she shouted, somehow knowing that he would not respond. In the last-minute preparation for opening day, she had cut him short on his exercise. Now gaining his freedom, he had a lot of energy to expend, so he would take advantage of every minute of it.

"Drat!" Sam cried out at the top of her lungs and stamped her foot. This was certainly a tangle. She should be present for breakfast, but she must capture Bob. If a guest decided to take an early morning trek and came face-to-face with the cat, all fury would break loose. The guests would most certainly leave, and they would tell their friends to avoid Montjoy Castle. Kevin would be in worse financial condition, and it would be all her fault. Frantic, she dashed into the maze.

Wildly running up one path and down another, she was soon hopelessly lost. Halting to gasp for breath, she looked up at the castle as if it would provide direction. The stone walls blandly stared back.

"Damn!" she burst out. "Where *am* I?"

"*I* certainly know where you are, from all that thrashing in the bushes."

Sam startled, whirling. "What—"

"You're going to help me let go of this cat." Kevin walked nervously into view, holding Bob's leash at arm's length. The bobcat docilely walked at his heel. She could have sworn that the animal was smiling. Her temper flared.

"You rotten, miserable—"

"Leave off your complimentary address, Samantha, and resume your responsibility," the earl stated.

"I wasn't speaking of you," she declared.

"I wonder," he fired back. "Now take this damned cat!"

"Do not curse in front of me, Kevin Montjoy," she warned.

"Don't play the innocent with me! I only echoed your own expletive," he retorted. "If you want to be treated like a lady, you must behave like one."

Sam set her jaw. "I am not in the mood for this manner of discourse."

"Ha!" Kevin exploded. "Apparently, you're not in the mood for controlling this kitty cat either. Take this!" He threw down the leash.

"No!" screeched Sam, diving for the strap of leather.

Luckily, Bob remained contentedly at Kevin's side, for in her haste, Samantha tripped and fell spread-eagled on her stomach. She stared at her cousin's brilliantly shined boot. Her anger flashed higher than ever when she thought she heard him chuckle.

He reached down to help her up. "Are you all right, Samantha?"

"No thanks to you!" She ignored his hand, hoisted herself

onto her knees, and rose, snatching the leash as she did so. "What are you doing out here, anyway?"

"I couldn't sleep."

"Sleep?" she cried. "What are you talking about?"

"Surely you know, Samantha. Sleep is an unconscious state, during which—"

"I am aware of that!" she snapped. "Do you think I'm a ninny?"

He grinned. "Then why are you asking?"

"How you do infuriate me!" She pretended to marvel. "Have you forgotten that we have guests to whom you must play the role of a perfect host?"

He shrugged. "I fail to see what that has to do with my sleeping or my morning stroll. However, given your warped mind, I'm sure you have conjured a connection."

"Good heavens, Kevin! I truly do not believe that it's necessary for me to teach you proper etiquette."

"You are correct." Mischief danced in his eyes. "I seriously doubt that an American could have greater knowledge of proper conduct in order to teach even the average Englishman, let alone a peer of lofty rank and birth."

"Ooh," she growled. "You do think highly of yourself."

"No more than would anyone of high, God-given station."

"God didn't give you your top-lofty position, Kevin Montjoy. Man did!" She crossly cleared her throat. "I do not know why we are standing here, wasting time. You must hurry to the dining room to greet your guests, and *that* is why your sleeping or walking is of no consequence! I shall return Bob to my room and quickly join you."

"Why the rush?" he asked.

"Must we go over this ground again?" she cried, exasperated.

He negligently lifted a shoulder. "No one will arise for another hour, at least. They're on holiday! Moreover, there are those who'll pretend to be aristocratic and lie in their beds until noon."

"I wouldn't wager on it," she advised. "Meet me in ten minutes in the dining room, Kevin."

He rolled his eyes skyward. "If I must."

"And furthermore," she added, "strive to be jolly, welcoming, and approachable."

"Jolly?" He laughed. "Ho ho ho! And who will be there to approach?"

Sam did not reply. Hurrying back in the direction she'd come, she, once more, became hopelessly lost. "Damn!" she muttered and shouted, "Kevin?"

He appeared within seconds. "Lost again?"

"Yes," she said shortly. "Will you help me out of this place?"

"You need some lessons in finding your way," he commented.

"Yes, but not now." She anxiously gazed up at the low riding sun that was beginning to burn off the morning dew. "We'll do it some other time. It's getting late."

"Very well, but you're wrong about the scheduling. Everyone will sleep much later."

"Just escort me from this maze, Kevin, and spare me your speculations."

"As you wish." He sighed and presented his arm.

Sam deigned to take it, fearing that if she refused, he might cut up stiff or lead her in a roundabout way. She smiled prettily up at him. "I shall pleasantly look forward to learning the secrets of the maze."

"Excellent!" He seemed pleased, but there was suspicion in his eyes. "I shall enjoy showing you."

They entered the house and turned to go their separate ways.

"I shall see you very shortly," Sam directed.

"I wonder if the kitchen staff has even begun to cook the meal," he taunted.

"Of course they have," she murmured, and she and Bob hastened up the stairs. The servants would be well aware that Lord Montjoy was up and about, and they would have commenced their daily routine, no matter what the hour.

Once more, vexation heated Samantha's blood. No one should have the power to turn a fixed routine topsy-turvy, just because of an accident of birth or circumstances. Thank heavens that America eschewed titles. Her mother had told her of how a certain faction wanted to make George Washington a king, following the War for Independence. The noble hero had turned it down flat. No, America would take only the good traits from its Mother Country and leave the bad, in particular a class system based on ancestry and not on effort. Where would that leave her high and mighty cousin?

She returned Bob to her room. "There you are, you traitor," she said, as the lynx resumed his position on the window seat. "I'm beginning to think that you like Kevin better than me."

The bobcat merely yawned and lazily lifted his foreleg to lick his paw.

"Perhaps that's the reason," she added, thinking she just might have detected a whiff of rum. "You're indolent, too."

Securely closing the door, she left the room and descended the stairs, finding Kevin alone in the dining room.

"I told you that no one—" he began.

She cut him off in mid-sentence. "It doesn't matter whether guests are present or not. We will have made the effort."

"Just don't expect me to wait for them," he cautioned. "I have work to do, and if you recall, I promised to take Miss Milton for a ride."

"Kevin, you wouldn't recognize work if it threw its arms around your neck," she said smugly, filling her plate at the buffet.

"Your great problem, Samantha, is that you cannot visualize work consisting of anything other than physical labor. Some people work with their minds instead of their muscles."

He had her there. She wisely retreated. "It truly does surprise me that no guests have arisen. The excitement of such an unusual holiday would have driven me from my bed."

"What you need," Kevin muttered, "is a man to drive you *to* your bed and cause you to act like a normal woman."

"I beg pardon?" she asked.

"Nothing," he said, as Mr. Milton and Fennimore entered the

room. "Well, Samantha, you've gotten your wish. Aren't you pleased?"

"Good morning, all," the cit greeted, bowing.

"Good morning." Sam smiled, and Kevin rose in a half-bow.

Fennimore, dropping a few paces behind his father, stuck out his tongue.

Sam's spirits flagged. She'd hoped that the little monster had been chastised into good behavior. Apparently, he had not.

"Please help yourselves to the buffet," she offered. "The drinks will be served by our staff, but we prefer to keep breakfast informal."

"Excellent, excellent!" enthused the businessman. "I like it that way, too. I'll have tea!" he called loudly to a footman. "The lad'll have milk. C'mon, Fennimore, let's belly up to the trough."

Kevin winced and shot Sam a nasty glare.

She swiftly lowered her gaze to her plate. "I hope you will find our food to be delicious, Mr. Milton."

"Who cares?" he asked jovially. "Food's food, and I can eat a lot of it. If it's good though, I'll eat a whole lot more!"

Sam felt a slight pang of panic as she saw Kevin's jaw muscle twitch, though she thought she could trust his unfailing good manners. Somewhere, however, there would be an end to the restraint. She prayed he would not erupt at one of the guests, Mr. Milton in particular.

The obese cit and his son filled their plates and sat down at the table. "I'm looking forward to this," the man stated. "I'm hungry as a cow in a hog pen!"

Sam produced the requisite low giggle, but Kevin merely looked confused.

"Don't get that, do you, m'lord?" he chuckled. "A cow in a hog pen! Cows eat grass and there's nothing but swill in a hog pen, so the cow's hungry."

"Ho ho ho," said Kevin.

"Our cook will be well rewarded by your enthusiasm, Mr. Milton," Sam said loudly, hoping to cover Kevin's response. "Nothing makes her happier than to see clean plates coming back to the kitchen. I imagine she'll indulge you in something very special."

"I'm the man to appreciate it!"

A footman approached with a silver tray, holding a steaming teapot for Mr. Milton and a frothy glass of milk for Fennimore. As if by magic, he suddenly pitched forward, the tray flying through the air, expelling its contents on the table and Kevin's sleeve. The servant fell to his knees.

Sam could only stare, speechless with shock.

"What the hell?" Kevin stood, dabbing his sleeve with his napkin.

Fennimore tittered.

"I'm sorry, my lord." The footman got up, frowning. "I'll fetch more." He picked up the once beautiful tray, now terribly dented, and began removing the shattered china and broken glass.

"Did you do that, Fennimore?" Mr. Milton demanded.

"Hell, no!" said the lad.

"You little scapegrace!" his father shouted. "I'll scrub out your mouth with soap!"

"You told me to act like Lord Montjoy and learn to be a gentleman," the youngster piped. "An' he said *hell.*"

Mr. Milton ground his teeth. "You're right, but— Don't change the subject! You tripped that footman, didn't you? Admit your guilt, rapscallion!"

Fennimore hung his head, the perfect picture of innocence. "Aw, Pap, it was an accident. I had m'feet out there in the way. I didn't mean for 'im to fall."

Sam made a mental note to make sure the servant wasn't injured and to apologize to him. The young footman hadn't hired on to be the victim of a naughty, spoiled brat. If he continued to be the butt of Fennimore's tricks, he might just seek employment elsewhere, and Kevin would be furious.

She cast a surreptitious glance at her cousin. He sat in stony silence, staring out the window. The milk on his sleeve had compressed the nap and left a chalky residue. She cringed. She'd certainly hear about this!

She focused on Kevin's slender, aristocratic hand with its faint blue veins. *Blue-blooded,* she thought. She allowed her gaze to rove upward to his face. Handsome, too, in a classical way. When her interest in the opposite sex had flowered, she thought that no man could be as well-looking as Davy Reed, a trapper who frequented her father's store. Davy had been tremendously tall and broad-shouldered, a rough-hewn frontiersman who could hold his own in any brawl or battle. Next to him, Kevin was . . . well, Kevin was an English lord. Her thoughts were jerked from the fantasy by Mr. Milton's booming voice.

"The boy and I'd like to do some riding, Lord Montjoy. Believe you said there'd be horses available."

"Yes," Kevin said reluctantly. "I planned to take your daughter riding, later in the morning. You can join us."

"No, no. Her mother wouldn't like that, ha-ha! We'll go right after breakfast and take a groom to show us the way, if that's all right?"

"Certainly, Mr. Milton. I'd accompany you myself and then escort your daughter, but I have estate business to attend."

"Think nothing of it, m'lord! Business comes first!" He nodded emphatically. "That's what I've always thought."

Samantha wondered if Kevin was telling the truth and decided to seek him out later to see if he truly was involved in estate affairs. He simply *must* understand how important he was to the business. Who would wish to pay exorbitant prices to stay in the castle if its owner eluded them? She sighed. The idea of the inn was a good one, but it would work only if Kevin allowed it to. They wouldn't always have guests like Fennimore.

Grimacing inwardly, she put on a pleasant smile and took up the waning conversation, neatly covering up her lack of speech.

Twelve

Kevin was grateful that Samantha had interceded and taken up the conversation. He was at his wit's end, dredging up something to say to Mr. Milton that was neither spitefully critical, nor an outright command for the Miltons to leave his premises. He had realized that the little brat, Fennimore, had deliberately tripped his footman, causing the breaking of fine china, the damage to heirloom silver, and whatever bumps and bruises the servant suffered. The boy should have been hauled from the dining room and whipped. If he had been the lad's father, that's what he would have done. Of course, in the case of *his son,* a birching would not have been necessary. *His son* would be impeccably behaved at all times. *His son.* Whatever made him think of something like that? *Frances.*

Ever since Samantha had arrived on the scene to turn Montjoy Castle inside out and upside down, he had neglected his almost-fiancée. In his heart, he'd hoped that Samantha's scheme would save him from the parson's mousetrap, but now that the play's first act had been executed, he wondered if it would do so. In fact, he doubted that he could bear the intrusion of such as the Miltons into his home. Frances, at least, was well spoken and perfectly behaved, but she would despise Samantha. If he married Frances, his cousin would have to go. But where?

No, he wouldn't allow that to happen. Samantha was Aunt Winifred's ward, and therefore, in a roundabout way, he was responsible for her. If he wed Frances, she would have to understand that Samantha and The Connection would always have a home at Montjoy Castle. He emphatically nodded affirmative.

"Then it is all right, Kevin?" Samantha broke into his reverie.

"I'm sorry, cousin." He grinned self-consciously. "I was wool-gathering."

"Mr. Milton has asked if you would mind his using your library for a few hours this afternoon. He wishes to write some letters."

"Business, you know," the cit added. "If a man's to succeed, he can't ignore his business for very long. Those are facts to heed, m'lord."

"Indeed, sir. You are quite right," Kevin said reluctantly, knowing that his admission would cause him to lose the rights to his second bastion of privacy, which now left only his bedchamber.

Samantha smiled at him with relief and also with sympathy.

"I won't disturb you, m'lord," Mr. Milton vowed. "You can work on one side of the desk while I use the other."

Kevin smiled wanly, determining to remove the estate ledgers to his chamber. Breakfast finished, he excused himself from the table and hastened away from the scene before anyone else could appear. If Samantha wished to linger over her tea and spend the whole morning being the hostess, she was welcome to it!

"Jenkins," he told the butler as he passed by. "I shall be in the library. Allow no one or nothing to disturb me."

The upper servant bowed his assent.

As he crossed the hall, he heard voices and footsteps above. He broke into a half-run, darted past an astonished footman, and dodged into the book room. Grinning with happiness, he shut the door behind him.

Before he had scarcely begun to work, there was a light knock on the door. Oh, no, he thought grimly. Who had the audacity to fly in the face of his wishes and interrupt him? There were only two denizens of Montjoy who would do so, unless of course there was an all-consuming fire: Samantha and his grandmama. He doubted that Lady Montjoy would leave her room to seek him. She was hiding from the guests, too. That left Samantha, the bold, little American baggage!

"What is it?" he shouted churlishly.

She entered, wide-eyed with shock. "My goodness, Kevin, what a horrible tone of voice!"

Kevin threw down his quill. "I left orders with Jenkins that I was not to be disturbed," he growled.

"I did not think it referred to me." She smiled brilliantly and sat down on the edge of his desk. "What I wanted—"

"No, I will not," he said firmly, anticipating her question. "I will not return to the dining room to remain there all morning as host. That is ridiculous, and I believe anyone would agree. So don't even ask me, Samantha, for I do refuse."

"But, Kevin . . ." she cajoled. "My dear sweet cousin."

"No!" he thundered. "I won't leave this room! I only have until mid-morning, when I must take Miss Milton for a ride. And I cannot even have privacy here in the afternoon! Oh, no! I have to play host to that red-nosed, blustering old Milton whom you have piled in on me! I intend to remove my ledgers to my bedroom and work on them there. Surely, no one would have the gall to bother me in my own chamber. No one but you, Samantha. That's why I believe I'll take off my clothes and go stark naked, this afternoon, as an incentive for you to leave me alone!"

"Kevin," she chided. "You would do no such thing."

He smiled wickedly. "Try me."

She eyed him warily. "I never know when you are joking."

"Well then, Samantha, you will just have to take your chances if you burst in on me. Now, is that all you wanted, or are there further assaults you wish to make on my fortress?"

"Truthfully," she admitted, "I've forgotten."

She might have ended her conversation, but she refused to depart. Contentedly swinging her legs back and forth, she studied the fire screen. "I imagine it will be quite cozy in here on a cold snowy day. And the castle and grounds would be ever so pretty. I love the snow."

"Then you are in the minority."

She ignored him. "We could decorate every room with holly and evergreen, and host very expensive holiday specials. We could serve mouth-watering, golden brown geese and pigs with apples in their mouths."

"Samantha." He held up a pleading hand. "Let us muddle through the summer first. We may not be in business by winter."

Her sparkling green eyes again reflected surprise. "You don't truly believe so?"

"Let us just say that I am not as convinced as you." He shrugged languidly. "When the newness wears off, we just might find ourselves with fewer customers."

"No!" She sat up very straight and motionless. "I have faith in the venture, and you must believe in it, too. After all, you are the one with the most to gain. If we are successful, you won't have to wed Lady Frances."

"Perhaps not, but it will be someone like her. I also need an heir," he mused. "Going into business has damaged my reputation. No matter how wealthy I become, I most definitely won't have my pick of ladies."

"That is ridiculous," she declared.

"Perhaps, but it's true."

She laughed shortly, without humor. "Then the women of England are more foolish than I thought."

He laughed. "Maybe I'll find an American girl."

Samantha sharply eyed him.

"That is," he expanded, "if I can find one who appreciates English lords."

His fair cousin stood and abruptly left the room.

A spotless, shining, black-lacquered carriage, with a fine team of dapple grays, proceeded sedately through the residential streets of London, looking for all the world like the conveyance of a grand royal personage. It almost was, for it was the coach of the Duchess of Walsingham, the highest stickler and the most powerful social arbiter the *ton* had ever seen. A visit from her was tantamount to a queenly progress, and was certain to cause the most redoubtable hostess to go weak in the knees. Who was the unlucky lady who would be her next victim? Those of the *ton* who witnessed the scene speculated as to whom the great harpy would terrorize. They were terribly disappointed when the coachman drew up before the door of the Danforth home. This was no good *on dit*. Her Grace had overwhelmed her daughter-in-law, Lady Danforth, and tucked her under her thumb years ago.

As her carriage came to a halt, the duchess efficiently surveyed her son's town house, making certain that the windows were clean and polished, that the tiny front yard and walkway were free of debris, and that there were no animal droppings in the street out front. All seemed to be well, a fact which truly stunned the lady. She could not remember the day when she had not been able to chastise her daughter-in-law for at least one dread offense. Indeed, she was slightly disappointed. Raking Marion over the coals was such sport.

A footman leapt down to dash up to the residence and knock on the door. When it was opened, he rushed back for his lady. First, he let down the step and dusted it with a small brush he kept especially for that task, in his magnificent silver livery. Next, he opened the door and made sure that there was no dust on the jamb. Satisfied, he extended his hand to his duchess.

Head high and nostrils drawn in a well-bred sneer, Her Grace descended. Although her chin was elevated, her gaze minutely scanned the premises. She was happily rewarded. Adorning one of the bricks of the walkway was a white spot of bird excrement. The duchess almost smiled with glee. She would open the conversation with this transgression. Then she would get to the meat of the matter. She waved at the seat she had vacated.

"Bring that newspaper, young man," she commanded.

He did her bidding, then escorted her to the front door, presenting the paper to the Danforths' staid butler.

The upper servant took it and bowed. "My lady is in the salon, Your Grace. If you will come this way?"

She nodded curtly. "I must inform you, my man, that there is avian offal on the front walk. See to it immediately."

The butler looked bewildered, but he bowed again. "Yes, madam," he responded, glancing questioningly at her footman.

"Bird shit," the servant mouthed behind his mistress's back.

"Ah." The butler nodded sagely. "You will come this way, madam?"

"I shall, and it is about time. I do not intend to spend the day waiting for underlings to serve me," she snapped. "Such incompetence!"

"Yes, madam." He strode down the hall in front of her and opened the door to the salon with an important, "The Duchess of Walsingham, my lady."

Lady Danforth was standing nervously in the center of the room, with her daughter, Frances, behind her. She curtsied so deeply she almost fell to the floor. The young lady's curtsy was more restrained, but none the less groveling.

"Get up," the duchess commanded. "Get up, I say! The two of you look like a pair of buffoons!"

They straightened, both looking cowed and fearful.

"Where is your spirit?" the duchess complained and motioned the butler to lay the newspaper on the sofa. "Fetch me a glass of sherry, my man, and then leave us."

When the duchess had ensconced herself on the sofa and taken a sip of her wine, she deigned to begin her commentary. "Marion, I am utterly appalled."

Her daughter-in-law shuddered.

"Upon your front walk is a sight so repulsive that it would shake a less stalwart person to the core. I speak of none other than avian offal!" She paused dramatically. "I hope you have had no other callers today. If you have, your reputation will be seriously endangered."

"W-what is it?" Lady Danforth stuttered.

"Avian offal!"

"I . . . I'm not sure what that is." She looked helplessly at her daughter for help, but the girl only shrugged. "We . . . we are both at sea, madam."

"Imbeciles!" ground out the duchess. "Pair of silly cows! I refer, of course, to bird-do!"

"Oh," the two females murmured lamely.

"Don't bother your empty heads about it," she advised severely. "I have already notified your butler. With any luck at all, it will be removed by the time I depart. Now, I shall move on to more crucial matters. Frances, has that young man, Montjoy, declared himself?"

"No, Grandmama." She picked at a small, pulled thread in her skirt. "Not yet."

"I assume he is interested in you for your money," she baldly stated. "Well, it seems that he is actually trying to *make* money! Perish the thought of a peer, and an earl at that, joining the work force like a common cit!"

"We know nothing of that," Lady Danforth gasped.

"I doubted that either of you did, since you would have been required to read the newspaper to find out." She picked up the edition and shook it at them. "Frances's fine earl is turning himself into an innkeeper!"

"I cannot believe it," Frances wailed.

"There must be something wrong," said her mother. "No nobleman would cast himself beyond the pale in such a fashion! You must be mistaken, madam."

The duchess glared. A deadly silence filled the room. Blanching, Lady Danforth stuttered, "I . . . I k-know you are correct, ma'am. M-my terrible shock precipitated that remark. Please do not take umbrage."

"Very well," the duchess regally granted and presented her with the paper. "You may read it yourself. It is his advertisement."

The lady perused the lines and shook her head. "I can scarcely believe it!"

"Let me see." Frances took the offensive paper from her

mother's hands and stared unhappily at it, groaning. "What does this mean, Grandmama?"

"It means that you did not catch your man, that's what it means!" she scolded. "He's grasping at straws to keep from marrying you."

"I did all I could!" she protested. "I was unfailingly polite. I hung on his every word as if he was the most brilliant gentleman in the kingdom. I often complimented him. I just don't know what else I could have done."

Her grandmother studied her. Frances wasn't pretty, but she wasn't downright ugly. She was precisely . . . plain.

Lord Montjoy was handsome, so admirably endowed that he could take the duchess's breath away, even at her advanced age. If he had wealth, he could have his pick of young ladies. As it was, desperately needing the money a bride's dower would bring him, he had turned his attention to her granddaughter.

"Do you really and truly want this man?" Her Grace queried.

Over the top of the girl's whiny voice, Lady Danforth came forth with the answer. "I am not so sure about him, now. Dabbling in trade will cast him beyond the pale. Frances does not want a socially shunned man to wed."

"Hm!" the duchess snorted. "I do not see a great throng of gentlemen milling around here in anticipation of receiving leave to court her in earnest! You have always had brains to let, Marion. We must be honest and admit that Frances is unattractive. If a peer is dangling about, you'd best snatch him by fair means or foul!"

"But if he is ostracized, do we truthfully want him?" her daughter-in-law moaned.

"Do you forget so easily? *I* can undo any prejudice against him! *I* can make anyone popular. Perhaps *I* shall even make innkeeping a fascinating pastime." She laughed. "It could become as fashionable as emulating odorous, snaggle-toothed coachmen!"

"Not for me you won't," muttered Lady Danforth. "I won't play hostess to the general public, and neither will my daughter!"

"You will do as I tell you," the duchess commanded.

Lady Danforth looked as if she were about to cry. Frances patted her mother's shoulder. "Grandmama, I'm not at all sure that I wish to wed Lord Montjoy. He . . . he's so handsome."

"So what is wrong with that?" she shrilled. "You should be happy about it."

"A gentleman who is as exquisite as Lord Montjoy will probably have . . ." She lowered her voice to a whisper. "Mistresses!"

"Then all the better!" She scrutinized her granddaughter's features. "Especially for you. A mistress will keep him so happy that he will never think to rue the day he wed you."

Tears glistened in Frances's eyes. "I want him to be fond of me."

"He'll be fond of your money. He might be fond of the children you give him. Maybe he will even be fond of *you* someday. Now, don't turn into a watering pot, young lady. I intensely dislike weeping. Do you not wish to hear your instructions?"

The two ladies obediently nodded.

"You must go immediately to Montjoy Castle," the duchess decreed. "See what kind of rig he is running. If his residence is full of vacationing cits, he may not be very pleased right now. Your presence will remind him that he only need wed you to set him up financially for the rest of his life."

They stared at her without response.

The duchess scowled back. "Also, you will take him a very expensive gift. Don't tell me it isn't proper! We shall take the chance of being forward. These are desperate times! So you will take the item, which will only serve again to remind him of our wealth."

Frances nodded, but Lady Danforth took a deep, pained breath. "I doubt I can talk Danforth into going to Montjoy Castle."

"Leave it to me, Marion," the duchess advised. "William is my son. He will obey me."

"I hope you are right!"

"Of course I am. I've ordered William about all his life. He will not change now." She imperiously lifted her nose. "In fact, he is almost as big a toady as you are, Marion!"

Lady Danforth did not speak up in her own defense, but she began to pout silently.

"What if this doesn't work, Grandmama?" Frances queried.

"Well, you could maneuver him into a compromising situation," the duchess suggested.

"But . . . but I want him to *care* for me," she lamented.

"Don't be ridiculous," said her grandmother.

Several days passed before the Danforths were ready to take to the road, despite the duchess's nagging them to lose no time. Lord Danforth had obeyed his mama in consenting to go, but only after he had concluded several matters of business. Lady Danforth and Frances had found it necessary to shop for countless accessories for their attire, as well as obtaining the earl's special gift, a silver and gold inlaid snuffbox.

"This is absurd," Lord Danforth grumbled, as they stood on the walk in front of his residence, preparing to set out. "I have matters of greater importance than this to attend."

"What?" his mother scoffed. "A card game? A wager to place in White's betting book?"

"Mother, whether or not you realize it, I am an independently wealthy man, due to my acumen in the world of investments."

"Balderdash!" sneered his mother. "Who gave you the money to play with, in the first place?"

"That is inconsequential," he returned.

"I think not, but we shall allow your statement stand as truth, if you will be silent and address yourself to the matter at hand." Turning to Lady Danforth and Frances, she stared piercingly at them. "Do you know what you are to do?"

They glanced at each other.

"Oh!" moaned the duchess. "I can see that you haven't the slightest hint. I should have planned to accompany you."

"Why are we going?" asked her son.

"Fools! You're trying to bring Montjoy up to the mark! Do you want your daughter to be an old maid?"

He shrugged. "If that's what she wants."

The duchess shuddered. "Be on your way! We can only hope that the earl knows why you are there and decides to comply. Begone! You are giving me a terrible headache."

They entered the carriage and set off down the street. Shaking her head, the duchess watched them until they were out of sight. Somehow, she knew they would be unsuccessful. They would return with no idea of why they had gone, and Montjoy would still be a free man.

Pursing her lips, she accepted the unpleasant truth. *She* was going to have to leap into the midst of this situation. Otherwise, nothing would be accomplished. She sighed and started toward her carriage, her minions practically falling over each other to ease her way. She would make plans immediately to storm the bastions of Montjoy's bachelorhood, and she would be triumphant.

"Well, what do you think, Kevin?" Samantha asked, standing in the hall and watching the workmen. "This will preserve your bachelorhood. No scheming females will encroach upon your domain."

He lifted a shoulder. "I doubt this will improve matters."

"Of course, it will," she disagreed.

The guests had invaded nearly every room in the castle. Kevin had been forced to remove his ledgers and personal papers from the library and set up an office in his sitting room. All had been well until one day, when he was surprised by Mrs. Milton and Delphinia peeking in his chamber door. They'd profusely apologized, explaining that they'd only been touring the castle. When The Connection experienced similar happenings, Sam had come up with the idea of erecting a locked, but temporary screen to block entrance to the family wing. This would allow the family to move to and from each other's rooms without having multiple doors to unlock. Watching one of the carpenters put the last nail into the project, Sam thought she was absolutely brilliant.

"Of course, since my room is located apart, I will not have this security," she mused, "but since the idea of the inn was mine, I shall suffer the repercussions."

"Oh, yes, be a martyr, Samantha," Kevin said. "And by the way, why is that cat on display? If guests saw him, they would leave at once."

She glanced down at Bob, who was rubbing his cheeks on Kevin's boots. "I know where the guests are. I'll have Bob tucked away in my room by the time there is any danger of their seeing him."

"Seems risky to me."

"I believe you're still afraid of him," she accused.

"No, I am not, although caution will always be in order." He reached down and scratched the bobcat's ears, as if to prove his point.

Sam couldn't keep from smiling. It was strange how her pet had developed a tolerance for Kevin. No, it was beyond tolerance. The animal continued to seek him out, and it couldn't be all due to liquor. Bob was stone sober, with no spirits in sight or scent, and he was permitting the earl to touch him.

He'd begun to be accustomed to The Connection as well, though he still growled if they came too near. That made things much more pleasant. Sam could visit the ladies' sitting room and bring Bob along for a change of scene.

The foreman of the carpenters approached the earl. "That's about all that needs to be done, m'lord, except for a lock. The locksmith should be here in one or two days."

Bob rumbled and the man stepped back. "Got a good bodyguard there, sir. Don't know why you'd need to worry about locks."

"The animal belongs to the lady," Kevin explained.

"And we do wish to keep his existence a secret," Sam emphasized. "Our guests wouldn't be very comfortable if they knew a wildcat was in the house."

"I won't tell, ma'am, and neither will my men. None of our business, you know."

She smiled. "Thank you so much. I knew I could depend on you."

"If you are finished, we'd best settle up," Kevin told him.

The man grinned self-consciously. "M'lord, can we barter? Our carpentry for a stay in your castle? I'd like to bring my wife here for a little holiday. She'd be so excited."

The earl glanced at Sam. "Of course we can work something out."

The carpenter bobbed his head. "My men are interested, too."

"We can accommodate you all," Sam effused. "In fact, we have other work that could be done in exchange. Then you could have a much longer stay."

He nodded eagerly. "Let me talk with the men, and I'll be right back with an answer."

"This is marvelous," Sam said as the foreman returned to his crew. "I cannot imagine why I never thought of the barter system. Think of what we can accomplish! There are so many repairs to be made."

"Unbelievable," Kevin declared.

She nodded. "It certainly is. We must make a list of it all."

"I wasn't referring to the work." He grinned. "I was in disbelief that your money-making, American mind hadn't come up with it long ago!"

She laughed and impulsively caught his hand, looking up into his flawless blue eyes. "We are going to win at this game, Kevin. I just know we are! You will not be forced to wed Lady Frances, or anyone like her. Furthermore, I don't believe that nonsense about losing your reputation, due to being in trade. Just wait and see!"

"Yes, Samantha, I shall." He lifted her hand to his lips and bestowed a brief kiss on her knuckles. "But don't claim victory too soon. It will be quite a while before we can predict if this enterprise proves lasting. Until then, I must hold on to all of my options."

With a pat to Bob's head, he strolled to the screen to assess the woodworkers' craft.

Thirteen

It hadn't taken Samantha long to modify her morning routine to suit that of the guests. Being the hostess/manageress of a luxury inn was a demanding vocation, especially as she interpreted the role. She must rise earlier in the morning than the guests, and stay up at night until all had retired to their chambers. She lingered over breakfast in order to greet the visitors with a cheery "Good Morning," and was present at all other meals. She arranged entertainment, although Kevin took charge of the equestrian activities. And on top of all the care required by the current company, she must answer and schedule reservation requests for future customers. As a result, she had little time for herself, or for Bob.

The bobcat did not like being alone, and exacted revenge by small depredations. His most frequent crime was chewing. When he gnawed the edge of a sofa squab and the lower corner of the drapery, Sam decided to give him free rein of her entire suite in hopes that greater territory would allay his boredom. Of course, this created difficulties, because the chambermaid could not enter the rooms without Sam's presence. Bob tolerated Martha and seemed on the verge of aloof friendship, but although Sam thought she could enter safely, the lady's maid was too wary to do so. This matter demanded that the servants adapt to Sam's schedule, a circumstance that was not always easy. But in the short amount of time that the inn had been open, Sam could see that any discomfort was worthwhile.

The first round of patrons had been replaced by new ones, except for Mr. Courtney and the Milton family, excluding Mr. Milton who had to return to his business enterprises. These clients were having such a good time that they wished to extend their stay. Luckily, Sam was able to accommodate them. She wondered how fortunate it was, however, when the next run-in with Fennimore occurred.

In order to exercise Bob unseen by patrons, she rose at day-break when only the servants were up and about. Taking him down the backstairs, she exited the service door and passed through the herb and kitchen gardens to the meadow beyond. There, he was able to engage in his exciting sport of rabbit terrorization. Having been raised in captivity, he didn't know what to do with the bunnies when he caught them, which came as a great disappointment to the gardeners, who were plagued by the furry beasts.

One morning, as Bob was sticking his paw down a rabbit hole, Sam caught a movement from the corner of her eye. Turning, she saw Fennimore Milton dart behind a tree. Her heart sank. Now that the boy had seen Bob, she had no doubt that he would blab it to all who would listen. She decided that she must attempt to cajole him into keeping his mouth shut.

"Fennimore!" she called cheerfully. "I see you!"

There was no movement from behind the big oak, but she could glimpse a thin strip of white shirt fabric along the tree trunk.

"I have a secret that simply screams to be told to a good little boy!"

He peeped out and, catching her eye, stepped from behind his hiding place.

"Come look at my special cat," she invited.

Fennimore strode forward. "That's a dumb-looking cat, Miss Samantha. It ain't got no tail. Did it get cut off?"

"No, that is why Bob is special. He's a bobcat. They don't have long tails."

The lad's eyed widened. "Where did you get him?"

"I brought him with me from America," she said, as Bob directed his attention to him and lifted a lip.

Fennimore halted. "He looks mean. He's turning a bad face to me."

"You must be very quiet and patient with him, if you wish to gain his friendship," Sam stated. "That is why I keep him a secret from guests. Most people want cats to cuddle up in their laps. Bob doesn't like to do that, so it makes them angry."

"I don't blame him," he piped. "I don't like people trying to hug me and pinch my cheeks. Last time m'grandma did that, I tramped on her foot and busted her toe."

Samantha inwardly cringed, but maintained her pleasant expression. "Then you understand how Bob feels, and why I allow only a very few people to see him. Would you like to be friends with Bob, Fennimore?"

He nodded soberly.

"All right. Stand very still, and I will let him sniff you, so he'll know you."

The child actually obeyed. He stood like a soldier as the lynx circled him, investigating. By the time Sam was ready to take Bob inside, the cat allowed Fennimore to walk with them and did not growl or show his teeth.

"You will keep this a secret, won't you?" she asked as they went up the backstairs. "If people find out about him, I'll have to keep him elsewhere. You wouldn't be able to see him again."

"I won't tattle! Does old Montjoy know about him?" he asked.

"Yes, the earl is Bob's only other friend, so that makes three of us who like Bob."

"I sure like Bob better than Delphinia's stinkin' old cat. It always wants to act like a baby and get in your lap. Bob's a good pet for men . . . and for you, too, Miss Samantha. You don't go around trying to act like a lady."

Sam supposed that was a compliment. "Thank you, Fennimore. I hope I'm your friend, especially since we share this *secret.*"

"Yes'm," he answered as they entered the hall. "Can I go out with you tomorrow?"

"Of course," she replied, "if Bob and I can depend on you to keep our *secret.*"

"You sure can!" he whooped and ran toward his room.

Samantha led Bob to her chamber, hoping against hope that Fennimore would keep quiet about the cat. Perhaps it would be just the thing the boy needed to control his high spirits and ill conduct. She knew she had taken a great chance, but she truly hadn't a choice in the matter. Fennimore had seen them, and therefore she'd been forced to come up with the scheme. The deed was done. She could only hope for the best.

Following breakfast, Samantha adjourned to the morning room, which served as her office, to converse with The Connection and the housekeeper about the day's meals and events. Lady Montjoy joined them on this occasion, sneaking down the servants' stairway and furtively scurrying through the hall to avoid the guests. Ever since her experience with Fennimore, Margaret had kept to her own apartments and ignored the visitors, although her champion, Mr. Courtney, periodically sent her flowers or chocolates. She prettily thanked him by note, but she did not grant him an audience. It appeared that she would never unbend enough to accept the customers.

After The Connection went on their way, Sam drew out her schedule of reservations. Strangely enough, the inn was to be either totally full or almost vacant. Sighing, she began to reply to reservation requests. She wished Kevin would aid her with the administrative work, but she guessed that she was stretching his share of the work to the maximum. He greeted new guests upon arrival and bid them farewell when they left. He sat at the head of the table for meals and took people riding most every morning. She couldn't honestly complain.

Wondering why everyone seemed to want one particular week and not another, she laid down her quill and rose, drifting to the little terrace that adjoined the room. In the meadow, she saw Kevin and Delphinia riding together, with only a groom to satisfy proper decorum. Frowning, she watched as the skilled equestrians set their horses into a canter. Of late, those two seemed to be spending a great deal of time together. It rankled, and she didn't understand why. She didn't want to ride a horse, or spend time at the pianoforte, but . . . She shrugged and turned away. *She* had *work* to do. She didn't have time for play. As she sat down at her desk, the butler silently entered.

"Miss Samantha, we may have a problem," he said worriedly. "My lord is out riding with some of the guests, so I thought it best to come to you, instead of Lady Montjoy."

"A problem? What now?" Sam groaned. The morning dilemma with Fennimore and this scheduling difficulty should have been trouble enough for one day.

"We have visitors," he went on, "Lord Danforth and family. There are no chambers available, and . . . well, I do not think that these guests expect to pay."

"Everyone pays, no matter what their rank," she said firmly. "We are not running a house of charity."

"Yes, miss," he nodded.

Sam quickly wracked her brain to come up with a way to house more patrons. There was one unused chamber, the future countess's room. Since it opened into Kevin's domicile, and boasted no internal lock, she could not house customers there. A brilliant idea struck her. *She* could stay in the countess's chamber and allow the guests to have her suite. Kevin could not object to extra money, especially when she promised that she would not disturb him.

"How many are there in the party?" she asked.

"Three, miss, the lord and lady, and their daughter, plus servants, of course."

She smiled brilliantly. "That's perfect. We have plenty of space available for the servants, and we shall house the family in my apartment. We'll set up a trundle bed in my sitting room for the daughter. These will be our first aristocratic clients,

Jenkins, and they certainly shall pay. No pay, no stay." She laughed at her little quip.

Jenkins did not find humor in it, Indeed, a pained expression settled on his face. "Miss Samantha, perhaps I'd best explain further. Their name is *Danforth.*"

"Danforth?" The name sounded familiar, but she couldn't place it. "Are they special friends of Lord Montjoy? Well, it doesn't matter. Business is business, and friends are friends. They will be charged, just like everyone else. We have no discrimination at Montjoy Castle."

The butler continued to look uneasy. "Lord and Lady Danforth, and their daughter, Lady Frances Danforth. The young woman is rumored to be Lord Montjoy's fiancée."

Her heart bounded to her throat. She was to meet Kevin's would-be fiancee. For no good reason, Sam had disliked the girl when first she had heard of her. This negative sentiment had ripened into pure loathing. Now Frances and her parents were here, at Montjoy Castle, probably expecting to stay for free.

"There is no official engagement," she coldly informed him. What to do? Actually, she could do nothing but what she'd already decided. She would not toss out an existing guest to accommodate the Danforth family, and these well-bred nuisances *would* pay!

"I will repeat, Jenkins, they will have no preferential treatment. We will look upon them just as if they were ordinary clientele. You were right in coming to me, though, instead of to Lady Montjoy." She lifted her chin in determination. "She would be terribly distressed by this situation. However, not being a part of this English social tyranny, I don't mind confronting the Danforths and telling them of our arrangements. And I don't care whether or not they stay, except that the extra money would be nice. In fact, they're supposed to be wealthy, aren't they? I shall charge double our usual fee."

Jenkins winced, gently shifting from foot to foot. "Miss Samantha, the staff and I love you sincerely. We believe you look out for our best interests. Because of this, I hope I can speak plainly."

"Please do," she nodded.

He hesitated briefly, then plunged ahead. "Miss Samantha, the class system, as you call it, is at the very core of British life. Whether you like it or not, you are a part of the privileged set. You must cater to the Danforths and treat them as if they were special, or your reputation will be damaged."

"I don't care," she said stubbornly. "Besides, if you look at it in those terms, you must assume that the Montjoys' distinction and mine, too, are already besmirched. That's what we get for attempting to earn an honest shilling. So, Jenkins, if you will invite the Danforths into the drawing room, I shall be along shortly."

"I have already done so." He bowed stiffly and left the room with a thunderous scowl of disapproval on his face.

When he was gone, Samantha ran to the mirror, anxiously hoping that her appearance was in good order. *Not bad,* she decided, smoothing back a stray tendril of hair and biting her lips to make them rosy. She pinched her cheeks, turning them into a healthy pink, and wondered all the while why her countenance was so important. It was rather ridiculous. Why did she care what the Danforths thought of her looks? By the time she was finished with them, they wouldn't like anything about her, anyway. Feeling a wee bit nervous, she left the room and proceeded to the drawing room.

Jenkins was waiting at the door. "Miss Samantha, I took the liberty of sending for Lord Montjoy. Perhaps we'd best fetch Lady Montjoy as well."

"I wouldn't dream of disturbing her. You shouldn't either. Think of how she hates being below stairs when cits are about." She smiled aloofly and swept past him.

Lord Danforth stood and raised his monocle to his eye as Sam entered. The ladies remained seated, regarding her with surprise and open suspicion. Sam curtsied.

"I am Samantha Edwards, manageress of this establishment.

I understand that you wish accommodations?" Without waiting for a reply, she forged on. "We have only one suite at the moment, but if the young lady doesn't mind sleeping on a trundle bed in the sitting room, you may rent it."

All three gaped at her.

"We also have plenty of room for your servants," she added.

Unexpectedly, Lady Danforth was the first one to recover from the shock. "We are Lord Montjoy's personal friends," she stammered.

"How delightful! I'm sure he will be so pleased to find his friends supporting his endeavor." She smiled pleasantly. "Now, about the rooms, we can ready them in a short time. Shall I fetch my registration book?"

"Where is Lord Montjoy?" Danforth demanded, puffing up like a bullfrog. "Why don't you fetch him?"

"At the moment, he is occupied with other guests," she said. "I'm sure he will greet you as soon as he may."

"Does he even know we're here?" he persisted. "I want him to know we are here!"

"Please be patient, my lord," Sam's voice was polite and soothing, but inwardly she was searching for the best words to use to frustrate these people. Seeing their outrage was very fine sport.

Lady Frances whispered to her mother, who, in turn, spoke out. "My daughter cannot sleep on a trundle bed. She is too delicate."

The remark permitted Sam to look openly at Kevin's would-be fiancée. She did appear frail. Her body was entirely too thin, and her skin had such a pale, translucent quality that it looked like it would bruise easily. Her hair was pale blond and her eyes, a pallid blue. Sam wondered if she was frequently ill. In Frances, it seemed that her aristocratic blue blood needed a good transfusion of a commoner's red.

"We must have three chambers," Lord Danforth insisted. "One for each of us."

"I'm sorry," Sam sympathized, "but we do not have such a vacancy. There is an inn in the village, which might suit you better. It is rather quiet on week nights, which might disappoint you, if you prefer to mingle and make merriment."

Lord Danforth was growing absolutely livid. "I refuse to stay in a public inn, when Montjoy's castle can serve our purposes!"

"That is completely correct," his wife ventured. "Merriment, indeed! Lord Montjoy will not be pleased when he finds how you have treated us. Neither will his mother. By the way, where *is* Lady Montjoy? Have you banished her and the other ladies so you may rent their chambers?"

"Lady Montjoy is resting," Sam told her, "but you may chat with her later . . . if you remain with us and rent the suite I have available."

"Now see here, young woman," Lord Danforth objected. "There is no reason why you cannot double up the other guests, so that we may have our requisite three rooms. Damn it! I am the heir to a dukedom!"

Samantha, having kept her sweet smile throughout the interview, became frigidly grave. "Lord Danforth, I do not care if you're heir to the throne. You must abide by our rules, or you may remove yourself and your family from this property!"

Lord Danforth glared at her and made fists. "You are a foreigner. You're American, I believe. And you don't know our ways! Let me tell you. You're making a mistake, girl, and you will pay for it. I intend to see that you are fired!"

Sam drew a deep breath. "Then you will be disappointed," she said, wondering if Kevin would back her up, and seriously doubting it.

"I think not!" Lady Danforth joined in. "My husband is a man of power."

He nodded viciously. "Montjoy will do as I say. In the very near future, I will own him!"

Lady Frances raucously caught her breath. As all attention was drawn to her, the combatants saw that she was staring at the earl, who was leaning against the doorjamb, his arms folded and his legs crossed negligently. Lord Danforth became even more florid; Lady Danforth gasped, her mouth hanging open like a dullard; Lady Frances wailed softly.

Sam wondered how much of the dialog Kevin had witnessed. He wouldn't like the way she had baited and toyed with the Danforths. She'd probably hear about that, in a manner which was not particularly pleasant.

If Kevin had listened to her, he couldn't have been deaf to Lord Danforth's words. He couldn't relish the man's assumption that he *owned* him. Knowing her cousin, she imagined that he must be furious beyond all belief. Yet he stood there, almost slouched, with a notably cool and casual expression. If he protested the idea of financial slavery, he wasn't showing it. He must not have watched the exchange.

Lord Danforth apparently decided that Kevin hadn't heard his defamation. He put his fist to his mouth, coughed, and raspingly cleared his throat. "You are a welcome sight, Montjoy. If I'd had to exchange one more sentence with this . . . with this impertinent manager-person, I'd have left in high dudgeon. She may be adept at dealing with the merchant class, but I do assure you that she has no knowledge of her betters. I have no idea what sort of rig you're running here, but if I were you, I'd waste no time sending her on her way."

"Indeed?" Kevin straightened, sauntering into the room and making his way to the liquor cabinet. "Have you been served, sir?"

"No!" he barked. "No restorative drink; not even a scrap of bread! All we've been provided with is a smart dose of her pert tongue!"

"That is correct," Lady Danforth seconded. "This person should never be placed in position of authority. We have never been so shabbily treated. Her manner is most obnoxious."

"Please, Mother, don't," Sam heard Lady Frances whispering from behind her parent's back.

"We have had a long and wearying trip," she plunged on. "We have not even been offered a glass of water!"

Samantha was tired of the slander. "Kevin, have you ever

known a guest to arrive in this hall without Jenkins offering a restorative repast?"

"Stay out of this, Sam."

She was taken aback. He'd never before made a diminutive of her name. But despite her surprise, she couldn't hold back her impudence. "How can I desist? I am right in the midst of it."

"This girl should be spanked black and blue," Lord Danforth recommended.

The ghost of a grin crossed Kevin's lips. "I agree, but she's a bit old for that."

Lady Danforth bristled. "Then fire her!"

"I can't. Brandy, my lord? And sherry for the ladies?" At their nods, Kevin turned his back and set out the bottles and glasses.

Samantha joined him. "Send these people away," she breathed, as he poured the spirits. "You cannot wish to become involved with them."

"I must keep all my options. You know that."

"You didn't hear what he said about you," she murmured, prepared to tattle.

"I heard him," he said calmly.

"Then why—"

"Shut up, Samantha. Here." He pointedly eyed the two glasses of wine. "Do serve the ladies, and then ring for a tray of refreshments."

She wrinkled her nose. "You didn't even pour me a drink."

"No," he acknowledged. "After you order the food, I want you to make room for these people."

"We don't *have* room."

"Make it," he hissed. "Now go about your business, and let me smooth this over."

"Kevin, you cannot even contemplate wedding that girl. She is the veritable inside of a toad!"

"Good God." He rolled his eyes heavenward. "The things you come up with amaze me."

"You'll be even more amazed if you continue to treat me like a servant," she warned. "I won't take this from you, Kevin Montjoy."

"My, my. Is that a threat? Samantha, do serve the drinks." Laughing quietly, he left her, carrying his and Lord Danforth's beakers of brandy.

Tempted to throw the sherry into the ladies' faces, Sam followed. Good reason, however, prevailed. She didn't care what the Danforths thought, but if she put her desire into action, her cousin would be absolutely livid.

"Don't forget the tray, Samantha," Kevin commanded as she started back to the liquor cabinet to pour herself a glass of sherry.

Her temper rose, threatening to spew forth. Gritting her teeth, she went to the bell rope and yanked hard, then started back toward the cabinet. The wine would do wonders for her present mood.

"Samantha?" Kevin interrupted her objective.

She stopped in her tracks, her back to him.

"The rooms?" he reminded. "Don't forget to prepare the rooms, and see that the Danforths' baggage is brought in."

She whirled, narrowing her eyes. "I informed these people of the accommodations we have available, and they turned up their noses before I even mentioned the price."

Kevin winced. "There will be no charge involved."

She threw up her hands. "Well, I might have known! Kevin, no wonder you are as poor as a church mouse! You have a warped financial sense. If we were going to provide our services free to some, we should have selected people who pinched all their shillings to afford a short holiday here, and not this rich, pompous dunce!"

"Dammit!" Lord Danforth shouted. "That's it! That's really it!"

"We have never been so insulted," cried his lady.

"Samantha . . ." Kevin began.

She tossed her head. "I will do my best to house these unexpected people, but I won't disturb our current patrons."

"Just see to it," he said weakly.

"We require three rooms!" Lady Danforth called after her as she went through the door.

"You will have three rooms," Sam vowed, under her breath. "You will have my chamber, my sitting room, and my dressing room."

She met Jenkins as she stalked across the hall. "Lord Montjoy desires a tray of refreshments," she told him. "And I will need several footmen and maids to make my rooms ready for guests. Someone must also locate two trundle beds or cots, since those people cannot sleep together. Bob and I will be moving into the chamber adjoining the earl's rooms."

He flinched with shock. ""But Miss Samantha! You cannot share a suite with Lord Montjoy!"

"Why not?" she said grimly. "Would you rather I housed Lady Frances there?"

"No, miss, but . . . But you just can't do it."

"Never fear, Jenkins," she stated. "Bob will dissuade any licentious advances on Kevin's part."

"Oh, miss," he begged. "That's not what I meant. It's the *idea* of it. My lord is an honorable gentleman and would not take advantage of such a situation, but gossip might commence. Reputations could be ruined."

"Thank you, Jenkins, for caring," she said, "but I have made up my mind. When I have made a decision, you know, I am difficult to budge. Well, I've made up my mind on this."

"Oh, Miss Samantha," he moaned.

With a caustic laugh, she started up the stairs.

Fourteen

Kevin watched Samantha flounce away and turned back to his potential in-laws. He felt like tossing Lord Danforth from his home, but he knew he must not do anything so rash. It was frightfully oversetting to hear someone say that they might own one. He was skeptical as to what the future would bring if he married Lady Frances. Lord Danforth apparently intended to keep him under his thumb, and was bold enough about it to announce it in public. Kevin set his jaw. Such a thing was not going to happen.

"Samantha will arrange for your rooms," he said, feeling as if he sounded exactly like an innkeeper, which he supposed he'd become.

"That was a most unpleasant young woman," Danforth stated, seating himself. "I hope you will severely chastise her, Montjoy."

"So do I," agreed his lady. "I was positively overset by her impudent remarks."

"Yes." Kevin nodded. "Any number of the comments uttered were most unfortunate."

Lady Frances sniffled into her handkerchief. Her mother stared at her hands, flushing deeply. Lord Danforth eyed him warily.

"Montjoy," he said, changing the subject, "we'll admit that we came to visit due to simple curiosity. Currently, there is a great deal of gossip about you, saying that you are renting rooms in your castle, that you've turned it into some sort of glorified country inn. Now in all honesty, I see that it's true."

"It is," he admitted. "Turning Montjoy Castle into an inn was my American cousin's idea. It's early times yet, but so far we're doing extremely well."

"It must be rather uncomfortable to have so many strangers in one's home," Lady Danforth mused. "Does Lady Margaret enjoy such doings?"

"Truthfully, no." He sat down in the only remaining chair in the conversational grouping, the seat next to Lady Frances. "My grandmother prefers to remain in our private family quarters."

"Poor Lady Montjoy! I cannot blame her." Lady Danforth shivered demonstratively. "It certainly would be disturbing to me. Why, the house must be filled with rich vulgar, social-climbing cits!"

Kevin's temper rose higher. His business enterprise was not the Danforths' affair, not at the present, at least. It was quite astonishing to find that they had the nerve to question and pass judgment on the concern.

Lord Danforth seemed to read his mind. "Don't come to the conclusion that we're prying, Montjoy. We've been good friends with you and your family for a long time, so we felt we could take the liberty of discussing the venture."

"Certainly," Kevin said stiffly, glancing at Frances to ascertain what she thought of this matter. The young lady was sitting demurely and properly, with her hands daintily cradling her glass of sherry and her head bent in submission. He decided to attempt to draw her out.

"What do you think of my country hotel, Lady Frances?" he asked.

Her gaze fleetingly met his, then lowered again. "It is not for me to say, my lord," she murmured.

"Surely you have some opinion?"

"No," she whispered.

"Don't be so mousy," her mother pressed.

Lady Frances smiled faintly, but remained with her head bowed.

"Our daughter is quite appropriately modest," Lord Danforth vaunted. "To be honest, she was just as concerned as we were, when we began to hear the scandalous prattle about you, Montjoy. But she so respects and trusts you that she would never address such an unpleasant topic."

A comparison of Lady Frances and Samantha flashed through his mind. His cousin would never be guilty of lacking an opinion or the confidence to voice it. Because of her liberated tongue, she was tremendously frustrating, but never boring. Thinking of her, he grinned. The Danforths believed he was smiling in appreciation of their daughter.

"Yes, indeed," fawned Lady Danforth. "Our Frances is always so eminently respectful."

"She knows a woman's place," crowed the father. "I am so proud of her. Never a word of criticism passes her lips. That makes for a peaceful home life."

Kevin fixed his attention on the young lady. "I know you must have some opinion, however, my lady, even though you are too demure to come forward with it. You may tell me. I'd like to hear it."

A touch of pink colored her pale cheeks. Her clasped hands trembled. She looked superbly uncomfortable.

"She is concerned about the social ramifications, my lord," answered her mother. "She fears that you will be shunned by polite society."

"Is that what you think, Lady Frances?" he queried.

She smiled placidly, all the while gaping at her hands.

"She is well aware of how fragile reputations can be," Lady Danforth went on. "She believes you are courting disaster."

Kevin's polite smiled faded. It was clear that the young lady was not going to speak out on the subject of his inn. In fact, he remembered on previous occasions that Lady Frances hardly spoke up about anything. What if he married her? Would her parents continue to be her spokesmen?

"You are taking a huge chance," agreed Lord Danforth. "It's entirely unnecessary, you know. Come to me for advice and aid. Just between friends, of course! That's safer and more discreet."

Kevin looked him straight in the eye. "I prefer to solve my own problems."

"Tsk-tsk. An admirable virtue! But don't be reluctant. A man often needs a bit of help from his elders, from time to time."

"That's right," Lady Danforth broke in. "And we are such dear friends, Lord Montjoy, that you must not be shy."

They were closing the noose around his neck. Accepting aid, either financially or otherwise, added a further degree of intimacy that would be hard to escape. He wouldn't consent to the offer, but that fact that it had been made assured him that they still considered him as a satisfactory suitor for their daughter.

Kevin surreptitiously watched Lady Frances during the dialog, in order to gauge her reaction, but as usual, the girl was expressionless, except for the soft flush. God, but she was so pallid! She had none of Samantha's rich coloration. Frances's complexion matched her personality . . . vapid and lackluster, while Samantha . . . He drew a deep breath. He shouldn't compare his cousin with this girl. It wasn't fair to Frances.

Conversation ceased as Jenkins brought in a tray of light refreshments. Appetite floundering because of the uncomfortable situation, Kevin passed up the repast, but the Danforths plunged in, the lord and lady eating a great amount, while Lady Frances chose only a small, crustless cucumber sandwich. He refilled his and Lord Danforth's glasses, returning to his chair as Samantha came through the door.

Rising, he marveled again at the difference between the two young ladies. Sami was much more eye-catching. Of course, her color was higher, probably due to the presence of the Danforths, whom she apparently disliked.

"The accommodations are prepared and ready for occupancy," she announced.

"About time," grumbled Lord Danforth, neglecting to stand, and therefore, relegating Samantha to a lower position on the social scale. "We've had to sit here in all our travel soil. Deuced uncomfortable, I say, and vastly unwelcoming."

Kevin frowned. The crotchety old goat should be glad that he had a room at all. He certainly shouldn't complain, especially since they'd had to go to so much effort to please him.

Kevin might have registered his aggravation by the wrinkling of his forehead, but Samantha voiced hers out loud.

"Lord Danforth," she said. "People who don't wish to make reservations have no call to complain. Our staff worked hard and fast to house you in the limited space we had available. If I were you, I believe I'd be more grateful."

Lady Danforth gasped. Lord Danforth began to puff up. Strangely, Lady Frances actually cracked a wee smile, before quickly guarding her expression once more.

With difficulty, Kevin overcame the urge to laugh. Samantha really was too bad. She'd gain an awful reputation from this type of conduct. He must warn her and try to put the fear of God in her. How would she ever find a husband, if she persisted in this kind of impudence?

"Do you wish to go to your rooms?" Sam asked with the gentle impatience a weary nurse might use to hasten recalcitrant children.

"Do not goad us," Lord Danforth growled. "We shall go in our own due time."

"I thought you were so uncomfortable in all your dirt," Sam reminded. "Furthermore, I imagine that Lord Montjoy is not particularly happy to remain in his riding clothes, but being the gentleman that he is, *he* is too well bred to complain about it."

"Impertinent wench!" Danforth began.

"Samantha," Kevin forestalled. "Come with me. I have a matter of importance to discuss. If the Danforths will excuse us?"

"Readily!" consented Lord Danforth. "You'd best talk about firing her."

"Oh, he wouldn't fire me, would you, Kevin?" Eyes brimming with delight, Samantha clasped his hand, stood on tiptoe, and kissed his cheek.

Lady Danforth leapt from the sofa. "Enough! I have never witnessed such a disgusting want of propriety, and I have never been so shabbily treated. Danforth, I wish to leave!"

Kevin felt the warmth of a blush creeping up his neck to suffuse his cheeks. He certainly did want the Danforths to hurry away. With them and Samantha at crossed swords, life would not be pleasant.

"At present, we shall remain," her husband proclaimed. "But, Montjoy, I do insist upon your disciplining the girl."

"How will you do that, my lord?" Sam giggled flirtatiously.

"Come with me." He tucked her arm through his and piloted her out of the room.

In the hall, she broke into peals of laughter. "Oh, what a hideous sourpuss that Danforth is, and his lady . . . she is the absolute rear end of a horse! The daughter just has to be weak as water and—"

"Shut up, Samantha," he cautioned, leading her past the butler and grinning footmen, and toward the library. "Jenkins? See the Danforths to their rooms."

"My lord," he appealed. "I—"

"No more!" Kevin commanded. "I have my hands full with this little witch."

Samantha snickered. "I fear I've been naughty, Jenkins," she said brightly as they passed.

"Naughty isn't the word for it," Kevin muttered, leading her into the library. "Destructive is more like it."

"Fiddlesticks!" she lightly protested. "That's rather strong."

"It's meant to be! Good God, Samantha, how could you be so obnoxious to those people?" he exclaimed. "They could be my future wife and in-laws, you know."

"Well, I certainly hope not. I doubt that you'd be very happy." She removed her arm from the crook of his elbow and strolled nonchalantly across the room to sit in his chair at the desk. "Kevin, I am being completely serious. Get rid of them! You are not their kind."

"Indeed I am, and please don't go off into a tirade about the social structure of this realm! I am an earl, and I am a part of the *ton,* unless I am ostracized, a fate I'd prefer not to experience. And I'm standing on the edge of that precipice right now." He slowly shook his head. "And you, Samantha, have already taken a step beyond the pale, but I believe we can save you by blaming your American upbringing."

She drummed her fingertips on the shining surface of the desk. "I don't want to be *saved.* I'd rather hobnob with servants, than with the likes of those artificial, cocky snobs. They are exactly as I pictured your aristocracy to be. I had begun to think that you might be different, but now I see that I was mistaken. I am disappointed in you, cousin."

"I'm sorry to hear that, but Samantha, you must face reality. We're civilized here, and thus we are blessed with sophistication and polish."

"Namby-pamby," she said in a singsong voice. "Effeminate."

"Think what you like," he snapped. "But it seems to me that you could contrive to be polite to my friends."

"If you think the Danforths are friends, you are sadly mistaken. They merely want to use you to get rid of that ugly daughter. They are so anxious to be shed of her, they will pay an exorbitant price." She narrowed her eyes and leaned forward. "How much are they offering you, Kevin? What is your price?"

"I've heard enough!" he cried. "I wish you to leave my library, Sam!"

"Oh?" She reflectively studied her nails. "Are you sending me to my room, *my lord?"*

He ground his teeth, thinking any number of epithets he could shout out, but none of them were suitable for a lady's ears. Whirling, he marched to the door. "To hell with it!"

Samantha's tinkling laughter followed him into the hall. He slammed the door as hard as he could. Tramping loudly to the stairs, he favored Jenkins with a hostile glance.

"I am going to my chamber, and I do not wish to be disturbed, even if the castle is afire!"

"My lord—"

"Do I make myself clear?" he demanded.

"Er . . . yes, but . . ."

"Silence, Jenkins!" he shouted and continued upstairs, banging the door to the family apartments and the one to his chamber.

"Sir!" His valet peeked from the dressing room. "In your sitting room—"

"Be still!" Kevin commanded and threw open the door to his small salon.

"R-r-r-row!" Bob cheerfully shrilled, leaping toward him.

"Goddam!" He caught the lynx in his arms, but not before Bob's claws pulled some threads from his coat.

The cat poked his face close to Kevin's and licked his cheek.

"This is enough! By damn, this is the last straw!" He disengaged Bob from his clothing and set him down on the floor. Samantha was going to answer to this! He tromped back into his bedroom, intending to send his valet after his infuriating cousin, but the dressing room was vacant. No doubt the man, fearing the cat, had fled as soon as Kevin had opened the door on the beast.

"Damn!" he shouted and strode into the hall and back to the stairs, nearly blinded by aggravation. He leaned over the railing.

"Samantha!" he roared. "Samantha! You will come at once to my bedchamber! And you'd best be submissive!"

"What in the name of God?" blared Lord Danforth, coming from what should have been Samantha's chamber.

His lady dashed after him. "I will endure no more! Insult on top of insult! What kind of a horrible place is this?"

"Yes, Montjoy!" her husband seconded. "Who is that girl? Your mistress?"

"For God's sake, no!" Kevin denied.

"Then why are you calling her to your bedroom?"

"O-o-o-h," Lady Danforth moaned, placing a limp hand on her forehead. "I think I am going to swoon!"

"Don't you dare," threatened Lord Danforth. "It will prolong our leave-taking! We are departing, Montjoy. Frances!"

Kevin's would-be bride tiptoed weakly from the room. "Please, Papa, there must be an explanation."

"There may be, but I don't want to hear it!" he railed.

"Come along." Lady Danforth grasped her daughter by the arm and almost dragged her down the stairs.

Samantha appeared in the hall below, smiling beautifully. "You wanted me, Kevin?"

"Harlot!" Lord Danforth accused and stormed down the stairs, herding his ladies before him. "Fetch my coach and baggage!" he directed Jenkins and his footmen.

"Pray tell what is going on?" Lady Montjoy and The Connection appeared in the hall.

"Kevin?" his grandmother asked, then immediately diverted her attention to the Danforths. "Oh, my goodness! Lord Danforth, Lady Danforth? What could be wrong?"

"Ask your whoremonger grandson! Ask his trollop!" Danforth bellowed.

"What?" Lady Montjoy gasped.

Lady Danforth eyed her with indignation. "I cannot believe you would allow your grandson to house his tart right under your nose!"

Kevin's grandmother promptly fainted into his arms.

"Take care of her." He told The Connection, gently laying her on the floor. "I must try to amend this misunderstanding."

"But what—" began Winifred.

"I'll explain later." Kevin raced downstairs, following the Danforths from the castle. "Please, my lord, my lady, I can clarify matters! Please wait."

"Let them go," Sam advised, catching up with him. "They aren't worth it."

He skipped down the front steps. "I'll clear your name, if nothing else."

"People like that won't listen anyway. Please, Kevin, don't degrade yourself."

Kevin ignored her. If the Danforths went away with this false image, he and she, The Connection, and the proud Montjoy family honor would be hopelessly ruined. He had to make them understand.

He intercepted them as they waited impatiently for their carriage to be brought around. "Lord Danforth, my lady . . ." He looked bleakly at the young lady. "Lady Frances. You have received the wrong impression. Samantha is my cousin. She isn't what you think . . ."

"Oh!" Lady Danforth shuddered. "You would compromise your relative! Gad, but I never dreamed you were so depraved."

"I don't wish to hear another word from your scandalous mouth!" Lord Danforth ordained.

"Papa, do allow him to enlighten us," Lady Frances begged. "I don't think things are actually the way they seem."

The coach arrived, and the footmen began to load the unopened baggage.

"Please, Papa!" the young lady whined.

Lord Danforth hesitated. "Well . . ."

Kevin was quick to begin his speech. "This whole tangle is a muddle of misunderstandings. You see . . ."

All of a sudden, a piece of fabric fell onto his head and draped itself across his eyes. "What the hell . . ."

Samantha burst into laughter.

Lady Danforth screamed.

Kevin ripped it away and found himself holding a pair of his unmentionables. What the . . . He looked upward and saw Bob balancing on his window ledge. In his mouth was another set of the garments. He watched in horror as the bobcat waved them to and fro like a flag.

Lady Frances swooned dead away. Her father caught her and loaded her roughly into the carriage, motioning his wife to follow. He turned to Kevin.

"I have never, in all my born days, seen such an exhibition. I came here in good faith, to apprise you of the gossip about you, which is circulating through the *ton*. I intended to assist you in overcoming this scandal." He removed a handkerchief and mopped his perspiring brow.

Bob must have decided to assist his lordship with his sweating countenance. With a playful toss of his head, he let loose the second item. Kevin's underwear came floating down from on high and alit on Lord Danforth's forehead.

"Son of a . . ." Danforth flung the garment to the ground and ground it with his foot. "Go to hell, Montjoy," he said shortly and leapt into his carriage. "Get us out of here!" he thundered.

The coachman snapped his whip and sent the team careening down the drive, perilously swaying from side to side.

"God damn!" Kevin sputtered, shaking his fist at the dancing, frolicsome cat on the window ledge, then turned to look for his next nemesis. "Samantha!"

Sam could hardly see through her tears of laughter, but she managed to locate Kevin's second pair of unmentionables. Picking them up, she shook dust from them, and extended them toward their owner. "Kevin, I believe these are yours?"

"Dammit!" Flushed scarlet, he ripped them from her hand. "This is not funny, Samantha!"

"Oh? If it is not, then hordes of people must be wrong." She gestured toward the castle.

A laughing servant or guest hung from almost every window, or had spilled out the doorway. Fennimore jumped and romped in the carriageway. The Connection had assembled, with Margaret supported by Mr. Courtney. They stood out as the only segment who were not chortling, except that Aunt Daphne wore the very faintest of smiles.

When Kevin glared at them, the servants quickly sobered from their merriment and hastened from view. Bob disappeared, then returned with a third set of personal linens and repeated his performance. This time, the undergarments landed on a topiary spiral, draping in such a way as to make them look rather shockingly occupied. Laughter recommenced, servants swiftly peeked out to guffaw, and Samantha giggled so hard she was forced to bend over and hold her sides.

Kevin did not retrieve his clothing. Wadding the others into a ball, he viciously threw them down. "Samantha," he growled and started toward her. "You are going to pay for this!"

Still nearly prostrate with glee, she took several steps backwards.

"I'm going to spank you like a child!" he jeered.

Seeing that he appeared very serious and quite capable of carrying out his attack, Sam pivoted, hitched up her skirts, and took to her heels. Quickly glancing back, she was pleased to see that she had a nice lead on him. He must have been surprised that she would actually try to escape.

In time with the strains of laughter, Sam ran around the side of the castle, hoping to be able to dodge Kevin in the formal plantings until she could reach the service door. She had almost gained the rose garden when an unforeseen event occurred. A rabbit, hiding in the thick, box hedge, startled and hopped across Sam's path, right under her feet. It seemed like she fell for minutes before she actually struck the ground. She bounded onto her knees, but Kevin, too close and speedy to stop, tripped on her leg and plummeted onto her.

"Ow!" Sam yelped as she sprawled out for the second time.

"My knee!" Kevin groaned.

She tried to wriggle away, only to find herself flat on her back and staring into his face, which was only inches away. "You great lummox!"

He looked back at her with a startled expression of surprise, then slowly grinned. "You are captured, Samantha."

"Let me up!" she wailed, flailing her arms.

He neatly caught her wrists. "I don't think I shall do that. Not yet, at least. Tell me, have you ever been kissed?"

"That is a very personal question, Kevin, one that I shall not answer!"

"Hm, maybe I can learn the truth in a different way." Leisurely, he lowered his lips to hers.

Fifteen

Startled, Samantha gaped. Kevin's eyes were closed, his dark fringe of eyelashes lightly dusting his cheekbones. *His eyes were beautiful,* she idly thought, before closing her own and drifting into the magic of the kiss, with throbbing pulse and breathless abandon.

She had never known a man's kiss, but she caught on quickly. Kevin was a marvelous teacher, even though he was causing her to be so unsteady at the knees. Aside from a natural desire to embrace him, she had to wrap her arms around his neck just to maintain her balance. It was wonderful, but it ended all too soon. Abruptly, Kevin lifted his head, leaving her lips still sweetly parted. It took him a moment to catch his breath, leaving her to wonder what had gone wrong.

"Good God, we can't do this," he finally said in a husky voice.

She blinked, feeling rather unfulfilled. "What?"

"We mustn't do this." He rose quickly, clasping her hands and helping her to her feet. "Can you imagine how we would have looked if someone espied us? It makes my blood run cold! Please accept my apology, Samantha."

Still cradled in the aura of the intimacy, she took a deep breath. "There is no need to apologize," she whispered.

"Indeed there is. I took advantage of you and the situation. I behaved badly. Being a gentleman (I hope!), who prizes honor, I must take the blame."

Reality began to dawn. He had kissed her, and now he was sorry that he'd done it. His thought process didn't make sense.

"Truly, no blame is involved," she assured him.

He ignored her declaration. "I promise that it will not happen again. I . . . I don't know what came over me."

"Kevin, shut up." She swayed, slightly light-headed.

He steadied her. "Samantha, are you all right?"

"I suppose so," she said dully, dropping her arms from his neck. Restlessly nibbling her lower lip, she smoothed her gown and tucked back a loose strand of hair.

"You don't sound very convincing. Is it because I took advantage? I am truly sorry for what happened," he reiterated. "Please forgive me."

Sam didn't want to forgive him, In her opinion, there was nothing to pardon. In fact, she had wished the kiss to go on and on. Suddenly, the immensity of emotion that the caress invoked imprinted itself on her brain. *She loved him.* Despite their frequent conflict, at sometime in their acquaintanceship, she had fallen in love with him. With that admission, her heart seemed to swell with affection.

"There is nothing to excuse," she assured him again, fondly reaching up to touch his cheek. His skin didn't feel as if his blood was running cold. It was very warm and slightly flushed.

"Don't, Samantha." He caught her hand and removed it. "I hope you'll pretend that none of this happened."

"How can I do that?" she questioned. "It did."

"Well, it shouldn't have, and nothing can come from it."

Her brain could not grasp the concept. "You must explain, Kevin. I'm afraid I do not understand."

"Oh, Sami . . . all right!" He led her on to the rose garden and drew her down beside him on a marble bench. "I don't know why we have to discuss this. You should know the answer."

"But I don't."

"Very well. Samantha, a true gentlemen doesn't kiss a lady without serious intent. We both are aware that, in the end, I will probably end up wedding an heiress."

"I don't know why you insist on believing that!" she cried, bosom aching. "The inn has been full ever since we opened it. You are going to be a wealthy man, Kevin, *without* an heiress's dowry!"

"That is all speculation," he insisted. "It's a gamble, and you know it."

"No! What *I* know is that you have no faith. If you expect the worst, Kevin, that is exactly what you will get!" In her ardor, she leaned toward him and clutched his thigh.

"Whoa!" He leapt to his feet, the motion disengaging her.

"What is it?" she shrilled, unnerved.

"You . . . you . . ." He swallowed hard. "Never mind."

"I thought you'd been stung by a bee."

"No." He exhaled slowly. "Let us drop the subject. In fact, let us cease this conversation. You are too dangerous to a man's self-control."

She frowned inquiringly. "What's that supposed to mean?"

He shook his head. "Samantha, there are times when you're impossibly naive and terribly dense. This is one of them."

"What did I do?" she demanded.

He stood, turned toward her, and hesitated, as if he were going to say something more.

"Kevin?" she prompted.

With a deep sigh, he strode toward the castle.

"You are the one who knocked *me* down!" she called after him, but he gave no indication of hearing. "Drat!"

With heavy footsteps, she followed him to the castle, but did not attempt to catch up. In his current mood, he would be unapproachable. And of course, she couldn't just throw herself into his arms and confess that she loved him. Before any protestations of devotion, she must convince him that he would not need to marry an heiress. Only time and a consistently full schedule of reservations would do that. At present, she could only strive to prevent him from making any irrevocable proposals.

She shook her head. On the other hand, did she truly love him, or was it merely the reaction to her first grown-up kiss?

She hadn't changed her opinion of England's arrogant, useless aristocrats. Kevin was better than most, but he still had that haughty air about him. No, she couldn't love a man who thought himself so much superior to most others.

It was a terrible tangle, one she was incapable of solving swiftly. In his arms, she knew the answer. Alone, she was not so sure.

First, she went upstairs to remove Bob from the balcony of Kevin's suite, only to find the cat inside and napping on the room's sofa. He did not wish to be disturbed, as evidenced by the lifting of his lips, but she was insistent and soon had him secured in her chamber and curled up on the bed. Not being able to ascertain how he had escaped from his confines, she decided that doors must have been left ajar, thus permitting entry.

She was lucky to have escaped Kevin's wrath about the undergarment episode. He'd been too distracted by the kiss to pursue it further. However, it was only a matter of time before he addressed the matter. She probably should play least in sight until some time had passed, and the event was not so raw, but she didn't feel like remaining in her chamber. Leaving the room, she descended the stairs.

As she proceeded to the morning room, Jenkins intercepted her with a sealed envelope. "Miss Samantha, a private messenger has delivered this and is instructed to wait for a reply."

She knew it was from a peer, because the letter was franked, but she hardly could be expected to recognize the name. She carried it with her to her desk, sat down, and opened it, while Jenkins hovered nearby.

"Oh! This is splendid! The Duchess of Walsingham wishes to hold a house party here!" she read with disbelief. "You see, Jenkins? We are not only attracting cits! Isn't that grand?"

"As you wish, Miss Samantha."

"I shall check my schedule." She opened her reservation book and scanned the dates. "Well, we do have a perfect time. Wait just a moment, while I pen a reply."

Assembling quill, ink, and stationery, she penned a response to the duchess's note. Her Grace and her guests would almost have the castle to themselves. Still booked would be the Miltons and Mr. Courtney, but surely they could not be a problem. Tingling with excitement, she handed the missive to Jenkins.

"Just wait till everyone hears of this!" she enthused. "Lord Montjoy should certainly have no more doubts about the success of this venture!"

She continued smiling after he left. Definitely too excited to balance her ledgers, she left the room and hastened upstairs to tell The Connection about the request. She entered the family salon and was happy to see Kevin there. Now all would hear and rejoice at once.

"You will never believe who has solicited reservations," she said smugly, grinning. "The request was even sent by private messenger, who waited for my reply."

"You look like a cat in the cream." Aunt Winifred chuckled. "We do not excel at guessing. Pray tell us."

Sam giggled. "It's a house party. The Duchess of Walsingham wishes to rent the entire facility. Now tell me we're not a success!"

Instead of happiness, her announcement brought scowls of dismay. "What's wrong?" she asked.

"The Duchess," groaned Aunt Margaret. "I shall be forced to go to table."

"Maybe not," said Aunt Winifred wryly. "When she hears of what has occurred today, she might cancel."

"If this isn't just what we need!" Kevin snapped.

"I don't understand," Sam appealed. "Have I done something I shouldn't?"

Aunt Daphne took mercy. "Samantha, dear, Duchess Walsingham is Lord Danforth's mother. Need I say more?"

Sam closed her eyes. "Oh, no," she moaned.

Duchess Walsingham heard of the reappearance of her son and his family on the day after they had come back to London.

Their early return angered her, for it signified failure, but she was not surprised that they hadn't been successful. She was well aware that all of her children had been born with defective intellects, especially George, who unfortunately was the heir to the coronet. He mucked up everything he tried to do. He must have muddled this, too, or they wouldn't be home this speedily. Ah well, knowing her son's penchant for trouble, she had already set a second plan into motion. But she still was curious as to why and how the Danforths had come up the losers. Quickly penning a note to invite them for dinner, the duchess presented it to a footman for delivery. She had no doubt that her family would do as the message directed. To the recipient, the letter was tantamount to a royal command.

That evening, waiting for the Danforths to arrive, the duchess was glad that her husband was inspecting one of his estates and would not be present. His Grace did not approve of her little intrigues. Without him rolling his eyes and looking long-suffering, she would be able to make her point and get her way without interference.

As the hour approached, she glanced out the window of the salon. George's carriage and team were standing at the curb, awaiting the exact hour to make their appearance. The duchess despised both early and late appearances.

As the clock was striking, she heard a bustle in the hall. Soon, her butler announced the guests. They entered the room and executed deep obeisances. Her impeccable butler went to the sideboard to prepare preprandial drinks, while the duchess motioned them to be seated.

"Pray tell me," she directed, after they had been served, "Why have you already returned from Montjoy Castle?"

"We have never been so insulted!" cried Lady Danforth and launched into a tale of horror, highlighted by such matters as an impudent girl, a love nest, terrible accommodations, cits, and unmentionables.

When she heard the story of the earl's undergarments, Her Grace laughed hard and long.

Fresh from her ordeal, Lady Danforth bristled. "It wasn't very funny!"

The duchess fixed her with a gaze that nearly reduced her to a puddle on the floor. "If I say it is amusing, then amusing it is!"

"Oh, Mother," her son sighed. "We have been through such an unimaginable experience that we are nervous beyond all belief. Just put yourself in our places. How would you like Montjoy's undergarments to float down upon your head?"

"It wouldn't happen," she stated. "No one, man or beast, would dare attempt such a thing. You are a fool, George, and a glutton for torture. Why didn't you put that girl in her place?"

"I tried!" he shrilled. "Nothing worked!"

"Fustian! I cannot believe that you would be intimidated by a young woman. Really, George, have you no gumption at all?"

"You weren't there, Mother! You don't know how it was," he asserted.

She lifted a severely sculpted eyebrow. "No, but do you think *I* would have had such trouble?"

He mumbled unintelligibly.

His wife broke in. "You should have seen our accommodations, ma'am. George and I were to sleep in *one* bed, and poor, dear Frances was assigned a *trundle bed* in our adjoining sitting room. That was all the girl said she had available. She refused to rearrange the chambers of *cits* to house us."

"You should have gritted your teeth and stayed. If you had, Frances might have been engaged right now, as we speak." The duchess eyed her granddaughter, who was sitting placidly, hands folded and head bowed. "Come to life, gel!"

Frances startled.

"Wake up!" cried Her Grace. "No wonder you've not snagged a husband! Who would show interest in a young lady who droops around looking like a dim-witted, dull-headed, totally boring dunce! For heaven's sake, show some spark."

The girl batted her eyelids as if she were awakening from a trance.

"What's wrong with you?" her grandmother cried. "Don't you like Lord Montjoy?"

"Of course she does," said Lady Danforth. "She thinks that he is—"

"Cease your prattle, woman! I asked your daughter. Has she no voice of her own?" She peered sharply at Frances. "Speak to me."

"Lord Montjoy is," she murmured, "very handsome. And he dances well."

The duchess waited a full five minutes. "Is that all you have to say?"

Lady Frances nodded.

"Do you even *want* to marry him?"

"I suppose I do. If only . . ." Voice wistfully trailing away, her granddaughter studied her hands, which were laced so tightly that her knuckles gleamed pure white.

"Frances, I wish you would talk openly to me. After all, I am on your side!" She paused to take a sip of wine and to give the girl the opportunity to speak out, but nothing was forthcoming. "You are beginning to exasperate me, my gel! The cat has your tongue, and I am not pleased by it."

"Yes, Grandmama." The young lady nibbled her lip. "Because Lord Montjoy is so terribly handsome, I wonder if he is the right match for me."

The duchess frowned. "I've been on this earth for more decades than I care to admit, and I've never heard such nonsense. Most females want their gentlemen to be good-looking. You are going to have to explain yourself."

Lady Frances cast a pained glance at her father.

Her Grace pounced on the gesture. "Is this a matter for ladies' ears alone?"

"Yes, ma'am," she muttered.

"Leave us, George," the duchess ordered.

When he had gone, Frances looked shyly from her grandmother to her mother and back again. She blushed deeply. "This is most difficult . . ."

"Must we pry everything from you?" Her Grace blared. "I am not very happy concerning this discourse! No wonder Montjoy is reticent. You probably can't manage one sentence when you are in his company. God only knows why you are so socially backward!"

Lady Danforth stepped in to assist her daughter. "Please, Frances. You must speak frankly to your grandmother. Indeed, she prefers it. Now, tell us why you fear his lordship's fine appearance."

The young lady onerously cleared her throat. "Gentlemen as exquisite as Lord Montjoy have . . . mistresses."

The duchess began to laugh. "Oh, my, that's rich!"

"It's not comical!" Frances unexpectedly blurted. "It worries me!"

Her grandmother chortled on. There was not much the other two women could do to stop her. She was too much their senior in rank, age, and more importantly, attitude. So although they were highly annoyed, they were forced to wait until the tears of hilarity subsided.

Finally, the duchess eased off and wiped her eyes, her recovery broken only by brief snickers. "Frances, my dear," she stated with a giggle, "you should hope that he keeps a mistress. That will save you from bothersome bedtime duties. It's a matter for rejoicing, not for weeping!"

Frances's brow wrinkled with thought. "But wouldn't people laugh about me and gossip behind my back."

"So what if they do? I'll wager that more than half of the married gentlemen in our circle of friends have tarts in their care. You must merely ignore it and hope that she takes care of his particular certain needs."

The girl eyed her doubtfully.

"Now, if that is all that concerns you, we shall call for your father and make our plans."

"What plans?" Lady Danforth asked.

"In good time! Fetch your husband, madam. I refuse to repeat myself," she decreed.

When her son entered the room, she waved him to seat himself. "I shall be brief," she told them. "Dinner is probably ready."

"I cannot fathom, Mother, what sort of scheme you have contrived," said Lord Danforth, "but whatever it is will probably come to naught. Besides, I'm not sure I wish my daughter to wed Montjoy. You should have gathered why I feel this way."

"It isn't as though there were numbers of suitors," she said roughly. "You'd best be satisfied with Montjoy."

"I suppose I am to have no say in the matter," he complained.

"That's right, George. I am older and far wiser." She aimed the next words to all. "I have already contacted Montjoy Castle, requesting to rent the entire inn for a weekend house party. The footman who carried my proposal should arrive at any time with an answer."

Her son groaned loudly. "Oh, no! We'll have to go back to that place?"

"Must we do this?" whined her daughter-in-law. "What can you hope to accomplish?"

"I shall succeed where you have failed," she boasted. "And while I am doing that, my guests will serve as a screen, to disguise my activities. What do you think of that, Frances?"

The young lady, having resumed her position of solemnity, her hands folded and her head lowered, quietly uttered, "That girl will be there."

"That is of no consequence." The duchess lifted a sculpted eyebrow. "Don't you remember our previous chat? She has no influence upon our mission."

"Mother, you had best know that I will be going under protest!" Lord Danforth announced. "And I won't be crowded, insofar as my bedchamber is concerned."

"George, you are becoming a total boor. No, I'll correct that. You are becoming a babyish boor!" The glare from her eyes was enough to pierce his skin. "You will do as I say. If not, you'll be sorry. Frances? Ring for the butler. I cannot imagine why our meal is so late. Ah, perhaps they were holding it until we had finished our scheming."

Before the young lady could reach the bell rope, the duchess's exemplary butler entered and bowed. "Dinner is served, Your Grace."

There was no further time for discussion of the Walsingham matter, so the family agreed to beg pardon from the guests and retire early. Instead of seeking their beds, they would assemble in the family salon. There, they could confer safely in private.

Sam had difficulty keeping her mind on the dinner ritual and the guests. The Connection had decided to take their meal in their quarters, leaving her and Kevin to maintain conversation. It wasn't easy, especially since the most notable event of the day was the incident of the unmentionables. Happily, the guests realized that what had happened was painful to the earl, so comment was kept to a minimum. Nor did anyone question Bob's breed. The onlookers must have been far enough away from him that they hadn't been able to see him well. Other than that, the evening was spent in the usual routine. Delphinia played the pianoforte and flirted with Kevin. Two young ladies from more recent arrivals attempted to set up a dalliance with him. When the majority of the older guests decided to try their hands at cards, Samantha excused herself and went up to the private salon. Shortly afterward, Kevin followed. As luck would have it, he began the discussion with the topic of Bob's antics.

Sam immediately leapt to the defense. "It was an accident. Bob has escaped only once before. That does not seem like a bad account."

"Once is too much," argued the earl.

"We have enough on our plates to discuss without delving into that," Lady Montjoy decided. "If Samantha's cat continues to be a problem, he will have to lodge elsewhere. Are we agreed?"

Everyone nodded, except for Sam. She didn't want Bob to be turned out of the house, but she thought it best to keep silent about it just now. As Aunt Margaret noted, they had a great deal to talk about in regards to the Walsingham reservation.

"There is a good chance that it won't come to pass, on account of the incident with the unmentionables," Aunt Winifred offered.

The muscles rippled under Kevin's jaw. Sam gritted her teeth. Why must everything come back to that?

"Also," she told them, "I informed her that there were several other bookings that prevent her from having the entire place to herself and her company."

"We cannot rely on that," Aunt Margaret stated, "so we must discuss this as if we were certain. First, her intent must be to snare Kevin, so we must guard against compromise. Secondly, if she fails at that, we may be sure that she will attempt to discredit us. Therefore, everything we do must be faultless. It's as simple but as daunting as that. Samantha, you have been acting as hostess. Are we prepared for the challenge?"

A stab of nervousness thrust through Sam's abdomen. Entertaining cits was one thing. Satisfying a high-in-the-instep duchess was quite another. In spite of her previous protestations against class distinctions, she was truly out of her element. Instinctively, she looked at Kevin.

"Can you do it?" he asked quietly. "Or do you care?"

In the beginning, she would have flippantly said that she didn't care. And truthfully, she wouldn't have given a fig for the outcome, or the repercussions. Now, because of the kiss, things had changed.

"I care," she murmured, "and I . . . I am not sure of myself."

Their gazes met. Kevin smiled crookedly. "I will help you."

The Connection was inquisitively watching them. Winifred spoke up first. "I will actively assist."

"I, too," announced Daphne.

Margaret studied the couple. "Samantha, *I* will be the hostess. You may support me."

Relief swept over her like a huge wave. "Thank you, Aunt. I cannot express how gratified I am."

Lady Montjoy nodded curtly. "We shall begin work tomorrow. If or when the Walsingham comes, we'll be ready!"

There were only desultory comments after that, before the conference broke up for the night. As she walked down the hall, Sam suddenly remembered the room change. Kevin was going to be furious, so soon after they had reached a delicate accord. She quickened her pace, hoping that she could reach her sanctuary before he left the salon. Thrusting open the door, she started in, but not before she heard a demanding male voice.

"Where the hell are you going, Samantha?"

With a wail, she darted inside, slammed the door, and locked it.

Sixteen

Kevin was brought up short by the sight he had witnessed. Surely he hadn't seen Samantha entering the chamber his future wife would occupy! But he wasn't given to hallucinations, and he hadn't imagined those wide, "caught-me," green eyes. The lady was up to something. As seemed to be happening frequently, he was to be her victim.

He started toward the door she had entered, then decided against it and went to his own room, his mind cluttered by random possibilities. As soon as he crossed the threshold, everything became crystal clear. To make room for the Danforths, Sam had moved from her own suite and occupied the future countess's. That also explained how Bob had so easily carried out his mischief. He'd gone through the sitting-room doors, which didn't fit well, and had gotten into some laundry that his valet had not put away yet.

Closing the door behind him, he glanced around quickly to ascertain that the manservant was not present, then he bolted the door. He would confront his vexatious cousin, and he wanted no witnesses. He strode into the sitting room and grinned. She could not escape the forthcoming encounter, for there were no locks on the adjoining doors. He would have highly enjoyed bursting in and taking her by surprise, but he was a gentleman, so he knocked.

There was no reply. Kevin quietly listened and could hear

not one sound. Aha! He would be able to walk through that door without blame! Turning the knob, he thrust it open.

Samantha sat on the edge of her bed, petting a yawning Bob and looking frightened. He went inside and paused, the room's distance away from her. "If your maid is here, dismiss her," he ordered.

She looked even more fearful. "What are you going to do, Kevin?" she asked in a small voice.

"Can't you guess?"

"I think so." Tossing her head, she regained her aplomb and spoke candidly, apparently girding herself for battle. "You intend to address chamber arrangements."

"How perceptive!" He applauded. "Fancy that! My, Samantha, but you are a brilliant individual."

She grimaced.

"Do you realize that this maneuver compromises us beyond repair?" he queried. "But then, perhaps that's what you want it to do."

"Certainly not!" The spice had returned to her tongue. "I accomplished this move in the spirit of practicality."

"That's rather ridiculous, don't you think? I hardly think it is practical for us to share a suite. I would tend to define it as scandalous."

She rose from the bed and assumed a defensive stance. Bob gracefully leapt down and came to Kevin, rubbing against the earl's legs.

"Bob indisputably likes you," she observed.

So the devious chit thought to change the subject? "Dammit, Samantha, I am not here to discuss Bob's peculiarities!"

There was a light rap on the door. She gaped wide-eyed at him. "It's Martha!"

"Get rid of her." He sped to the sitting room and closed the door, putting his ear to it.

"Come in!" Samantha called.

There was the bustle of entry.

"It's been a hard day," said the maid. "First that move, then m'lord's underbritches!" She chortled.

"Please do not remind me," Samantha begged.

"We servants could hardly eat supper. We'd take a few bites, then we'd start laughing. Even Mr. Jenkins guffawed, and I've never seen him forget himself like that!"

Kevin began to seethe. It was bad enough to think of the guests and the Danforths. So the whole staff was giggling?

"Do not speak of it again," Samantha commanded in such forceful tones, that he was surprised. "Lord Montjoy is terribly angered and embarrassed by it. Whoever mentioned it would probably be fired."

"Yes'm," she replied. "I'm sorry, miss."

"Just remember what I have said," Samantha directed, "and warn the others."

There was a long silence. Kevin could picture the abigail standing before her mistress with her head bowed and her lip stuck out in an attitude of abject servitude. Finally, Samantha broke the hush.

"It was very funny, I know, and I don't mean to admonish you, Martha. I only want you to be very careful of your surroundings when you mention it."

"Yes, miss." The servant recovered her cheeriness. "Shall I help you undress now?"

"No!" cried Samantha.

There was another silence. Kevin grinned, visualizing Samantha's dismay at the thought of donning her nightgown and knowing that he was standing by. She'd probably blushed scarlet.

"I am not ready for bed, Martha. I must take Bob for his nightly walk."

He was disappointed that she had a ready excuse. It would have been interesting to hear her fight her way out of that one.

"I will undress myself," she informed the maid. "Go on with your evening and do not worry about me."

"Are you sure, Miss Samantha?"

"Indeed, I am."

"Then I might take a little walk with m'beau. I'll lay out your nightclothes before I go."

"I can do that!" Sam protested.

There was quiet again. The maid must be performing her duties, in spite of what her mistress insisted upon. The door abruptly opened, nearly sending him sprawling.

"So!" Samantha cried. "Eavesdropping, my lord?"

"Good God, Samantha," he grumbled, catching his balance.

"There is absolutely no excuse for this," she announced. "If you persecute the servants for what you have heard, I shall make things very difficult for you."

"You don't have the power to make things difficult for anyone," he couldn't help saying.

"Oh? Just watch me! For a good start, I possess the fact that you are standing right now in my bedroom." She smiled, fluttering her eyelashes. "What do you think of that?"

"Not much," he admitted.

"Well then, Lord Montjoy, what do you choose to discuss?" She lifted her chin in a rather imperious fashion. "Or maybe nothing, since I do hold you captive by my knowledge."

"Don't you dare threaten me," he reproached. "Get your cat's leash, and we'll take him outside."

She nodded. "Very well."

"We'll meet at the service door."

He left her, unconcerned that she would elude him. Without a lock on the sitting-room door, she was helpless prey. So he was not surprised when she joined him minutes after they'd parted.

"Where do you usually walk?" he asked her, as he fell in step.

"The meadow. It seems safer than the gardens."

"For being seen by guests, yes." He frowned. Didn't she realize what could happen to her if she went out alone in the night?

"Do I detect something wrong in that?" she asked.

"It isn't unknown for poachers and gypsies to trespass on

my land," he stated. "Other felons could do it, too. I doubt that they would consider you a lady, or themselves as gentlemen."

"With Bob along? Ha!" she scoffed. "No one could harm me."

"No? Criminals often carry weapons," he fired back. "They would kill Bob and have their way with you."

"That's terribly farfetched, Kevin," she chortled, passing through the gate to the field and bending to release Bob.

"Nevertheless, I forbid you to do it."

"Forbid?" she gasped, straightening. "Forbid!"

"That's right," he asserted. "I am your guardian."

"Aunt Winifred is that, Kevin. Actually, I am too old to have a guardian."

He sighed. Why must everything end in an argument? He felt like shaking her. Was she too naive to realize what harm could befall her? Traipsing alone at night! How idiotic could she be?

"Samantha, whether you like it or not, I am responsible for you. After all, I am the man." As soon as the words left his mouth, he realized how childish they sounded. But it was too late to take them back.

She smirked. "If I needed a bodyguard, I'd scarcely choose an English earl."

He bit back a curse. "You would mightily benefit by reading a history book, madam. You would learn that English earls, and other peers as well, led many armies to victory. Compared with that, safeguarding one obstinate female does not seem to be that great a chore."

"All that glory is from the past." She eyed him impishly. "Come, Kevin, be sporting! You know that nothing will happen to me."

"The main thing I do know is that you are the most infuriating woman I've ever met. Tell me, Samantha, do you spend an hour each morning deciding what you will do to derange me the most?"

She trilled, slipping her arm companionably through his. "Let's walk."

"So you refuse to answer? Very well." He grinned. "You may be concerned for your cat, however. I haven't seen him for some time."

"I am not worried. He will come when I call, but there is a thing that troubles me." She soberly looked up at him. What should I expect from the Walsingham house party?"

"The worst?"

"Yes, I suppose so, if there has to be a worst."

He considered his answer, guessing that she instinctively feared the *ton,* whether she would admit to it or not. A mental vision arose of society's tabbies with their claws unsheathed and ready to pounce. Samantha wouldn't stand a chance.

She seemed to read his mind. "Don't spare me."

He shrugged. "Depending upon who is invited, they will probably try to make you appear rustic and ignorant of propriety. They'll make fun of you."

"I see," she murmured. "They'll set out to eat me alive."

More images struck him, igniting his anger. The thought of her standing alone to face the *ton* was overwhelming. He set his jaw. No one would hurt her if he had anything to say about it.

"They may attempt to discredit you, but they won't succeed," he said, as much to himself as to her.

"No?" She laughed hollowly. "And who will stop them?"

"Me," he said simply, and the truth seemed to clout him between the eyes. He was in love with this impossible widgeon. Good God, when had that happened?

He halted under a tree and turned her to face him. "I told you I would assist. Do you doubt me?"

She smiled wistfully. "I don't want to, but we were speaking of the hostessing duties, not of me personally."

"Those are the least of your worries." He tilted her chin with his fingers. The moonlight filtering through the leaves made intriguing, lacy shadows on her face. It was more than any man could withstand. Lost to all else, he bent his head and kissed her.

Samantha responded, slipping her arms around him in a sweet embrace. At that moment, he wished with all his heart that the inn would be a success, so that he need not marry an heiress to rescue the family fortune. In the next moment, something fell with a hideous scream onto his shoulders and nearly scared him to death.

"God help us!" he shouted, jumping backward and sending Sam reeling.

There was the sound of a great rending of cloth as his coat ripped. His tormentor clawed its way up, repositioning itself. A fuzzy face with sticky whiskers pushed past his cheek.

"Goddamn!" Kevin exploded. "Bob!"

Samantha let loose a gale of laughter.

"Get him off me!" he bellowed.

Giggling, she lifted the cat from Kevin's shoulders.

"He has ruined my coat!"

"Now, now," she soothed. "The damage appears to be in the seams. I shall mend it."

"It will never be the same!" He caught his breath. Nothing else would ever be the same. The first kiss, in the garden, might be construed as an accident, but not this second one. Not twice in one day.

"Put the leash on him," he directed her, brushing his coat. "It's time to go in."

Silence reigned as they walked to the castle. Kevin was thinking his own thoughts, and he assumed Samantha was lost in hers. Was she reflecting on him? He really did not want to know. If he learned that she loved him, he'd have an extremely hard time not giving way to his love for her. He must consider only his familial responsibilities. Loving her was a luxury he couldn't afford.

As they entered the castle, she touched his forearm. "Kevin?" she said softly.

He brought her hand to his lips and kissed it lingeringly. "We can't, you know."

In the dim light, her eyes sparkled unnaturally bright, as if they were filled with tears. Pulling her hand away from his, she dashed up the servants' stairway with Bob galloping along beside her.

Kevin turned and strode away to the library to partake in a large glass of brandy.

Sam raced to her chamber, swiftly unleashed Bob, and threw herself onto the bed. Her emotions had never been in such a turmoil as they were today. On the one hand, she was in love with Kevin, but on the other . . . How could she love a man who was so opposite from all that she prized? He could boast as much as he wished about noblemen leading armies. She knew that they had, but those men were in the minority. English lords were effete. Even Kevin himself proved that. In his very last words to her that evening, he had admitted that he was unable to follow his real feelings. That was cowardly, wasn't it? Besides, she couldn't wed an Englishman. She had to return to America, because she owned property there. But oh, if those things were not true . . . She burst into tears.

In the morning, Martha found her still lying, fully dressed, across the bed, her cheeks streaked with dried tears. In a dither over whether to wake her mistress or attempt to make her more comfortable, she cracked open the draperies to let in more light. Sam awakened and rolled over, holding her head as if her brain was in danger of exploding through the top of it.

"Oh, Martha, my head is splitting."

The abigail scurried to serve her.

Sam moaned. "I doubt that I am able to appear at breakfast. I cannot understand it. I am never ill."

"Then bed is where you should be. Let me help you undress." The abigail was already reaching around to undo the tapes of her gown.

"I don't know what I'd do without you," Sam admitted, remembering how, just a short time ago, she had maintained that she certainly did not need a lady's maid.

Martha helped her into a white lawn nightgown, plumped the

pillows, and sat her up against them with a cup of hot tea. "Now, miss, I'll fetch some headache powders."

"Thank you." She nodded, sipping the brew. "You are taking such good care of me. When you go downstairs, please inform Jenkins and Lord Montjoy that I shall not be down this morning."

"Yes, miss. Shall I fetch your breakfast, too?"

"No. Not yet."

When the servant left, Sam drained her cup and fell back upon the squabs. Being coddled by a lady's maid was the height of luxury. It was too bad that her head hurt too much to enjoy it. Closing her eyes, she briefly dozed, only to wake up because of a nightmare, in which Kevin was standing at the altar with Lady Frances and Delphinia on each arm. Fiddlesticks! Was he to invade her dreams as well as her waking moments?

When Martha returned, Sam took the powders and began her second cup of tea. "Did you see Lord Montjoy?"

"No, miss. I told Mr. Jenkins, as he was going from the kitchen to the dining room. He promised to tell m'lord."

"All right. I wonder if any of the guests have come down," she mused.

"I know Miss Milton has. Mr. Jenkins was fetching chocolate for her. I don't know about any others, but I can find out, if you want me to."

"No, that isn't necessary." A stab of jealousy impaled her heart. "I believe I shall go down to breakfast, after all."

Smiling knowingly, Martha began to assist her.

Hurrying through her morning ablutions, Sam soon descended the stairs and hastened to the dining room. She was glad she'd changed her mind about breakfast. Kevin and Delphinia were the only ones present. Head still aching, she seated herself across from the girl and adjacent to her cousin. She bid Jenkins to fetch her a breakfast pastry and a cup of tea.

"Headache better?" Kevin asked.

"Yes," she fibbed.

"You should join us for a ride," Delphinia said smugly. "One's education is sorely short, if one doesn't learn to ride."

Sam thought of the members of the *ton* who would assemble at Montjoy Castle. No doubt all of them would know how to ride, but there wasn't time for her to master the skill. If she tried, she would only be a laughingstock.

"Riding is such a pleasure," the girl went on. "I don't know how you can bear to remain ignorant of the sport, Miss Edwards."

"Yes," said Samantha, snidely. "I'm sure I don't know how to make my way through life without riding. One appears to such great advantage in a riding habit."

"That's right," Delphinia soberly agreed. "Take, for example, my habit, with its hat and saucy blue plume. The feather dances flirtatiously, does it not, my lord?"

"So do you," her brother chortled, entering, "or at least, you try to. But you only succeed in making yourself look idiotic, Finny."

"Shut up!" she gasped. "And do not call me Finny! What are you doing here?"

"That's a stupid question, Finny." He took a plate and began to fill it at the buffet. "Why are you always so dumb?"

"I'm going to tell Mama about you, you urchin!" Delphinia threatened.

"Waste of breath." He sat down beside her and began eating the huge servings he'd taken. "You know she won't flail me. Besides, what I say is true."

"I want you to go away," she muttered. "I cannot bear you, and neither can anyone else. You are an embarrassment to the family."

"Miss Samantha likes me, don't you, ma'am?" Fennimore boasted.

Sam smiled and nodded.

"We have a secret, and you can't hear about it, Delphinia." He wrinkled his nose. "Nobody trusts you to keep your mouth shut."

"I don't want to know your old secret. Ow!" she cried. "Quit kicking your legs! You struck me . . . probably on purpose!"

Sam caught Kevin's eye and smiled. Delphinia surely didn't know how juvenile she appeared when she brangled with her brother. She wondered how the girl would conduct herself when Duchess Walsingham and her guests arrived. Even though she had yet to receive a confirmation from the lady, she couldn't resist the thought of telling about it, just to see Delphinia's reaction. Catching a break in the brother/sister tit for tat, she spilled her news.

"They will be coming when I am here?" the girl cried.

Sam nodded triumphantly.

"Oh, my! What shall I do?"

Fennimore snickered. "You'll probably go on just as dumb as usual."

"Oh! I must tell Mama to lock you in your chamber, little brother," she said angrily. "Perhaps she'll send you back to London. You would only embarrass us because of your lack of etiquette."

"Lord Montjoy?" the boy begged. "Will you shut her up? She's making my food go sour in my stomach."

"Perhaps it would be more pleasant to speak of other things," Kevin suggested.

"That's right!" Fennimore stuck out his tongue at his sister. "If you don't quit bothering me, I'll throw up in your lap."

"You disgusting excuse for humanity!" she returned, and the two of them didn't cease bickering until Sam's head hurt so badly that she excused herself from the table.

Fennimore trailed into the hall after her. "Are you getting ready to take Bob out, Miss Samantha?"

"Unfortunately, no. I slept too late, so he had to be satisfied with his indoor arrangements."

"Can I see him? Please?"

She hesitated.

"I'll be good," he vowed. "I'll be perfect!"

Still, she vacillated. With the headache, she didn't much feel like supervising Fennimore. But he was awfully cute and beguiling, even though she couldn't trust the rascal to stay out of mischief.

"Look." He pulled a mangled piece of toast from his pocket. "I saved this to feed him."

"Very well," she allowed, unable to turn him down. "But you must do exactly what I say. You might have gotten along wonderfully outside, but we don't know how he will react to you when you invade his lair."

"Yes'm!" He took her hand and fairly dragged her up the stairs.

In the upper hall, she again had thoughts about permitting him to enter the family enclave, but it was too late now. Taking his hand, she led him through the door into the private precinct, hoping that she didn't meet any member of The Connection, who would surely frown on admitting the boy into their realm. Hurriedly, she jerked him into her chamber.

Fennimore's face lit up as he saw Bob padding toward them. "I like 'im, Miss Samantha. I really like 'im!"

"Stand very still and let him sniff you" she said.

Bob was more interested in scenting the boy's pocket than in smelling the rest of him.

"Can I give it to him?" he asked.

"Be very careful not to let him nip your fingers," she cautioned.

Fennimore removed the toast from his coat and started to extend it, but Bob's head snaked out and took charge, chomping down solidly.

"Ooh!" the lad exclaimed. "He's fast!"

"He certainly is. Now stay away from him while he eats."

Fennimore backed up. "Can I look around and see where he lives?"

"As long as you don't make a mess."

Sam went into the sitting room and sat on the sofa, which commanded a fine view of much of the suite. Fennimore did appear to be minding his manners. She could only fault him when he came to her.

"Where's that door go?" he probed pointedly, and before she could answer, he threw it open. "Wow! Look at that bed! Whose is that?"

"Shh! Stay out of there!" she shrilled. "That is Lord Montjoy's room. You cannot go in."

"Think he'd let me see it sometime?"

"I doubt it," she candidly told him. "Lord Montjoy is a very private person."

"You and he could sneak in here and talk to each other, and no one would know," the boy eagerly mentioned.

"But we don't." Sam assured him with a confidence she did not feel. Why hadn't she thought of this before she'd brought Fennimore to her chamber? If he tattled, she and Kevin both would be ruined.

"Fennimore," she spoke in as secretive a voice as she could. "You must tell no one what you have discovered. You see, this sitting room was once a secret passageway. Old castles had lots of secret places."

His mouth dropped open. "I'll bet there are more than this, aren't there?"

"I don't know," she confessed, "but I'll try to find out for you."

He chuckled. "What if there was a secret passage to Delphinia's room. I could scare her."

Samantha wished she hadn't brought up the subject. "If you did that, they wouldn't be a secret anymore, and Lord Montjoy would probably have them locked up. You must keep quiet about it."

"We have lots of secrets, don't we, Miss Samantha?"

"Yes, we do," she acknowledged. *And I wish I had never gotten myself into a conspiracy with you,* she silently added.

He grinned from ear to ear "This is fun! Are there any more discoveries to make?"

"Not that I know of."

"There's probably an attic. Let's go look!"

Luckily, Bob joined them at that moment and allowed Fennimore to pet him. The cat was also interested in a game of ball. Fennimore became so engrossed in play that he seemed to forget his exploration. Sam hoped he would continue to do so. Forever.

Seventeen

Duchess Walsingham accepted the reservations. On the day the party was to arrive, Sam was almost beside herself with concern. She inspected the house once by herself, again with Margaret, and a third time with Daphne and Winifred. At last, she was satisfied. There was some degree of shabbiness in certain areas, but hopefully the guests would look upon them as quaint.

Samantha was not the only young lady who was excited by the party. Delphinia had never been so nervous. This type of opportunity did not come every day for a cit's daughter, and she meant to make the most of it. She and her mama sent away to London for further additions to her wardrobe. Her abigail styled and restyled her hair to see which fashion was most becoming. With The Connection in greater circulation, she carefully studied their deportment and polish, even asking questions of the friendlier Daphne.

Neither was Kevin as calm as he looked. Externally, he was cool and sophisticated. Inside, he was tense. He knew that no member of the *ton* would approve of him being in business, and he wondered how they would behave toward him. He was certain that the duchess had a very definite reason for arranging this fete, and he assumed it was one last chance to bring him up to the mark for her granddaughter. The noble family must be truly desperate to find a mate for Frances.

The Connection was as overset as everyone else. Margaret, being a countess with a position to uphold, was the most fidgety.

Like Kevin, she was certain that going into business had cast her family beyond the pale. Unlike him, she believed that his chances with Lady Frances were gone, especially after their previous travesty of a visit. The duchess and her friends must be coming to laugh and gloat. She wished that Samantha had told Her Grace that there was no vacancy, but that was beside the point now. She was glad of Mr. Courtney's support. He, at least, understood her fears. When the first of the carriages was seen on the drive, he was at hand to escort her to the entrance hall and to leave her at Kevin's side.

With the family arranging themselves into a receiving line, Sam found herself on the end. Thus, she was fully able to witness the duchess's arrival and to count it as one of the most annoying spectacles she'd ever seen.

The Duchess of Walsingham was a tall, slender woman with ramrod-straight posture and piercing blue eyes. Her haughty, thin nose was held high. Her mouth curled in an expression of distaste, and her jaw muscles quivered. In all her born days, Sam had never seen such a disagreeable person.

The duchess made a quick path through the line. When she reached Sam, she withdrew a lorgnette and held it up to study her, just as if she were a piece of offal which had unbelievably been left on the carpet. Unhurriedly, she scrutinized her from head to toe.

Perspiration beaded on Sam's upper lip. She knew that Her Grace was deliberately trying to make her uncomfortable, but that made it no easier. When she thought that she would truly expire from intimidation, the woman moved on.

After that, greeting the other guests was relatively simple. The Danforths tried and failed to ape the duchess. One young man attempted to look down her bodice. Several people were actually friendly, one married couple in particular, who claimed to be Kevin's friends. But no matter how they behaved toward her, she knew she had been through an ordeal. And it was just beginning.

When the entire assemblage had passed and began milling about and having refreshments in the drawing room, the welcoming line dissolved. Kevin immediately joined Sam. "Well, what did you think?"

She grimaced. "It was awful."

"Surely not! Weren't the Hopewells pleasant?"

"Yes. They were just about the only ones. By the time they came along, I was exhausted." She sighed. "The duchess appears prepared to hate me."

Before he could comment, Lady Montjoy came by on Mr. Courtney's arm. "Come along, children. We've managed this far. Let us not tarry."

"Must I really?" Sam asked when she had gone. "I am only the manager."

"You are also a member of this family."

"I imagine only the Danforths and the duchess know that," she countered. "Please, Kevin, my nerves are raw."

"I want you to meet Drew and Corinna," he expressed. "I think you will like them. I surely was glad to see them arrive. It's strange that the duchess invited them."

"Maybe they do not approve of your business, and she plans to use their influence to drive you into the fold."

He frowned. "I hadn't thought of that."

She was sorry she'd planted the doubt and ruined his relief to see his friends. "That's silly of me," she rebuked. "I vow I cannot trust anyone!"

"Come with me, Samantha."

Feeling guilty for possibly destroying his confidence, she consented. "Just keep me away from the duchess."

He grinned. "I shall guard you against that virago."

"Don't forget." She slipped her arm through his elbow. "If you leave me stranded, I shall make a run for it!"

"You deserve being left," he swore. "After some of the tricks you've played on me! Tell me, can you ever again look at Lord Danforth without visualizing my unmentionables on his head?"

At least he was able to joke about it now. She giggled. "Bob was actually the true culprit."

"Suffice it to say that you *and* Bob have overturned my sophisticated demeanor."

When they entered the drawing room, they were laughing with the easy manner of those who know each other well. This brought scowls and raised eyebrows from most of the guests. Andrew, Viscount Hopewell, detached himself from a small group of gentlemen and came to meet them, but Corinna was helplessly affixed to the duchess and Lady Montjoy.

"It seems that my wife is trapped," Kevin's friend apologized, directing his words to Samantha.

She smiled, suddenly unsure of her conversational ability.

He addressed his next comment to Kevin. "Well, my friend, I know better than to ask what you have been doing of late."

Kevin lifted a shoulder and grinned. "I suppose it is obvious."

"Some of it, perhaps." Lord Hopewell pointedly glanced from his friend to Sam.

She realized that she still possessed Kevin's arm. Cheeks warming, she reluctantly dropped her hand to her side. Touching Kevin had been a comfort, but she didn't wish to add to the gossip.

"Samantha is my cousin," Kevin announced. "Did you know that?"

"Of course. Did you ever know the *ton's* grapevine to lack details?"

"Ha!" Kevin scoffed. "Why not? It frequently misplaces the truth."

Lord Hopewell grinned lopsidedly. "For some strange reason, I expect that this is going to be a very entertaining party."

The two friends went on, their discourse spiced with such innuendo that Sam couldn't translate. She let her gaze wander around the room, fastening immediately on Delphinia, sitting by a window, hemmed in by two young gentlemen. She wondered if the men were honestly interested in the cit's daughter, or if they were merely toying with her. As she peered, another young man disengaged himself and came straight toward her. He bowed deeply.

"You beautify the room, Miss . . ." He shrugged, grinning. "I'm sorry. I don't remember your name."

Samantha started to tell him, but Kevin interrupted her and made the introduction.

Sam smiled, curtsying. "How do you do, Lord Lawrence? I must confess that I did not recall your name either. I welcomed too many people in too short a time. I will pardon you, if you will forgive me."

"Certainly, Miss Edwards." He bowed again. "My day would be ruined had you not absolved me."

She was taken aback. What foolishness! The handsome Lord Lawrence dropped a notch in her estimation. If the most of the *ton's* bachelors spouted this kind of nonsense, she wanted nothing to do with them. She glanced at Kevin to determine, by his expression, what he thought of Lord Lawrence's flattery, but he had returned to his conversation with Lord Hopewell.

"I hope you will enjoy your stay at Montjoy Castle, my lord," she remarked.

"With your presence, I know I will. When I received my invitation, I vacillated about whether or not I would attend. Curiosity prevailed, and here I am!" He lazily smiled. "Had I known that such a lovely lady would be here, I would have had no qualms about attending."

"I am glad that you chose to visit," she said politely.

"Your kind words have delighted me beyond all belief," he waxed on. "I believe someone said that you are American?"

She nodded.

"You must tell me about your country. I have long held an interest in the colonies . . . Do excuse me! I mean the United States, of course. Are you from Virginia?"

"I was born and raised on the Ohio frontier," Sam explained.

"My word!" He feigned great shock. "A comely lady who has overcome great challenges. After that kind of background, you must be especially happy to remove to England."

"Not necessarily," she said coolly. "I loved my home."

"Alas!" he cried. "I have offended you. Once again, I must

beg your pardon. I suppose I judged you according to the way *I* would feel. If I were a native of the wilderness, no doubt I would embrace the same sentiment."

Sam wished he would go on his way. He was the kind of obnoxious, opinionated, and arrogant nobleman she had expected to meet. Lord Lawrence probably represented the norm. Kevin was different . . . or was he? Deep inside, he might be just like this man. She sighed. How many times had she questioned her cousin's masculinity?

Lord Lawrence was speaking, drawing her from her silent speculation. She heard only the last of his commentary, "Perhaps you will show me the garden, Miss Edwards."

"I'm sorry, but I must put that off till later," she declined. "And now, if you will excuse me, I must go about my responsibilities."

"My heart will break," he teased. "Can you not spare me ten more minutes?"

"I'm sorry. I cannot."

He took her elbow. "I will not take no for an answer."

"Lord Lawrence, please!" She jerked away.

He looked contrite. "I did not mean to frighten you."

"You are not *frightening* me," Sam vehemently denied. "But you are making a pest of yourself."

His eyes darkened with irritation. "I've never heard that complaint of myself. Perhaps I should examine my character."

Sam inwardly winced. She did not want to start out on the wrong foot with a guest, but she instinctively distrusted this man. Good etiquette, however, overruled her hesitance.

"Lord Lawrence," she disclosed, "my choice of words was unfortunate. I did not intend to insult you, but I have numerous responsibilities to tend to today. I suppose I am a bit edgy."

"I am relieved." He bowed. "We shall resume our discourse at another time?"

"Yes, of course." She fastened a smile on her face. "I shall look forward to it."

Hastening away from him, Samantha left the drawing room,

relieved that no one else tried to stop her on her way out. In the hall, she was astonished by the mountains of baggage which awaited distribution. These people packed more for a short party than she had when she'd crossed the Atlantic. Such wastrels! Were clothing and parties all that they cared for?

Shaking her head in disgust, she approached the butler. "I have never seen such a display. One would think that these people planned to stay for a year! Do you have it all under control?"

"Yes, Miss Samantha."

She watched as Montjoy's footmen and the guests' servants made trip after trip up the long stairs. "This is so ridiculous."

At length, she made her way to the kitchen. The hall might be as busy as a hill of ants, but the cook and her assistants were even more bustling. Feeling terribly in the way, Sam left after a few minutes.

At least Montjoy's staff was rising to the occasion. She wished she was. Feeling sneaky, she slipped up the stairs to her room. It was an absolute relief to escape the noise and the crowd. She looked longingly at the bed. Why not? With a large amount of guilt, she kicked off her shoes and lay down across it. Almost immediately, she dozed.

Making the final adjustment to his neckcloth, Kevin surveyed his appearance in the pier glass mirror. He nodded, satisfied, and wished that he was half as pleased with the occasion. He was not looking forward to the dinner, nor the evening afterward.

The Duchess of Walsingham's fete was strange, at best, and there definitely was something in the wind that he didn't understand. Was it actually supposed to be an engagement party? Perhaps that was why many guests had looked so disgruntled when he walked in with Samantha on his arm. He'd asked Drew if he perceived what the duchess had up her sleeve, but his friend had not known. He supposed he'd just have to wait it out, and be very cautious as he did so. He didn't trust the duchess at all, and wouldn't put it past her to drum up an intrigue in order to capture him.

Pondering the matter, he left his chamber and descended the stairs to await the guests in the drawing room. As he entered, he was surprised to see that the duchess was already present. He bowed.

"Madam, you are quite lovely, tonight."

"Fustian!" She sipped her glass of sherry and rudely scrutinized him. "You are not interested in the appearance of an old woman. Moreover, I am too old to be lovely. Grand maybe, but not lovely."

"Yes, ma'am." He crossed the room to the sideboard and poured himself a glass of the wine.

"Montjoy," she began, "you are probably wondering why I have put in an early attendance. I will not mince words."

He immediately hoisted his guard. As an elderly duchess, she need not be quite so conventional as others, because of her rank and age. Good God, it was hard telling what she might say!

She lifted her chin and assumed a well-bred sneer. "I am concerned about your attentions to my granddaughter. Having declared yourself—"

"Now just a minute!" he interjected. "I have made no promises!"

She looked as if she didn't like his response, but he wasn't sure what she held in contempt. His refusal to admit to asking for Frances's hand, or his interrupting her? Maybe both. He smiled cynically. If a duchess could be outlandish, so could an earl who had cast himself beyond the pale.

"You have created expectations," she stated.

"I don't think so!" he fired back.

"Do not shout at me, Montjoy," she threatened, "else I will conclude my bargain with another gentleman. Now, to the point! I wish you to wed my granddaughter, and I am willing to bestow a large sum of money upon you, if you do."

He stared at her.

"You will be a wealthy man," she promised, "and as we know,

marriage does not particularly mean that certain . . . er . . . activities must cease to exist. I can assure you that Frances will look the other way. So you see, Montjoy? You cannot lose."

Gad, but she was uncouth! Many *ton* marriages were matters of business, but no one came right out into the open like this and discussed extramarital affairs. Suddenly, it all struck him funny. She was bartering for possession of him, just as she might for a doll in a shop. What would she do next? Inquire about his price? He couldn't restrain a grin.

"Do you think this is amusing, young man?" she stated. "I assure you that it is not! Name your price!"

He began to chuckle.

"I'm sorry. Am I interfering with business?" From behind them, Samantha's voice contained a veritable fountain of suppressed laughter.

If looks could kill, he would soon be attending Samantha's funeral. The duchess appraised her with pure hatred. Kevin knew that he should be angry at Her Grace for expressing such animosity toward his cousin, but he was simply too full of mirth.

The duchess's bosom heaved. "I am not certain what is going on, Montjoy, but I am not pleased."

Kevin bit down hard on the inside of his lower lip to keep from laughing. "I do beg your pardon, Your Grace."

"You may be attempting to make your living like a tradesman, young man," she snapped, "but that does not mean you should act like one! I am no longer sure that you are right for our Frances."

Lady Montjoy entered at that moment, looking worried. "Is everything all right?"

"No, it is not." She sniffed. "Your grandson is behaving like a churl. He has no respect for his betters."

"Oh! Kevin?" his grandmama entreated. "That hardly sounds like you."

"It is my fault," volunteered Samantha. "I caused him to laugh in an inopportune moment."

Margaret clicked her tongue. "Shame on you both! They meant no harm, Your Grace. Ah, the vagaries of youth!"

"Margaret, you always were a silly woman," the duchess pronounced. "But I can scarcely believe that you deem him a callow lad. He is a man and an earl, and he'd best be conducting himself with maturity."

Lady Montjoy's mouth dropped open.

Further conversation was halted by the arrival of the large majority of the guests, along with Jenkins and one of his footmen to serve the preprandial drinks. The duchess marched off to greet her friends, while Lady Montjoy drifted after her. Kevin was left alone with Samantha.

"That evil old woman!" Sam disparaged. "Accusing you of disrespect!"

He grinned lopsidedly. "Actually, I suppose she is correct."

"She is not your better!"

"She's that, too." His smile widened. "She is a duchess, while I am nothing but a puling earl."

"Fiddlesticks! She is a rotten egg," she retorted. "I cannot bear her!"

"Strong words." Kevin's friend, Andrew, his wife on his arm, entered the exchange. "I would be greatly daunted if they were aimed at me."

Samantha blushed. She did manage to greet the Hopewells before she began to withdraw. Kevin caught her hand.

"Everything is being taken care of, Sami. You need time to relax."

She paused, but he sensed flight.

"I have never met up with a rotten egg, Miss Edwards, but it sounds perfectly ghastly," Drew teased.

"Oh, yes, it is," she assured him. "Happily, I imagine that you will go for the rest of your life without smelling that particular, horrid odor. In the Ohio country, where I come from, food was sometimes scarce, so people got in the habit of hoarding all they could. It was not unusual to crack open an egg and find it spoiled."

"Ohio," the viscount mused. "The name has a mysterious ring."

"It sounds fascinating," agreed his wife. "Won't you tell us about it sometime, Miss Edwards?"

Sam nodded and seemed to settle a bit, but dinner was called before Kevin could be sure. Reluctantly, he left her to escort the highest-ranking lady, the duchess, into the dining room. As they entered the hall, he looked back to see if his cousin was coping with the complicated protocol, but she was lost in the crowd.

"Well, Montjoy, I see you have overcome your misguided merriment," the lady remarked.

Kevin wasn't exactly sure how to answer that observation, so he remained silent.

"I hope you are pondering what I have told you. By wedding Frances, you will eliminate all of your troubles. Moreover, if you act now, I believe we can surmount this stigma of trade."

He set his jaw. The duchess was making herself and her proposition very undesirable. He loathed this assault. Was she stupid? Didn't she understand that her harassment was driving him in the opposite direction?

"What is your answer?" she goaded. "I would like nothing better than to hear your announcement this very eve."

"Then you will be disappointed, Your Grace," he muttered.

"Your cousin is causing this confusion, isn't she?"

Kevin did not reply.

"If your cousin wants to play innkeeper at your expense, you may buy her a place to do so. You will be able to afford it," she urged. "And your grandmother and aunts can reside with her."

He wished that propriety would allow him to tell her to shut her mouth.

She pounded on. "It is best that your female relatives dwell elsewhere. Having more than one mistress of the house is inadvisable. Frances must be the one to whom the servants listen and obey. Montjoy! Do you comprehend what I am saying?"

"Yes," he said shortly.

"Then why will you not respond?"

He looked her straight in the eye. "Madam, I will not be coerced. In fact, your harassment is spurring me in the exact opposite direction."

She narrowed her eyes. "This *harassment,* as you call it, is my way of jogging reticent people, who refuse to act for their own good."

"Well, it is not the way to achieve results with me."

"Montjoy, you are a stubborn man," she grumbled. "That is probably the reason you are in dire straits this day. You will not be reasonable."

That was the final straw. He would not marry her granddaughter. He might be tossing his financial future to the wind, but having money was tantamount to being ruled by the duchess. He would not willingly place himself under her thumb. It was finished, and he doubted that he would ever be sorry for terminating it.

He took the duchess to her place at the table, unfortunately adjacent to his own, and seated her. "Duchess, I will give you my answer. No, I will not wed your granddaughter. It is out of the question."

She loudly caught her breath. "What did you say?"

Other guests were now within earshot, but he did not care. If she could be audacious enough to speak so blatantly, so could he. He repeated, "I will not marry Frances."

There were several tumultuous gasps, which he ignored. He took his place at the head of the table and unfolded his napkin. His hands trembled slightly. He had done it now! He hoped his grandmother would understand.

He glanced down the table at Frances. It was obvious that she had heard. She had bowed her head and was frantically blinking back tears. He was sorry that she was so downcast. But it was just as much the fault of her manipulative grandmother as it was his own.

He returned his attention to the duchess. Her face was ugly with displeasure. He wouldn't have been surprised if she had leapt up and tried to thrash him.

She glared. "You will be very sorry for this day's work, Montjoy. I am very serious about that. I will ruin you."

"I doubt you can do that," he mildly retorted.

"No?" A sneer suffused her face. "Just wait and see. I will destroy you . . . and everything you hold dear."

"Duchess Walsingham, you cannot do that," he said cynically. "I seem to be doing a good job of it by myself."

She snorted. "You don't know the half of it, Montjoy. You will see. You will see *very soon.*"

"Good!" he declared savagely. "I dislike waiting. Attempt to do your damage, Your Grace. You may find that many people will not heed you. You *do* have a reputation for maliciousness, you know."

With that, he plunged his spoon into the delicious turtle soup and began to eat, totally ignoring the lady and her sour expression.

Eighteen

Samantha realized that something noteworthy had gone on at Kevin's end of the table, and from the look on the face of the Duchess of Walsingham, she guessed that her cousin had displeased the repulsive virago. She hoped the cause was what she craved . . . that Kevin would dispense with all notions of wedding Lady Frances Danforth. Studying the girl, who seemed to be teary-eyed, she guessed that it must be so.

She didn't have the chance to learn anything definite, though. Dinner was certainly not the place to inquire, and Kevin was instantly surrounded by people as soon as the men joined the ladies in the drawing room after the meal. Annoyingly, Sam herself was besieged.

Lord Lawrence, whose unwelcome attentions she had spurned earlier, had renewed his assault. Some young ladies might be delighted to be so pursued, but she was not. The man was the very epitome of an arrogant, conceited aristocrat, and for the life of her, Sam couldn't seem to escape him. Moreover, along with his revolting, top-lofty personality, he possessed a dark side. She instinctively did not trust Lord Lawrence. And she couldn't understand why he was so interested in her. In an attempt to evade the nobleman, she followed Delphinia to the pianoforte and volunteered to turn the pages of the music the girl selected to play. Her offer, however, was superseded by a young lord who seemed to be rather taken with the cit's daughter, and she was thrown back into the company of the objectionable lord.

"Are you pretending to dodge me?" he asked with a smile. "Your shyness is most becoming."

"I am not timid," she vowed, "and my conduct is not pretense."

He chuckled in disbelief. "Charming. Charming, indeed."

Samantha sighed. Could nothing discourage him? She did not wish to be sharp with Lord Lawrence and thus risk censure of the business, but he was driving her to it. Moreover, he had the breath and the look of a man who'd been imbibing too freely of liquor.

"Sir," she said, "I'm sure that your attentions would be mightily welcomed by someone else."

"By whom?" he retorted. "That vulgar cit's girl?"

Sam could no longer hold her temper. "You are a fine one to speak of vulgarity! Your own behavior in plaguing me is greatly offensive. Your manners are certainly wanting, far more than I have ever witnessed on the part of Miss Milton."

Color rose in his cheeks. "I am sorry you've received that impression of me, Miss Edwards. I assure you that my regard is meant only for the best. Do forgive me."

She took mercy. "Very well, but please direct your attentions elsewhere."

"It will be difficult." His lips curled in an oily smile. "Whether you know it or not, Miss Edwards, you are an extremely attractive young woman."

Not a lady? Woman, as he used it, seemed a disparaging choice of words, but she did not intend to question it and give him an excuse to continue the conversation.

"Please excuse me, Lord Lawrence," she said. "I've matters to attend."

Samantha turned, just as Fennimore, followed by Martha, dashed into the room.

"Come back, you scamp!" the abigail cried.

"I have to talk to Miss Samantha!" he squealed, dodging as she grabbed for him.

Seeing the combination of guilt and excitement mirrored in his face, Sam had a terrible, sinking feeling. Somehow, she knew that the boy's agitation had to do with Bob. She bent, catching his shoulder, and saw the coiled leash he held behind his back.

"Fennimore, what is it? Does it have to do with *our friend?*" she asked, even though she was certain of the answer.

Nodding miserably, he hung his head. "I'm sorry, Miss Samantha. I only thought to help! You were busy. I knew you'd be late taking him out, so I . . ."

"He is loose?"

"Yes, ma'am." He wiped tears from his eyes and snuffled his nose. "I let him off the leash and he ran around, having fun. But when it was time to go in, he wouldn't come. I called and called; I chased him. I tried everything, but he wouldn't mind me."

"He is free in the area we usually go?" she queried.

"Yes'm. I was going to keep trying to catch him, but then I decided I'd better fetch you."

"You did right, Fennimore." She straightened. "I shall go immediately."

"I'll help," he proffered.

"No. It might be best for me to go alone. If he is overset, he might not respond if others are present." She patted his head and took the leash. "Thank you for telling me. That was a brave thing to do."

"*She* wasn't going to let me." The lad scowled at Martha.

"I don't trust that rascal!" shrilled the lady's maid. "He is the devil 'imself come to earth!"

"Hush," begged Samantha. "People are staring. Go on your way, both of you. I shall quickly return with Bob, and see you upstairs."

As Fennimore and Martha hastened from the room, Samantha glanced at Kevin in hopes that she would be able to tell him where she was going, but he was still in the center of a crowd. The Connection was similarly occupied. Ah well, probably no one would miss her.

"May I be of assistance?" quizzed a deep voice behind her.

She whirled, frowning. "No, Lord Lawrence. I must do this myself."

"This Bob is a pet?"

"My cat. Now, please, leave me alone!" Turning on her heel, she stalked toward the door.

Happily, he didn't follow. She hurried to the service door and let herself out into the night. In the distance, an owl whooed. A whispery breeze smelling of rain lifted her hair. It was an eve that might frighten a young lady all by herself, but Sam, accustomed to the dark forests of the frontier, paid it no heed. She was only hoping that she could easily seize the bobcat and return him unseen to her chamber.

"Bob!" she began calling, as she reached the meadow. "Bob, come here!"

The lynx did not bound up to greet her, but she thought she heard scratching in a nearby tree. "Bob! Get down here right now!"

"I am glad you are hailing a cat, instead of another gentleman. I fear I'd be jealous."

"Damn!" Sam swore daringly. "Lord Lawrence, how many times must I tell you to leave me alone? What are you doing here, of all places?"

"I followed you." He closed the distance between them. "I realize now that you do not wish me to approach you in public. Such a thing would only incite the wrath of such as the Duchess of Walsingham. No, we must secretly carry on our little game."

"What game?" Sam backed up several steps.

"The sport of love, of course." He laughed lightly.

"What nonsense!" she sneered. "I am playing no game with you, Lawrence. You'll have to play by yourself. Now, get out of here!"

His smile faded. "I do not think I'll do that."

"You'd best have second thoughts!" she warned, continuing to step backwards.

Lord Lawrence, gloating, pursued.

It was obvious that he did not intend to give up, and there

was nothing positive that she could do, other than taking to her heels. She refused to resort to that ignoble means of escape. She curled her fists into small, rigid knots.

"Bob!" she shrieked, desperately wishing the cat would appear and strike fear into the heart of Lord Lawrence. Her pet, in his aggressive stance, was an awesome beast to behold. He must be above her. She could plainly hear the swish of leaves.

"Bob!" Her spirits sank when she heard the beating of wings, as a large owl flew from the tree. Bob wasn't there at all! She was on her own as Lord Lawrence mounted his attack, springing forward like a wild animal.

Her fists proved useless. With a quick snatch, Lord Lawrence caught her wrists and twisted them behind her back. His face loomed lower and lower toward hers.

Samantha wriggled in his tight clutch. Jerking her head to the side, she deflected his sloppy kiss from her mouth to her ear. She tried to kick him, but he was standing on the toes of her shoes. He grasped her wrists with one hand, and with the other, pulled her chin around. Sam screeched with fury until her protest was cut off by his lips. Plundering her mouth, he pressed hard until he forced her teeth to part.

"Enough!"

Her heart leapt for joy as she heard Kevin's voice. Her cousin yanked the man away from her and squared off against him. Her elation turned to fear. Kevin couldn't know how to fight. He had lived the sheltered life of a pampered aristocrat. Lord Lawrence must have had the same upbringing, but somehow she believed him to be capable of injuring the earl.

"No!" she wailed as they paused briefly, glowering at each other. They slowly began to circle, two sets of cold eyes staring rigidly at each other.

"Stop this at once!" she begged.

Simultaneously, Kevin launched a practiced blow to the jaw that sent his opponent reeling. He followed up, grasping Lord Lawrence by the neckcloth and striking him again. He loosed his grip and let the villain fall to the ground.

Sam stared openmouthed. "That's all?"

Her cousin shrugged. "I could pick him up and hit him again."

"No!" she cried. "This is sufficient. How did you learn to do it? It is . . ." She broke off, deciding that Kevin wouldn't wish to be favorably compared to an American frontiersman.

His reply was cut off by Lord Lawrence staggering to his feet, revitalizing, and drawing a small pistol, which he pointed toward Kevin. "I'll get you for this, Montjoy."

All of a sudden, the air seemed filled with fur and snarling. Bob sprang onto the scene and pounced on Lord Lawrence, knocking him down. The gun flew out of his hand and disappeared into the darkness. Standing over his prey, Bob gawked down at him, clicking his teeth and plainly enjoying the man's torment. Slowly, the cat closed his mouth around Lawrence's neck, teeth sinking into the man's neckcloth.

"Help me, Montjoy, help me!" screamed the fallen nobleman. "This creature from hell will devour me! Help me!"

"Bob," Kevin commanded, catching the lynx's collar. "That's enough."

The bobcat obediently spit out Lord Lawrence's cravat, and along with that, his neck. The peer heaved a great sigh of relief and looked up at his intended victim. "I only meant to be friendly."

"Your interpretation of friendliness is not mine!" Sam snapped. "Get out of here! Leave us and leave the castle!"

"It's nighttime," he whined.

"You should have thought of that before you accosted me!" She crinkled her nose in profound distaste. "If you do not go away, I will turn this cat on you!"

"That is your little kitty cat?" he pouted. "I could have you jailed for harboring a dangerous, wild animal."

"Oh?" Sam angrily marched toward him, but managed only one stride before Kevin captured her, pulling her back against him and encircling her in his arms.

"He isn't worth your effort, Samantha."

He was right. Chin high, she merely looked with disdain at Lord Lawrence, but it was difficult to maintain the enraged expression when she was so warm and secure in Kevin's arms.

"Be gone by early morning," Kevin told the man, "or I will not be responsible for your safety. If Miss Edwards orders this cat to attack you, you will be seriously injured."

"You'll be sorry," Lord Lawrence growled and sped toward the castle.

"A threat!" Sam worried. "He might really mean it."

"I am not afraid of him." He drew her closer against his chest, his breath ruffling her hair.

She shuddered. "He might hire thugs."

"I can take care of myself," he assured her, "and I can take care of you."

"But . . ."

"Hush, Samantha." He kissed the top of her head.

She felt as if her knees had turned to water. Any opinions she'd ever held about English lords seemed to float away on the breeze. Kevin was not unmanly. The blows he had landed on Lawrence were precise and devastating. How had she ever considered him as effete? She had been very, very wrong.

Kevin sighed. "If only it weren't for . . ."

"For what?" she murmured.

"Money," he said ruefully. "If it weren't for money, we could . . ."

"Yes?" she urged, turning in his arms and looking up at him.

"Nothing." He dropped his hands to his sides. "We'd best take Bob in now."

"But what were you going to say?"

He remained silent.

"Kevin!"

"Let it be, Samantha." He bent to hook the leash on Bob's collar.

The lynx let forth a husky purr and nuzzled Kevin's coat.

"Oh, very well. I came prepared, as usual." Kevin removed

a small, very slender flask from his inner pocket and removed the lid.

"What are you doing?" Sam cried.

Bob had already sat back on his haunches and was swatting playfully at the container. Grinning, the earl held the bottle to his lips. The cat gulped greedily.

"I cannot believe this!" Sam shouted. "You are feeding him alcohol!"

"He likes a bit, now and then."

"Give me that leash!" She jerked it from his hands. "For shame!"

Kevin chuckled.

"It isn't funny," she vowed. "Spirits cannot be good for him."

"I doubt if a little nip, now and then, will hurt him," he countered, "and it's definitely healthy for me. It keeps me on his good side."

"Perhaps, but now he's had enough. Let us return to the castle."

"As you wish." He offered her his arm.

Sam accepted. As they returned to the garden and strolled along the brick path, she gazed up at him. "Kevin? It seemed at dinner that you and the Duchess Walsingham were at odds."

"That is true."

She could have wrung his neck for withholding information. "May I ask why?"

"Samantha, you are shameless. You are the nosiest human being I have ever known." He shook his head. "I informed Her Grace that I would not wed her granddaughter. I did not appreciate her attitude or her attempts to manipulate me."

Sam's heartbeat increased. If he would not marry Frances Danforth, then . . .

"I'd as soon wed Delphinia Milton. In fact, I believe I'll explore that option." He shrugged. "Can you imagine how financially stable the family would be, if I married her?"

"Damn!" Sam cried, stopping and stamping her foot. "A

bride's fortune is unnecessary! Why do you refuse to get it through your thick skull? This inn is making you a wealthy man."

"It could fail—"

"Well, it isn't going to! I want to hear no more of that defeatist attitude." She pursed her lips in pique.

He doggedly hung on to his opinion. "No one can predict that uncertain future, whereas if I married Delphinia, all of us would live very comfortably."

"Not I!" Sam dropped her hand from his arm. "I refuse to live on the spoils of marital warfare. I shall remove to Portsmouth and join Polly in her business."

"No, you won't!" he exclaimed. "You'll remain right here!"

Sam did not wish to bandy words with him, so she did not inform him how wrong he was.

"You will not remove yourself from your family," he emphasized.

She was unable to allow that statement to live on. "I won't remove myself from my family, just from this location. I shall stay in touch."

"I won't let you leave," he threatened.

"Oh, you won't?" She set her jaw. "We'll just see about that!"

"Dammit, Samantha! Why must you fail to accept reality?"

Holding back tears, she led Bob through the service door. So he'd decided to forget Frances. What about Delphinia? Why wouldn't he believe that his financial troubles had ended? Why? Why couldn't he see that she loved him? He was the one who refused to discern reality!

She was gritting her teeth very audibly now. The backstairs were in sight, thank heavens. She must get away from him.

"Samantha," he said, gripping her elbow.

"Let me go!" she shrilled. "First Lawrence, now you! Why must everyone attempt to control me! I won't have it! Especially from the man I love—"

Bursting into wrenching sobs, she dashed up the stairs, with Bob scampering beside her.

* * *

Kevin gaped, too stunned to do anything but watch her flight. She loved him? His heart felt as if it would explode. He loved her, too. But he was practical enough to realize that he couldn't give her what she deserved. Miserable, he walked through the corridor of the service area and passed through the green baize door to the front of the house.

Strains of laughter and music filtered from the drawing room. As luck would have it, the guests were still at play. It was too bad they hadn't decided to go to bed early. He debated retiring, himself, but that would have been an unpleasant trick to play on The Connection. The duchess and the Danforths were probably rather difficult to entertain, after he had refused to fall in with their plans. He wished they would leave, but he doubted if that would occur. The Duchess Walsingham was too proud to flee, especially in front of her guests. She would remain at Montjoy Castle for her allotted time.

He hailed his butler. "Jenkins? Assign a man to keep an eye on Lord Lawrence, until he leaves in the morning. He's up to no good. I had a bit of a discussion with him, but he may not have learned from it."

"Yes, my lord."

Kevin entered the drawing room to find the guests occupied with cards and Delphinia's singing. Halting just inside the door, he paused, listening. If he ended up wedding the cit's daughter, he would, at least, be well entertained. He wondered, however, if he wasn't too late in displaying marked attention to her. Young Howard, Lord Kimball, was turning the pages of her music and fawning over her like a moonstruck calf. Curious, Kevin quietly circled the room and came up behind the couple.

"I don't know when I have heard anything so beautiful," Kimball was saying.

Delphinia blushed. "How you do run on, my lord. I consider my music only passable, at best, though I greatly enjoy it."

"Why, it is the best of the best, Miss Milton," he cried. "I am overcome with its beauty . . . and most of all with yours."

The girl smiled shyly and lowered her gaze. "How you do flatter me."

"When you return to London, may I dare hope that I may call on you? I would like that above all things!" he effused.

"I would like it, too," she whispered, rendered dreamy by his words.

Kevin moved on. Delphinia was as good as taken. He'd never seen a man so smitten. Ah, well, there were many more cits' daughters. He should have no trouble in finding one.

His grandmama and Mr. Courtney were sitting nearby, engaged in rapt conversation. The two certainly seemed to get along marvelously with one another. He wondered if their friendship would ripen to a greater thing.

"Hello, dear Kevin." Lady Montjoy looked up, slightly flushing, as he approached. "Where is Samantha?"

"She doesn't feel well," he told her. "She has gone to her chamber."

"I see." She eyed him curiously, before dropping the subject. "Mr. Courtney has been telling me the most fascinating things about Egypt. Won't you join us?"

They both regarded him with such disinterest that he knew they must wish him to be somewhere else.

"Thank you," he replied, "but I have several matters to attend."

They looked relieved.

He completed his circuit around the room and came back to where he had started. Everyone seemed to be entertained. Even the duchess was occupied with a hand of whist, and surprise of surprises, Lady Frances was demurely talking with a bachelor gentleman.

Andrew Hopewell strolled up to him. "Is your intended occupied elsewhere?"

"Yes, it seems as if Lady Frances has another beau." He

grinned. "I'm glad. I've been a disappointment to the Danforth family, to say the least."

Lord Hopewell raised an eyebrow. "I wasn't thinking of her."

Kevin looked askance at him. "Miss Delphinia Milton?"

"Don't be ridiculous," Drew laughed. "I'm speaking of your cousin. Samantha."

Kevin felt his cheeks growing very warm.

"Am I right?" asked his friend.

Samantha. Had his feelings for her been so easily discernible? He took a deep breath and exhaled it slowly.

"Sometimes, one cannot indulge such feelings," he told him.

"Why not?" Drew demanded.

"What is my usual answer?" he said bleakly. "Money."

"I wouldn't give that a thought. It looks as if you have an extremely good business here. It should make you a wealthy man, but even if it doesn't, you shouldn't allow money to prevent you from being happy." He chuckled "Unless the lady has a great fondness for luxury."

Kevin grinned "Not Samantha. She doesn't even want a lady's maid. We overcame her resistance and forced her to have one, anyway."

"Then there you are."

He shook his head. "If the innkeeping doesn't work out, I wouldn't be able to give her what she deserves."

"Kevin! You just told me she shuns luxury!"

"I know, but—"

"Perhaps you'd best let *her* decide if she wishes to marry you," his friend suggested. "She is aware of your circumstances. Let her make the choice."

"Well . . ." he mused. "I suppose I could. Yes, maybe I shall."

There was a long silence.

"Go!" Lord Hopewell urged. "Ask her and ease your mind. Do you know where she is?"

"She's probably in my sitting room." Kevin wondered if

Samantha was still weeping, and felt wretched. Because she loved him, he had made her cry.

"Your sitting room?" his friend gasped. "The sitting room that's part of your bedchamber? I believe you'd best ask her as soon as possible!"

"It does appear rather scandalous, but I assure you . . ."

"Go to her," Drew prodded. "If you don't, I'll announce where she is to all these people!"

"That's blackmail," Kevin objected.

Lord Hopewell's eyes twinkled. "Exactly so, and I'll do it, Kevin. I really will."

"Well, then . . . You win! I'm going right now." Abruptly, his heart suddenly feeling very light, he sped from the room.

Sam was exactly where he thought she'd be. She nearly jumped out of her skin when he burst into the room, and Bob leapt from the window seat with a hearty growl. "Kevin! What is it?"

"I'm in love with you, Sami!" He hastened to the liquor cabinet and removed a partial bottle of rum. "I want you to marry me!"

Her mouth dropped open. So did Bob's. He crossed the room in one pounce and sat down on his haunches, grinning up at his lordship. Kevin held the bottle to the cat's lips. With a blissful expression on his face, the lynx began to indulge in his favorite libation.

"No!" cried Sam. "And yes!"

Kevin eyed her, perplexed. "What kind of answer is that?"

Her eyes sparkled like perfect jewels. She giggled. "No to the rum, and yes to the marriage. Oh, my, I didn't think you would really ask me!"

Then she was suddenly in his arms. Nearly as speedily, Bob drained the bottle. Kevin dropped it to the floor, so he could give Samantha his full attention.

"It was money," he revealed. "I didn't want to ask you to wed a pauper, but Drew convinced me that you should make that decision."

"I must give him my heartfelt thanks," she murmured.

"Of course, I worried also about your opinion of English lords."

"Whatever for? I have always held them in great esteem."

"Samantha!" He kissed her hair, then lifted her chin.

"At least, I have the highest admiration for one English lord, in particular," she whispered. "Oh, Kevin, I do love you so very much!"

"And I, you." He brought his mouth down upon her sweet lips to kiss her thoroughly. As he did so, a cheerful animal leapt upon his back and clawed its way to his shoulders. A furry face with sticky whiskers shoved between them.

"Bob!" Samantha cried in protest.

"He only had a small draught," Kevin said. "I suppose I'll have to send for more."

"Yes, it would seem so."

"What?" he exclaimed. "You are advocating the use of spirits on this animal?"

"Well," she said, turning her face from the strong scent of rum, "I really do want my kiss, and that seems to be the only way I shall get one."

"Excellent!" Kevin agreed.

As if to appease her, Bob lapped her cheek with his tongue.

"Not that kind of kiss," she remonstrated. "I can scarcely breathe from the fumes."

"I'd best keep that in mind." Kevin stepped away from her and swung the bobcat to the floor. "I'll not stand any competition from you, sir."

"Hurry!" Samantha exhorted. "Get the rum."

But more rum was not necessary. With a great yawn, the cat padded to his favored window seat. Climbing up, he flopped down, and with a loud burp, closed his eyes.

"Hm, it seems he is satisfied with the amount that he had," she reflected.

"Well, I am not." Taking his future bride into his arms, Kevin managed this time to kiss her without interference.

About the Author

Cathleen Clare lives with her family in Ironton, Ohio. She is the author of nine Regency romances, including *An Elusive Groom, Lord Scandal's Lady* and *A Priceless Acquisition.* Cathleen is currently working on her next Zebra regency romance, *A Family Affair,* which will be published in November 1998. Cathleen loves hearing from her readers and you may write to her c/o Zebra Books. Please include a self-addressed stamped envelope if you wish a response.

BOOK YOUR PLACE ON OUR WEBSITE AND MAKE THE READING CONNECTION!

We've created a customized website just for our very special readers, where you can get the inside scoop on everything that's going on with Zebra, Pinnacle and Kensington books.

When you come online, you'll have the exciting opportunity to:

- View covers of upcoming books
- Read sample chapters
- Learn about our future publishing schedule (listed by publication month *and author*)
- Find out when your favorite authors will be visiting a city near you
- Search for and order backlist books from our online catalog
- Check out author bios and background information
- Send e-mail to your favorite authors
- Meet the Kensington staff online
- Join us in weekly chats with authors, readers and other guests
- Get writing guidelines
- AND MUCH MORE!

Visit our website at
http://www.zebrabooks.com